Flatmates

Life in the Brohouse – Book 3

By Carmen Black

Published by Scarlet Lantern Publishing

SCARLET LANTERN
Publishing

This is a work of fiction. Names, characters, businesses, places, events and incidents are either the products of the author's imagination or used in a fictitious manner. Any resemblance to actual persons, living or dead, or actual events is purely coincidental.

This book contains sexually explicit scenes and adult language.

1

RACHEL

I groan while heaving my giant suitcase out of the baggage carousel, nearly slamming it into the inpatient crowd of people standing to my right. An elderly man looks over his shoulder while I try to balance myself. His eyes narrow into a dark scowl and I offer him a small smile, probably appearing meek and lost in this huge airport. The man's eyes go up and down my body, as if he's scrutinizing my clothes. I clutch my purse closer to me, trying to cover up my sweater and jeans combo. His eyes land on my tennis shoes and he clucks his tongue, his eyes narrowing into disdainful slits.

"Sorry," I say softly. For what, I don't know. It's not like I wanted to arrive in Paris wearing the typical American attire- jeans and a t-shirt. However, the flight from Colorado to France is too long to be dressed in a pretty floral skirt and crop top and I wanted something I could sleep in.

Maybe I should have taken the time to change in the bathroom.

"Rachel, are you coming?" I hear Seth call from the benches.

I am very thankful for the excuse to leave. "Yeah!" I shout back, turning my back to the angry looking man and dragging my suitcase towards Seth, sitting on the bench, looking irritated while guarding our pile of luggage. Hunter must be looking around for some snacks while Lucas is calling the taxi service.

Seth taps his fingers against his jaw, scowling at the crowd of people surrounding the baggage carousel. His legs are propped on Lucas's Louis Vuitton suitcases and I grimace, wondering if I should be the one to tell him to get his dirty tennis shoes off the $5000 bag.

"I hate waiting," Seth mutters while leaning back on the bench.

I bite my lip as the heel of his muddy shoes digs into the pristine leather. "Well," I start, grabbing his feet and throwing them off the beautiful bag. Before Seth can complain, I toss myself into his lap and wrap my arms around his neck. "It's not so bad waiting with me, now is it?"

Seth purses his lips, looking me up and down. His gaze is filled with affection while his arm circles around my waist and his fingers stroke my messy, curly hair behind my ear. "No. I guess not." He smiles wickedly while tugging on a curl. "Although, you have looked better."

I scoff and smack his shoulder. "The flight was long," I say while tickling his ribs.

Seth laughs, bouncing me up and down while trying to bat my hands away. "Stop," he gasps.

"How do they expect you to sleep in that tiny little chair? And don't get me started on the movie choices."

"Stop!" he laughs, his face turning red as he giggles.

"It wouldn't have been that bad if you had allowed me to buy you first class," I hear a familiar voice say from behind.

I glance over my shoulder, finding Lucas standing behind me with his arms crossed. He raises an eyebrow at us. My eyes rake over him, taking in his pristinely gelled hair and his clean dark jeans and button-down shirt. He rode with us in economy, yet obviously he took the time to change while I was waiting for my suitcase at the carousel.

My gaze wanders to the ladies standing behind him, speaking a foreign language I don't know. It's definitely not French; the intonation reminds me of Italian, while the words seem more Slavic. Croatian perhaps?

It doesn't really matter what they are speaking, but it matters where they are looking. They smile to one another while gazing at Lucas, their eyes lingering on his shoulders and his well sculptured bottom. They shift from side to side; their black stilettos clacking on the floor. Their legs are at least a mile long if not longer and somehow they are wearing beautiful floral dresses that accent their beauty.

I frown and look down at my clothes once more, feeling extremely self-conscious.

I am definitely going to form some sort of complex while I'm here. Everyone is so beautiful and I'm-

"I think I'm going to like this place," says Hunter while coming up from behind us.

I tilt my head up, my mouth hanging open in both offense and hurt while watching him look around. I can't believe he's been checking out the women while I've been here with Seth on luggage duty.

Hunter smiles while holding out an armful of packaged food. "Their snacks are amazing. Do you want some?"

My mouth shuts and I swallow whatever hurt I felt. Right. Hunter is only talking about the food. I peruse through his findings, frowning at the croissant filled with chocolate and the baguette sandwich.

"You could have just waited," I hear Lucas say, the irritation tainting his tone. "Those are going to be at least three times less expensive once we leave the airport."

Hunter shrugs. "I'm hungry. You don't want to see me when I'm hangry."

Seth nods while grabbing the baguette sandwich.

Well, I guess that decision has been made for me, I think while grabbing the chocolate croissant.

"I can vouch for him," says Seth while stuffing his face with food. "He's definitely an asshole when he's hungry."

Lucas sighs and when I turn around, I see him rubbing his head. The girls from before have thankfully left and the crowd around the carousel is slowly dissipating. "We should probably go," I say while pushing myself off Seth. "The taxis are probably all taken at this rate." I look around, finding a bus sign to my left. Pointing towards it I say, "Maybe we should get tickets-"

Lucas grabs my finger and pulls me towards him. "Everything has been taken care of," he says while lacing my fingers with his and pressing a kiss against my forehead. "Don't you worry about a thing." Lucas looks at his clock, his eyes widening. "Actually, he should be here by now."

"Thank God," says Seth while jumping up from the bench. He slings his bag over his shoulder while Hunter grabs his suitcase.

"He?" I ask, wondering if Lucas called a friend I didn't know about.

It's crazy to think that this isn't Lucas's first trip to Paris. Apparently, his parents stay here frequently. They even have an apartment here and his mother's family owns a hotel. I haven't really discussed Lucas's family with him, other than he pretty much hates his father, doesn't have the best of relationships with his mother and he tries to avoid both at all costs.

Lucas's past and familial life are a mystery to me.

We lug our suitcases out of the airport and towards the taxi pick-up and drop-off. The heat smacks me in the face and I'm desperate to be rid of my sweater while I hold a hand up to my eyes, shielding my gaze from the sun while looking around for a man carrying a Lucas Brent sign.

My hand slowly lowers when I find the man. He's holding a small white card with Lucas's name on it, written in beautiful calligraphy. The man smiles and waves his white gloved hand delicately, slowly lowering the card and placing it under his arm, donned in an immaculately pressed suit jacket. Behind him stands a long, black limousine.

"Well, what are you waiting for?" asks Lucas when I don't immediately follow him towards the chauffeur.

"That's our ride?" I rasp while pointing at the limo.

"How are you shocked at this point?" Seth whispers in my ear. "It's Lucas."

He's right, I shouldn't be shocked. But I am. I've never ridden in a limo before. Not even for prom. And I don't know anyone who has an on call chauffeur in another country.

"Come on, you," says Seth while grabbing my elbow and pulling me after him.

I should be thankful he's leading me. I'm too shocked to move on my own.

"Welcome, Mr. Brent," says the chauffeur in a sexy French accent. "It is good to have you back again. Will your parents be joining you?"

Lucas hands the chauffeur his suitcase. "No. I'm afraid they are spending their summer in Caicos."

"Ah. That's a shame." The chauffeur takes Hunter's suitcase and Seth's bag. His smile seems forced as he looks between us. "But it looks like you've brought some friends with you. Madam, may I have your bag?"

I blink and look around. "Me?" I ask, realizing that I'm being stupid. Of course he means me.

The chauffeur chuckles while holding out his hand. I drag my suitcase forward, my gaze lowering towards the frayed fabric and the scuffs on the side. I really should have ignored Seth's protests and changed. I most likely look like a hairy greaseball after that flight and now I'm going to be sitting in a fancy limo.

I force a smile as the chauffeur takes the suitcase. "Thank you," I murmur.

"Alright then," says the chauffeur while opening the door. "In you go. I'll handle your bags, and then we'll be on our way. Please help yourself to some champagne."

"Champagne?" I repeat while slowly stepping towards the entrance.

"Party time!" shouts Seth while slipping inside and dumping his body in the far corner.

"There should be some Red Bull, as well," says Lucas. Looking over my shoulder, I see he's talking to Hunter, who simply shrugs and stuffs a croissant into his mouth.

"I'm fine with water."

I take a seat next to Seth while Lucas and Hunter sit across from us. The limo is large and wide with black leather seats I could fall asleep in. Lucas opens the small fridge near him while grabbing several glasses resting on the small table.

"Anyone?" he asks while holding up a glass.

"Me," says Seth while holding out his hand.

Lucas turns to me, but I'm not so sure. My gaze goes to Hunter, knowing he's the only one that can't drink with his new sobriety. I don't want to do anything to mess that up.

But I also want the champagne.

Hunter nods. "Its fine," he says, as if he read my mind. "Go ahead and have a glass. It won't hurt my feelings or anything." He takes another bite from his snack.

Hunter had so many issues earlier this year. First, his mom's cancer relapsed, and he began drinking too much. He was abusing his pain medication for his shoulder. Then, he started doing drugs. How and when he started, I didn't quite know. It wasn't until his mother died that he finally began turning things around for the better. He was beginning to put on weight; beginning to look like the Hunter I knew, the Hunter I fell for.

I don't want to ruin what he's achieved.

Hunter reaches for me, grabbing my hand and giving it a gentle squeeze. "It's not like we're in a club or anything. I won't be triggered."

I nod. My lips twitch into a smile. "Alright. A glass for me, too."

Lucas pours me a glass while I stare out the window, watching the chauffeur come around the limo and getting into the driver's seat. "Everyone ready?" he asks while starting the car.

"Ready!" Seth shouts while holding up his glass, filled with the bubbling liquid.

I hold up my glass while Lucas hands Hunter a water bottle.

"Alright," begins Lucas, holding up his glass and looking between us. "Here's to a fun summer."

"And to my internship," I add.

"And my marathon," Seth pipes in.

"Cheers!" we shout in unison while the chauffeur pulls away from the airport.

***

It takes nearly an hour to arrive at our final destination and I feel both woozy from the lack of sleep and the champagne. My head lulls from side to side while the chauffeur slows the car in front of a beautiful area of

European style apartment complexes. Deep down, I understand why the airport is so far away from everything, but why all the traffic? Don't they have subways? Don't most people cycle?

Apparently not.

I practically roll out of the car as soon as the door is opened. I groan, stretching my arms over my shoulders while looking at what will be our neighborhood for the next seven weeks. The apartments are stained in various colors of white, grey and yellow with detailed balconies jutting out from the sides. Pink flowers cascade down the length of the long bars.

Looking up, I see a couple sitting in one, sharing a bottle of wine. A woman holds a Yorkie in her lap. Large sunglasses cover nearly half her face while she sips at her glass, gazing at something in the distance. Turning around, I gasp seeing the Eiffel Tower in the distance through the alley of beautiful apartment complexes. The park is about a fifteen minute walk away and from where I stand I see many people sitting on blankets, picnicking in front of the beautiful structure.

"This is amazing," I say while clapping my hands together. "We have to go to the tower as soon as we unpack."

"And Notre Dame," adds Hunter while taking my suitcase from the chauffeur.

Seth groans. "I can't believe you two are already talking about site seeing. All I want is a shower and a nap."

I cross my arms and tilt my head to the side while watching Seth trudge from the cobblestone streets onto the sidewalk. "You, of all people, want a nap?"

Seth makes a face. "I couldn't sleep with you elbowing me in my ribs and Thor here snoring in my ear." He juts a thumb in Hunter's direction.

"Again, I offered to pay for first class," says Lucas, taking out several euros from his wallet and paying the chauffeur.

Hunter, Seth, and I scowl in his direction, although in retrospect, first class would have been nice. My seat could have been made into a bed, the movie choices would have been better, and I would have gotten a proper night's sleep. Instead, I'm this mess of a person in the most romantic city on the planet.

"Well, if you think this is amazing," says Lucas, taking out his keys and shoving them into the large door. "Then you should see where we're staying."

My eyes widen and I quickly grab my suitcase before running after Lucas. I'm already imagining a quaint little balcony with flowers overlooking a lovely view of the tower. Maybe even a refrigerator stocked with the best wine in the world and cheese.

We cram into the elevator, and I step from foot to foot, feeling giddy and inpatient as Lucas rambles on. "There's a room for each of us. My parents usually use this place when we're having a get together with friends."

"Your parents have friends?" asks Seth with a raised eyebrow. "I thought they had business associates."

"It's all the same to them," says Lucas. "The grocery store is only about five minutes away and the metro is about ten."

"The metro?" asks Hunter.

Lucas sighs. "It's pretty much what they call the subway here."

The elevator opens, and we follow Lucas out and down the hall until we reach the very end. My eyes widen when he opens the door. I really need to start thinking bigger when it comes to Lucas. The place is on the top floor, with a whole terrace for our use, covered in pink and yellow flowers. Glass doors cover the whole length of the wall, which can be seen as soon as we enter the foyer.

The foyer is tiny, barely big enough for me and Lucas with all our luggage. Seth and Hunter wait outside while I follow Lucas's lead and kick off my shoes. Following him inside, we immediately enter the kitchen. An island stands at the center with four stools surrounding it. The living room is to my right, with a large flat screen TV and a giant sofa. To my left is a dim hallway, which I suppose is where I'll find the rooms. My gaze lingers on the terrace, taking in the unobstructed view of the Eiffel Tower. There are outdoor sofas arranged in a circle and I immediately want to grab a bottle of wine, plop my butt in one of those sofas, and never leave.

"It's perfect," I say, turning my gaze to Lucas and smiling brightly.

"Come," says Lucas, taking my hand and tugging me towards the hallway. "I'll show you your room."

I giggle while he pulls me towards him, enjoying the feel of his hand in mine, while I ignore Hunter and Seth stumbling into the apartment. Their struggles resonate from behind as they try to fit their bodies into the small foyer while dumping their bags.

"This place is fucking great!" Seth shouts from behind.

There are four doors in the narrow hall and when Lucas presses the switch near one, a chandelier lights the hall. The crystals twinkle and glisten, and I can't pull my gaze away from them as Lucas leads me deeper into the apartment.

"So, seeing how you're the lady of the house, I figured this would meet your standards more." Lucas winks at me and opens the door, displaying a large room with a canopy bed draped in white linens. To the right is a large window and on the other side is a small balcony with a round table and chair. The same flowers decorate the table and I'm tempted to ditch the boys and spend the rest of the day sketching while sitting on my very own balcony.

Turning around, I go to thank Lucas, but I stop, my eyes widening in surprise as I push him to the side, seeing a giant tub and vanity behind him. Lights circle the mirror and a pink cushioned chair sits in front of it. I plop myself down and flick my hair over my shoulder, gazing at the mess through the mirror.

But, it doesn't matter.

I'm in Paris with my guys and I'm staying in the most beautiful apartment I had ever seen.

I wish I could stay here forever.

I smile brightly at the reflection in the mirror, watching as Lucas comes up from behind and nuzzles my neck. "Do you like it?" he breathes in my ear.

I shiver, turning towards him and pressing my lips against his. "Very much," I whisper before capturing his mouth once more. His hand tangles in my hair, pulling me closer to him until I'm on the tip of my seat. My arms circle his neck. His fingers run through my hair and I gasp, feeling his tongue intertwine around mine, making my heart stutter. I know I should pull away and start unpacking, yet I'm unable to move from his warmth, and the way his teeth slightly graze mine is making a pit in my stomach.

I pull him closer to me. His feet stumble forward, nearly toppling over me. The chair tips with his weight while my legs spread. A desperate need claws at me, demanding I have him between my legs here and now.

"And what do we have here?"

I open my eyes and turn. My lips slip from Luke and I smile sheepishly up at Seth and Hunter standing in the doorway, both with a knowing look on their faces. "Starting without us, are we?"

Seth grabs his shirt and pulls it over his head, tossing it on my bed before striding towards us. He grabs my shoulders and turns me around. He kisses my forehead and my nose before running his tongue along my bottom lip. I feel Lucas's warmth ebbing away and stop myself from reaching out and grabbing his shirt. Hunter comes to my other side and kisses my neck, sucking lightly at it while stroking my hair. I hear water gushing behind me and end my kiss with Seth to look, finding Lucas kneeling in front of the bath and holding his hand under the water.

"Maybe we should all wash up first?" he says without bothering to turn around.

The man really is amazing. It's like he could read my mind.

"Really, Lucas?" Seth smacks his hands against his legs. "I'm trying to get my rocks off here."

Lucas rolls his eyes while Hunter throws off his shirt. "I could go for a bath," Hunter says with a shrug. "I probably smell like sweat and airplane farts anyway."

I sputter, pressing a hand against my mouth to stifle my giggles. Well, there goes the mood.

Lucas scowls at Hunter. "Really, Hunter? We're in the most romantic city in the world and you're talking about airplane farts?"

Hunter shrugs again. "Hey, man. You know people were farting on that airplane. Especially that guy sitting in front of me. Didn't you-"

Lucas holds up a hand. "Stop."

Seth points a finger at Hunter. "I thought that was you."

Hunter smirks and crosses his arms in front of his broad chest. "Nah, man. You would know if it was me."

"You do have a point," says Seth while stroking his chin.

"Enough fart talk," Lucas says, his tone irritated while he takes my hand and pulls me towards the tub. "After you, my lady," he says gently.

I giggle and unzip my sweater, shrugging out of it before pulling my shirt up and over my head. Hands press into my shoulders and I realize it's Lucas, behind me undoing my bra. His fingers stroke up and down my arms before settling along my hips, dipping into my jeans and stroking the top of my panties.

"You should relax before we go site seeing," he whispers.

It's hard for me to focus on his words when his fingers are unbuttoning my jeans, pulling down my zipper. I feel lips on my neck, finding Seth on my right side, nuzzling my shoulder.

"I guess I can make some room for romance," Seth murmurs.

Hunter comes into my view, stripping his jeans and boxers from his legs and getting into the bath. My eyes gaze longingly at his muscled chest and washboard abs, wanting to run my hands up and down them. Lucas tugs at my jeans while Hunter reaches for me. I push my pants down, kicking them away along with my underwear before stepping into the bathtub and resting myself between Hunter's legs.

I lean back against Hunter, moaning when his fingers slide against my inner thigh. Seth and Lucas kneel on either side of me, stroking up and down my arms. Their hands slowly make their way to my breasts and I suck in air, the sound like a hiss to my ears as they tug and pinch at my nipples. I nuzzle my bottom closer towards Hunter's shaft, enjoying the feeling of the twitching member against my back and Hunter's stifled moans.

Hunter pushes my hair away, pressing kisses against my neck while his fingers continue to tease me. They slide up and down my inner thigh rhythmically. I whimper, jutting myself out, wanting him to thrust his fingers into me. Seth rises from my side, stepping slowly into the tub and crouching in front of me. I watch him through half-open eyes as he licks his lips. His cock is hard and twitching, and I reach for him, running my index finger over the sensitive bit of flesh at the top. He shudders and leans forward, taking a nipple into his mouth.

I cry out as I feel Hunter slide his fingers upwards against my clit at the same time Seth sucks and prods my nipple with his tongue. Out of the corner of my eye, I see Lucas slowly stand, his hand running up and down the length of his hard cock. I lick my lips and open my mouth, watching Lucas step forward. He places his dick in my mouth and I suck on it tenderly, running my tongue up and down his length.

His hisses urge me on, and I suck harder.

I suck like his dick is a tasty lollipop, all for me to enjoy.

"Fuck," Lucas groans, running a hand through his hair while thrusting into his mouth.

I grind my bottom against Hunter's cock. His kisses on my neck grow more desperate. A part of me wonders if there will be hickeys all over my nape when we're done. Another part of me worries what my new boss will think when I come into work with hickeys all over my body.

And then there's a part of me who doesn't give a fuck.

I toss my head back against Hunter's chest, feeling a finger slip inside me while his thumb continues circling around my nub. Lucas's hand grips the bathtub's rim while he continues shoving his dick deeper into my mouth. Seth nibbles on nipple and my legs widen and wrap around his waist, pulling him closer to me.

Lucas's hand slips and he swiftly turns into the side, tumbling into the water, which splashes all over the tiled floor. I quickly sit up and grab Lucas's hand. "Are you alright," I ask.

Lucas laughs, his face a mixture of joy and pleasure. "I'm fine," he rasps between fits of giggles.

"Maybe we should take this to the bed?" Seth suggests while nodding towards my canopy bed behind us.

I nod and watch Seth step out of the tub. He reaches for Lucas, helping him steadily out of the tub. Both men take my hands and I wobble into a standing position. My legs tremble and feel like jelly. Lucas picks me up swiftly and I straddle him, seizing his lips immediately while he carries me to the bed.

He throws me down onto the bed, and I watch him crawl on top of me. His hard shaft rubs against my leg before nestling himself between my legs. I bite my lip against my cries, tossing back my head as his tongue circles around my nipple for a brief, wondrous moment. My legs tighten around him. My whole body tingles with want and need as he continues licking and sucking his way down the length of my body, before his seductive tongue presses against my clit.

My whole body spasms and my hands clutch the bed sheets beneath me. "Lucas," I cry, my head tossing back and forth as he continues to lick me.

I feel more lips on either side of me, and when I open my eyes, I see both Hunter and Seth kissing me, stroking me. I feel so hot, like someone has dipped me in fire; the most pleasurable fire in the entire world.

Lucas lifts his gaze to mine with a mischievous gleam in his eyes. I have no clue what he has planned for me, and I feel the thrill of it coursing through my veins, sending pleasurable shivers all over my body. He nods at Hunter, and before I know it, he's on top of me, kissing me for a brief moment before rolling me over on top of him. His dick rubs against my backside and I have half the mind to sit on it and end this sweet torture, but Lucas grabs my thighs and hoists me towards him until my womanhood is right above his head.

I grip the headboard. My face is probably the color of a cherry with how embarrassed I feel at this position, but all shyness leaves me when I feel Lucas's tongue against my clit and his fingers going in and out of me.

"Do you like that?" Seth whispers in my ear.

I can hardly breathe, let alone speak. "Yes," I rasp.

I feel Hunter move up behind me. His hand swats my bottom and I flinch, biting back a cry while I glance over my shoulder, wondering if he's going to swat me again. My eyes widen, finding him bent over, his hands pushing my butt cheeks apart.

"Hunter, what-"

I pause while I feel his tongue slide against my other hole and my hands tighten on the headboard, feeling even more mortified and turned on in this position. I grind my teeth to keep from shouting out as his tongue continues to poke into me. My grasp becomes white knuckled on the headboard. I can feel myself getting close. My whole body feels so tight, like I'm about to explode into tiny little pieces.

"No more," I say, tapping at Lucas's shoulders and trying to move my butt away from Hunter. "I can't. No more."

Lucas immediately stops and Hunter rises, looking worried.

"Are you alright?" Lucas asks. I move off him and help him sit up in the bed. He strokes my face tenderly, looking me over as if checking for any injuries. My whole body tingles from his touch, wanting and needing more.

"Did we cross a line?" asks Hunter.

"No, no," I say with a smile. "I want you." I kiss Lucas, then Hunter, and finally Seth before I say, "I want you inside me. I don't want to come just yet."

The bros chuckle and Hunter grabs my hips, pressing his large dick against my cheeks. "Why don't you just say so," he says before slamming his dick into my ass.

I pant, arching my back and grabbing his hands while I feel him press in and out of me. With each thrust, I'm unable to stifle my moans, growing louder and longer. I fall forward onto the mattress in front of Lucas with my ass in the air as Hunter thrusts in and out. His movements become more frantic, and I can feel his dick pulsing inside me. Lucas and Seth pump their cocks in front of me, and I push myself up, opening my mouth like a bitch in heat and sliding my tongue along my lips.

Seth shudders and thrusts himself inside my mouth. I suck on him, my tongue circling around his head and playing with him before releasing him and moving to Lucas. As I suck on Lucas, Seth whimpers, poking my cheek with his leaking dick.

"Rachel," Seth murmurs, his voice needy and wanting.

I grab his cock, giving it several strokes before releasing Lucas and sucking on Seth. Lucas strokes my cheek. I find myself unable to keep up with the both of them while Hunter continues to thrust into me, his movements becoming erratic.

"Fuck, Rachel, your ass is so good," Hunter mutters. "So tight. My dick loves it."

I feel myself becoming wet at his words and I grab both Lucas and Seth's dicks and open my mouth wide, trying to take both heads into my mouth at the same time.

Seth tosses his head back in bliss and I hear Lucas's hiss, but it's short lived. Unfortunately, I'm not a porn star and my mouth just isn't that big, but it's the thought that counts, right?

"Fuck, I'm going to come," Hunter shouts, slamming into me deeper and harder.

My head presses into the mattress as he takes me. I'm unable to do anything else but accept him. My whole body feels both pain and pleasure, and I desperately want to cum. I feel Hunter's hands slid over my hips, pressing against my clit.

"Hunter," I moan, my whole body shaking. "So good."

"Fuck, Rachel!" Hunter shouts, and I feel him thrust into me once more, releasing his load into my ass. His hands are tight on my hips, holding me still before pulling out of me.

Seth grabs my shoulder and turns me around, pressing me down onto the bed. "My turn," he says with a smirk while rubbing his dick along my clit. "I'm going to make you feel so fucking good."

Lucas hands him a condom and I writhe against him, watching him rip open the wrapper with his teeth and place the condom on his dick. My legs part for him, waiting anxiously for him to enter me. Lucas sidles next to me and I open my mouth, running my tongue along his leaking dick.

"Are you ready for this?" Seth hisses.

Lucas thrusts into my mouth and all I can do to answer is suck him in and enjoy his hard length in my mouth.

Seth presses inside slowly. It's like torture waiting for him to slam into me, pumping inside me at a painstakingly slow pace. I thrust against him, trying to get him to go faster, harder, but all Seth does is chuckle and press a hand against my hips, deciding the pace for me.

Lucas continues thrusting into my mouth and I nearly gag when I feel him pushing his shaft all the way in, his hard member taking up the entire space. I try to keep calm. I try to focus on sucking and licking while taking both men deep inside me. Lucas's movements become faster, harder and I grab hold of his shaft, trying to slow him down while simultaneously trying to urge Seth to thrust deeper into me.

Lucas strokes my cheek. "You like sucking on my dick, mon cheri?"

I shiver. His voice sounds amazing, deep and sultry. And I love the way he says mon cheri with a French accent.

"You want to suck it all night long?"

I open my mouth, taking him as deep as I can. My tongue slides against his shaft as he pulls out, dipping into his slit briefly before focusing on the twitching, tender bit at his head.

"God, that feels good," Lucas hisses. "You're so good at sucking cock. I bet you love it."

I take him in again. My body writhes against Seth's and I feel him gasping above me. His hand slips between us, pressing against my clit, and my body tightens around his cock, earning a moan. My mouth moves faster against Lucas, while Seth's thrusts quicken. He grinds against me, his fingers tugging at my clit, and I feel my body soaring higher and higher. I suck and thrust, feeling as if my body is being pulled here and there.

Lucas thrusts deep inside me, and I gag, feeling his cock twitch. "So, fucking good," Lucas gasps, his fingers tightening on my hair and dragging me closer to his dick, using my mouth as if it were nothing more than a hole. "I'm gonna..." he cuts himself off, clenching his jaw as his movements become more frantic, more desperate. "I'm going to come," he shouts.

Lucas stills, letting out a shout while I feel his cum filling my mouth. He pulls away from me and I swallow his load. Seth's fingers grab my jaw and he brings my attentions back to him, claiming my lips with his and thrusting his tongue inside. He rolls us over until I'm on top, straddling him. My fingers lace with his and he thrusts upwards into me. Hands come from behind, and I find Hunter behind me, pinching my nipples while Lucas slides his fingers around my clit. I lean into Hunter, my hands tighten on Seth while Lucas claims my lips. I meet each and every one of Seth's thrusts. My cries grow louder, longer, until all I can hear is me screaming as I feel my body cascading over a cliff.

"Rachel, more!" Seth shouts while I grind against him, unable to stop my body from moving and taking what it wants.

I give Seth more. I give him my entire body. Ripping my mouth away from Lucas's, I scream, feeling my whole body shiver as I fly over the edge, cascading down a cliff of bliss. "Yes!" I scream, thrusting against Seth over and over again. "Yes!"

Seth's hold on me tightens, and he stills underneath me. His mouth hangs open as he moans his release. I watch him fall back into the bed, his head lulling from side to side while his hands become slack.

I roll over, finding my place between Seth and Hunter. Lucas reaches over Hunter and strokes my shoulder while I nuzzle against Seth's chest. "That was amazing," I whisper while grabbing Hunter's hand and putting it around my waist.

"So fucking good," Seth rasps with a slight nod, his chin knocking against my head.

"You're the best," says Hunter before kissing my temple.

"Definitely amazing," Lucas yawns.

I know I should get up and begin on my long list of things to do. I want to unpack, get the lay of the land, find out how to get to the Louvre on my own, figure out the whole metro system, and do some site seeing.

But I can't seem to pry my body from the bed. And it's so warm and snuggly here.

My eyes close. "Should we take a little nap?" I yawn.

"Only a small one," says Lucas.

"I'll set the alarm clock," says Seth.

I already hear Hunter's soft snoring from behind, soothing me into a deep sleep.

***

I groan while rubbing at my eyes. The birds are chirping outside. The sun's bright rays seep into the room. I blink away the sleep, feeling like I've slept years rather than an hour. Looking around, I see Hunter still burying his head into my pillow while Lucas stands, grabbing his shirt on the floor and pulling it over his head.

"What time is it?" Seth asks.

Lucas looks at his phone, confusion marring his face. He blinks and rubs his eyes before looking again. "It's two."

"That's funny," I yawn while standing. "Didn't we arrive at two?"

Seth chuckles. "You think we slept a whole day away?"

I frown. "That can't be right. That would mean we," I pause and slowly turn towards Lucas, my heart thumping hard in my chest. "That would mean we," I repeat, thinking of my list and all the things I wanted to get done before my internship begins.

Lucas nods. "We slept twenty-two hours."

"What?" Seth and I shout in unison.

Hunter springs from the bed, looking around the room before settling his wince on me. "Why are you being so loud?"

"We slept twenty-two hours," I say while crossing my arms.

Hunter groans and grabs the pillow, burying his face into it while muttering, "And I want to sleep at least another twenty-two more."

I rub my temples while pacing back and forth. "This is bad," I mutter. "So bad. My list is shot. I won't get everything done in time."

Seth steps into my path and grabs my shoulder. I try to shove myself out of his hold, but he's too strong. "Hey," he says and the adoration in his gaze makes me pause and take a deep breath. "It'll be okay. We'll help you."

"I will not," Hunter mutters from the bed.

Seth rolls his eyes. "I will help you."

"And me," Lucas adds while taking my hand.

"We'll just save the site seeing for later. Besides," Seth says with a shrug, "what do you really need to get done? Some unpacking and a look at how to get to work? That's not such a big deal."

I sigh and tug at my hair. "Well, I need to unpack, pick out what I will wear for tomorrow, figure out how to get to the Louvre and find the staff entrance." I grimace. "Since it's now Tuesday, I have a meeting at four with the manager to have a tour of the museum. Seeing how I have no clue where to go and I'm still in my birthday suit, I doubt I will make that meeting, which will probably put me in a bad situation with-"

"Stop," says Lucas while turning me around. "Breathe. We'll figure it out. It's not that big of a deal. Now get dressed and I'll order some pizza for us."

Hunter bounds out of the bed. "Pizza?" He asks while looking around. "Who said pizza?"

I scoff. "We're in France. We're not going to eat pizza. Surely we can go to some cute café and have something yummy there."

Hunter's eyes widen and he sticks out his bottom lip in a pout. I swear, if he was a dog he would be a golden retriever with his long blonde hair and his docile attitude. I open my mouth, about to insist on the need to eat like the locals and enjoy the culture as much as possible when my stomach stops me, gurgling very loudly.

Hunter, Lucas, and Seth's gazes lower to my stomach and I cover myself, feeling very embarrassed. "Fine, we can order pizza," I grumble while grabbing a t-shirt on the floor and throwing it on. It obviously isn't mine. The fabric ends around my mid-thigh, but it's comfortable and I decide I'm not going to change.

"Alright, pizza it is," says Lucas while typing into his phone.

Seth sighs and shakes his head. "I can't believe we missed a whole day. How is that even possible?"

I dump my body into the chair in front of the vanity, my mouth hanging open at horror at my reflections. Dark bruises cover my neck and I look worse off than I did yesterday with dark bags under my eyes and my curly hair in a tangled mess.

"Hunter, what the hell?" I shout while pointing at my neck.

Hunter smirks and shrugs while rolling out of bed. "I couldn't help myself."

I groan and press my face into my hands. Just great. I'm going to need several tubes of concealer to cover this mess.

Sleeping a whole day, a neck covered in hickeys… I'm not prepared for my internship to begin tomorrow.

2

LUCAS

I pad softly into the kitchen. It's still seven in the morning and I don't want to wake the others. I hear the shower running, wondering briefly if Rachel would like someone joining her for a quickie. Although, after yesterday's little freak out, I doubt she would be up for anything. She was so nervous and scattered brained. Unfortunately, she didn't make it to her tour, and she was even more nervous about how that would look to her intern manager.

If I were her, I wouldn't care.

But then again, we are completely different people.

One thing I really like about Rachel is she's a hard worker. Something I should probably work on. Although, it's hard when everything's been given to you on a silver platter. I've always known what I am supposed to be and what I am supposed to do. Nothing is my choice. Not my studies, not my career, not my future.

Nothing.

Sure, my father allowed me to choose my college. He allowed me to choose my friends, my clothes, and my sport. But it's all fake. It all creates a false illusion that I'm in control, when really it's quite the opposite. Next year is my senior year and I'm expected to take the LSAT and apply to a law school in the east coast where he can sink his talons into me even further.

After next year, I'm officially no longer a free man.

I lean against the counter, frowning at the Eiffel Tower while I let that settle. I can't believe the time has flown by so quickly. It was only yesterday I was moving in with the bros, living essentially in a dump compared to my usual pristine, golden platter life.

And now it's all about to end.

I feel my cell vibrate and pull it out, rolling my eyes when I read: *Dad.* Speak of the devil. He's always calling me when I'm thinking about him. He knew I was going to Paris. He was probably calling to check up on me. I grimace, remembering our conversation on the phone. I had told him I won the writing contest, and he had brushed it off and told me about a position that had just opened up in Samuel's office.

In Paris.

Obviously, I lied and told him that I would take the apprenticeship at Samuel's firm. Now, I'm beginning to think I should have told him the truth. At least then I wouldn't feel so guilty, spending my summer writing and enjoying Paris with Rachel and the bros, not working on my future law career.

Oh, well. It's not like he's ever going to find out. He's too busy to really double check every lie I tell him. It also helps that there's a whole ocean between us. I doubt he'll drop everything to come all the way out here.

Rachel stomps into the kitchen and I smile as I watch her tug at the snug, black pencil skirt while carrying her pink pumps. Her black suit jacket is undone and her curly hair is wet and sticking to her face. A blush sits nicely upon her cheeks and she looks around, appearing frazzled for a moment before groaning in disdain and running back to her room.

So much for not waking the roommates.

She runs back in, carrying a giant black purse. Her whole outfit is black as if she's going to a funeral and not her first art internship.

"Coffee?" I ask while reaching for the cabinets.

"No," Rachel moans, pouting and shoving on her shoes. "I don't have time."

I chuckle and shake my head. "Running late again?"

Rachel's shoulders slump forward. "Don't tease me. I'm already having a hard enough time as it is."

I stride towards her, stopping and taking her chin with my fingers. "You have nothing to worry about. It's all in your head."

"I know. I just want everything to be perfect."

"Well, it won't be." I press my lips against hers and stroke my fingers tenderly against her jaw. She leans into the touch. Before I can deepen the kiss, she pulls away.

"No more," she says with a hard look and a quick wag of her finger. "I have to at least be on time. Tonight." She pokes my nose, then grabs her bag and turns on her heel. My gaze lingers on her ass while she strides towards the door, feeling my cock awaken. The skirt hugs her curves perfectly and all I want to do is grab her hand and throw her onto the table and fuck her senseless.

I grab my cock as the image repeats in my head and wonder if the lube is still where I kept it in the drawer next to the refrigerator.

Rachel turns around and her eyes go to my hand grabbing my cock, currently tenting my sweats. She chuckles and shakes her head. "Tonight," she repeats, the one word filled with so much promise.

I nod, my hand slipping away while I watch the door shut, closing off the wonderful view I have of her ass. I place my hands on the counter, focusing on the coolness and hoping it would calm me down. The sex from the other day was fantastic, and I kept wanting to relive it.

Paris is a wonderful, beautiful place with so much potential for romance. I can't wait to show it to Rachel. Especially, since this might be my only and final summer with her. At least then, we'll always have Paris.

There's a knock on the door and I smile, sauntering towards the door and wondering if Rachel has changed her mind. She doesn't need to be at the Louvre until eight. I'm sure she's realized we have at least fifteen minutes of playtime.

"Did you change your-" I stop, my heart deflating as I see a face in the doorway; one I definitely wasn't expecting.

"Alex," I whisper, watching the blond enter without being invited.

"Lucas," Alex says in greeting while his green eyes search the room. He chuckles and spins around, rubbing the back of his head. "I was expecting a woman to answer the door."

I frown and cross my arms. "The woman just left. What are you doing here?"

I haven't seen Alex since our prep school days when we both lived in New York. After we graduated, we went our separate ways with Alex obviously following the plan his parents set out for him: a prestigious med school followed by an intern program and a position at his father's side. Alex came from old money, just like me, and had family residing all over Europe, particularly in Sweden. When we were boys, we used to come here all the time and get up to mischief.

Now we just send a congratulatory email every now and then.

Alex doesn't answer and continues entering the apartment, starting the espresso machine and pulling out two cups. He's dressed like he just finished a run, but unlike Seth, who will run in anything, Alex wears, from head to toe, Puma. I also know Alex is on his school's track team, and if he's here, I can only suspect he plans to run the marathon, as well.

I scrunch up my nose and peak around the corner, praying Seth remains in his bed. It's unlike him to sleep in so late, but maybe the jet lag and sleeping for twenty-two hours has messed up his internal clock. Knowing Seth, he would attack like a guard dog if he saw a rival here, drinking our coffee, getting all close with me.

Seth could be both possessive and competitive. Two traits I really think he needs to work on.

"Alex, seriously," I begin when the espresso machine finishes and Alex hands me a cup. "What are you doing here? Did you leave anything here?"

Alex downs his espresso in one swig and shakes his head. "It's not that."

"Then what?" I chuckle and rub the back of my head, feeling awkward. It's strange to be around Alex after three years of hardly talking. I would love to catch up if it wasn't for Seth sleeping in the other room. "It's not like you to-"

"Your parents are coming to Paris."

I frown and slowly lower my cup. My heart feels like it's completely disappeared from my body. I'm finding it difficult to breathe let alone continue standing. "What?" I breathe while leaning against the counter.

Alex nods. "I heard them speaking with my parents in the country club. They're coming."

"And why are you telling me?" I cross my arms, straightening myself and jutting out my chin. Everything will be fine. They're probably just coming for the weekend. Probably just taking the private jet and want to meet me for some coffee and some lovely conversation that would likely spiral into a yelling match. "Why should I care?"

Alex smirks and tilts his head to the side. "You tell me. I spoke with Samuel the other day."

I grimace.

"He says you're not interning with him this summer."

I feel whatever hope I had left slowly dissipate and my mind goes into overdrive, wondering how I'll explain the situation to my parents if they do discover my lie. I know whatever I say, Father will be angry and Mother will cry, turning the discussion to her problems and 'oh, why do I have such an ungrateful son'.

Although, why would Alex come all this way to tell me this? It's not the worse news in the world. So what if my parents come and discover that I'm slacking off this summer? It's nothing they're unused to.

"Ok," I nod, ready to be rid of Alex. I cringe when I hear footsteps. I hope it's not Seth. I pray to all the gods in the world that it's not Seth. I don't want to be dealing with him getting all heated and explosive before my parents arrive. "Thanks for the notice. I'll figure it out."

"That's not all."

I groan. "For fuck's sake. What else could there be?"

"Your parents were talking about some contest you won." Alex waves a hand in front of his face, trying to think of the words, but I already know what he's going to say.

"Yeah, I won a writer's contest, go on," I press, wanting him to get to the point.

"Well, your father was pretty angry and said if he found out that you lied to him again, and you're not interning with Samuel," Alex pauses and I wonder if he wants me to give him a drum roll or if he enjoys being this dramatic.

"Well, spit it out," I say, grimacing at how loud my voice is. I glance over my shoulder, hearing more footsteps.

"He's going to cut you off, Lucas."

I blink. "That's it?" I ask, stifling the need to roll my eyes. "That's the big thing you had to tell me."

"It's a pretty big deal, Lucas."

This time I permit myself a much needed eye roll. "Please," I drawl out. "You must be kidding me. You know how many times that man threatens to cut me off?" I chuckle and grab Alex's shoulder, edging him towards the door. "They won't do it. They still need their only son to go to all their stupid little soirees and charity events." I open the door and motion towards the hallway. "If they were to cut me off, they could say goodbye to all that."

Alex shakes his head. "No, they're serious, Lucas."

I scoff. "They're always serious. Doesn't mean they'll do it."

"Your father did mention the parties and the charity events. They say with your piss-poor attitude, it's better that you're not there. It will give you more time to study and focus on better things."

I frown. "What?"

"They will do it, Lucas. That's what you need to get into that thick head of yours." To emphasize his point, Alex knocks his knuckles against my head.

I bat his hands away. I'm still finding this whole situation crazy. Father is actually talking about cutting me off? Essentially disowning me? All because I won a writer's contest and now he's worried I'm wasting my time in Paris enjoying the arts and the brief freedom I have left.

What a fucking asshole.

"Alright, so what should I do?" I ask, watching Alex walk into the hallway. Great, now he wants to leave when I want him to stay and provide me with some advice.

"I don't know, man," calls Alex while walking briskly down the hall. "That's up to you. I just wanted to let you know. Can't see another one of my friends go down."

I grimace, remembering our friend Tom, who went against his parents and got disowned. I don't know what happened to him after that. I haven't thought of him until now and the idea of disappearing off everyone's radar makes a shiver ripple down my spine.

I close the door and walk back into the kitchen, finding Seth downing a cup of espresso. "Was someone here?" He asks while pushing the button for more.

I shake my head, not wanting to explain. This is my battle to fight; my problem to fix. I don't want to involve Rachel and the bros in my family troubles. Nor do I want to admit that I had a potential rival over for espresso.

Well, it's not like I invited him, but I doubt Seth would see it that way.

I release a frustrated sigh while dumping my body into the sofa, wondering what I should do. I take out my cell, flipping through the contacts. Father probably called to inform me of their trip; maybe he wanted to set up a time to meet with Samuel at the office. That definitely seems like him.

I scowl at Samuel's contact.

There are hundreds of things I'd rather do than call Samuel Allen. Skydiving? Cliff jumping? Pick up litter? Clean the toilet? All those options would be better than calling Sam, who was like a brother to my father and an uncle to me. And he is definitely just as much of an asshole as my father.

I flip back to my father's contact, wondering if I should just call him and come clean; let him know I am staying with my friends. That I still intend on taking the

LSAT and going to grad school. Maybe I could just explain I need this down time for myself in order to prepare for all the stress adulthood has waiting for me after graduation.

I groan.

Knowing my father, he will never accept it.

He doesn't care if I'm stressed, exhausted, or burnt out. He doesn't care if I have different ideas and morals than him. No, my father doesn't care at all about me. To him, I'm not a person. I'm just a tool to use in order to raise his status and ego. That's the only reason why he and Mother had me. There's no love in our family, no respect.

I could just continue with my plan; have a fun summer with Rachel and the bros, ignore my parents and pretend Alex was never here. Most likely nothing would happen. Or, Father could cut me off, disown me.

And then what?

I wouldn't be able to stay here. We would all have to find a different apartment, a tinier one that is far away and in a shady area. Seth still wouldn't be able to afford it. We wouldn't be able to get a job to pay for anything since we're on a tourist visa. We would be completely and utterly fucked.

And then what about school? What about our apartment on campus? I would have to take a part-time job. I would most likely lose my SUV. I groan and rise from the sofa, stomping past Hunter and entering my room, slamming the door behind me.

This isn't supposed to happen. Nevertheless, I find my fingers stabbing into my cell, dialing the number. I scowl at my window, at the Eiffel Tower mocking me in the distance. I had hoped to take Rachel there on a date. Just the two of us. A romantic candlelit dinner followed by a kiss at the top of the tower.

"Hello?" comes Samuel's low tone on the other line.

3

HUNTER

It's six in the morning and I twiddle my thumbs while I sit across from my computer on the bed, waiting for Dr. Forrester to answer on the other line. She said we could continue our routinely meetings over Skype. Unfortunately, with the time difference, I have to be up at the crack of dawn.

The screen fades from black to Dr. Forrester's face and I force a smile while she pushes her ear buds into her ears. "Hello, Hunter," she says with a smile. "How are you today?"

"Well, it's not quite day," I say with a small yawn. "I haven't really done anything besides sleep so I don't know if I have much to discuss."

Dr. Forrester chuckles and she bobs her head up and down. "I see the jet lag has gotten to you."

I wince. "Yeah."

"Don't worry, you'll get over it soon enough. Have you had any triggers or upsets?"

I shake my head. "No. The whole gang had some champagne, but I was fine. I just stuck to water." I sigh, lowering my gaze and picking at my fingernails. "I'm just worried I'm going to be a big bother here. Rachel has her internship. Seth is busy prepping for the marathon. Lucas has his whole writing… thing. But I have nothing."

Dr. Forrester's brows push together and she stares back at me with concern. "You don't have nothing. You have your friends, your health-"

"Yeah, but I don't have football. I don't have a job; nothing to keep me busy or take up my time."

Dr. Forrester shrugs. "Maybe that's a good thing. Maybe that will open you up to new hobbies; to something you didn't think you would enjoy."

I purse my lips. "I don't know, Dr. Forrester."

She leans into the screen, her elbows resting on the table while she looks me in the eye. "The thing you should focus on is sticking to a routine, making sure that you have your friends' support so you don't relapse. Maybe try running with your friend or meeting this Rachel after work for coffee. Try taking a French cooking course and attempt remaking the dish at home."

I make a face. "I don't know if that will help. Last time I tried making more than just eggs, I nearly lit the whole kitchen on fire."

She chuckles. "Well, at least it's something. You should do something new. Learning something is always good for you."

An hour later our session ends and I lean back in my chair, staring up at the ceiling while thinking about what Dr. Forrester said. I scrunch up my nose, knowing she's right about learning something new. Problem with that is how do I go about it? Or what if I figure out in the next few days that I absolutely hate Paris? It's not like I'm an art nerd or I love history. I don't know anything about France other than they eat croissants.

What if I ruin Rachel's time here?

I sigh and shake my head, knowing negative thoughts are never going to get me out of this room, let alone the apartment. I hoist my body up and trudge out of the room, feeling my head sway from too much sleep. Lucas brushes past me and I frown, watching him stomp into his room and slam the door.

"What's his deal?" I mutter while entering into the kitchen, finding Seth leaning against the counter and drinking an espresso.

Seth shrugs. "Who knows?"

My eyes linger yearningly on Seth's cup and I point, asking, "Can I have one of those?"

Seth sighs, turning around and working with the espresso machine while I gaze out the long glass window, displaying a beautiful terrace and beyond that the Eiffel Tower. "Did Rachel already leave for her internship?"

I wince, hearing the grinder turn on for a moment, followed by the boiling of water. "I suppose so," Seth shouts over the sound.

"Do you know when she gets off?" I ask while leaning against the island.

Seth taps my shoulder and gives me the coffee. "Probably around four or five."

I take a sip, savoring the bitter taste and instantly wishing I asked for a double. The only way I'm going to get through this whole jet lag thing is by drowning myself in coffee. Seth shifts and I watch him grab his keys, heading for the door.

"Heading out for a run?" I quickly ask, feeling awkward while setting down my cup.

Seth makes a face, resting his hands on his hips. "What's with the interrogation? You know I go for a run every day."

I rub the back of my head, wondering if I should just wait for Rachel to get back or find something else to day. But football involves running. It wouldn't be so strange to pick it up with Seth and it would give me a morning routine I could stick to for the next few days.

I shrug, knowing I had nothing to lose by simply asking. "I was just wondering if I could join you. That ok?"

Seth's face contorts into a mixture of annoyance and intrigue. I have no clue what's he going to say. I know he used to go running with Rachel. I don't know if they went running together anymore given I was pretty much gone last semester, either out partying or at my dad's.

"Okay," Seth finally says after several minutes of me watching him, waiting. "But I need to train for the marathon."

I nod and quickly turn on my heel to change.

"You have two minutes and then I'm leaving!" Seth calls after me as I rush into my room. I strip down to my underwear and grab whatever shorts and t-shirt are close to me. I hear Seth's footsteps and scramble for my shoes, reaching for my keys on the nightstand before running out. I hear the door open and quickly race after him, shoving the door open. Seth is nearly to the staircase, stretching his arms over his shoulders as he waits impatiently for me.

I stop in front of him and he shoves a finger in my face. "If you can't keep up, that's on you," he says while taking the first steps down. "I gotta win this marathon for coach."

I nod and follow him down. "Fair enough."

We walk down the staircase in silence and I watch Seth stretching his arms over his head, tilting his neck from side to side. As we reach the landing, he lifts one leg behind him, grabbing the ankle and stretching. I copy his movements, wondering why this is the first time I've gone running with Seth. I think, when we first hung out, I would go with him, but the guy was too fast and I couldn't quite keep up.

I make a face. It's most likely going to be the same this time.

Seth shoves the door open and as soon as we are out on the sidewalk, he's running towards the Eiffel Tower. I pick up my pace, sidling up next to him. It's slow, which I'm thankful for, given that I am a little out of shape from spending the last several months either doing drugs and drinking or going to therapy. My physical therapy for my shoulder has helped me keep a bit of my figure, but otherwise I feel like I've let me body go compared to how it once looked. I'm a bit thinner. My muscles are there, yet I'm not as strong as I once was.

I guess I could focus on that this summer. Getting back into shape, feeling more confident in my own skin.

As soon as we reach the Eiffel Tower Park, Seth picks up the pace. I grind my teeth, urging my body forward. My arms pump at my sides and my hands fist, fighting through the need to stop. I concentrate on my breathing, and the trees surrounding us, shaped into large green cubes. I dodge other runners, chatting easily with their friends in French. I hear a bit of English, yet it's hard to focus on anything but the burn in my muscles.

This is probably exactly what I need.

As soon as that thought enters my mind, Seth surges forward and I'm scrambling to keep up. My breathing rasps, my fists tighten and I feel a stitch forming in my left side. There's no way I can run that fast. Maybe if it's for a minute or two, but I doubt Seth had a couple minutes in mind. I slow my pace until I'm no longer running, but standing, heaved over, and trying to regain my breath. Seth is already several feet ahead of me, the distance growing more and more with each passing second.

Well, there goes that plan.

With a groan, I straighten myself and stumble forward. I breathe in deep, closing my eyes and enjoying the sun on my face and the wind whipping through my hair. I had forgotten to tie it back in my attempts to catch up to Seth. Moving forward, I walk briskly, knowing I can still run in the park, I'll just have to do it at my own pace and rhythm.

Stretching my arms over my head, I practice the exercises my physical therapist gave me for my shoulder. It's still stiff and at times and I'm unable to lift my arm more than eye level, but it's better than before. The pain isn't as bad.

I continue walking, taking in the people running through the park. There's a group of people near a tree, standing around a large picnic blanket. Several girls are sitting while smoking, passing round a bottle of liquor. They laugh and sway against each other. It must be a party still continuing from last night.

My hands shake and I swallow as memories flood me. I try to look away, focus on the scenery, urge myself back into a run, but I can't pull myself away. I remember the feeling of the bottle in my hand, downing the burning liquid while Mille, Drew, and Jerry laugh around me. Millie holds onto my arm, pressing her large breasts against me, trying to lead me into another room. I remember Drew and Jerry tugging me into a bathroom, a white substance on the toilet.

My teeth grind and I feel myself shaking as I remember Jerry swinging his bat at me. *"Where's our money, Hunter?"*

A chill ripples through my spine, leaving me cold. I step back, away from the group of kids and quickly turn around. I gasp, holding up my arms as Seth rams into me. I brace myself, feeling him collide with my body, but thankfully I'm a heavy dude and remain rooted to the pavement. Seth groans, stumbling backwards onto his ass and he lies there for a moment, his chest heaving while he regains his breath.

"What the fuck, Hunter?" He rasps while pushing himself up. "You should know better than to step out in front of someone!"

I give him my hand, pulling him to his feet. "Sorry," I murmur, looking away. I feel bad. I should know better. I always hate it when someone interrupts my workouts, or doesn't know the rules of the gym. The most important one being, don't get in my way.

"I could have gotten seriously injured."

I nod. "I know. I…" I wince, still feeling cold all over as I recall throwing my phone into the snow back in Aurora; ignoring the call from my father, telling me Mom had passed away. Tears prickle my eyes and I wipe them away, hoping Seth doesn't notice. "I wasn't thinking," I quickly say.

"Obviously."

"You know what, I'm just going to go," I say, turning on my heel. I can't stand myself right now. I can't stand these memories, haunting me all the time. I'm a pain not only to myself, but my friends and family.

"No, Hunter," I hear Seth shout from behind. "Come back. I didn't mean it like-"

I raise a hand, waving it slightly while shouting, "It is fine." I sniff and I feel my heart twinge with pain once more. I don't know what has come over me. I don't know what it is that triggered me. The memories? Nearly hurting Seth? The group of kids partying away?

I could really use a drink right now.

I press my palms into my eyes and shake my head. No, I tell myself.

Lucas most likely has wine and beer in the fridge, that dark voice whispers in the back of my head.

I grit my teeth, feeling the urge to give in, but I know I can't. I know I need to fight it, keep busy.

Stay out of the apartment.

I slow my walk back home, trying to make a game plan in my head to keep myself from Lucas's refrigerator. I already made Rachel and the bros worry about me last several months. I couldn't do that now. We're in a completely different country for one. How would they even be able to find me? Help me?

No, I need to keep busy. I'll take a shower, and wander around to get the lay of the land. I nod to myself, probably looking like an insane person, but I don't care. Afterwards, I'll meet Rachel at the Louvre and we can go for coffee.

Yeah, I smile to myself. That sounds good. I just need to keep myself busy for the next seven hours.

4

SETH

I watch Hunter go, feeling guilty for the way I treated him. It wasn't that bad. I'm just being an asshole, because I'm stressed out about the marathon. I sigh, watching him go and wondering if I should chase after him. The dude was going through a lot. With last semester being an absolute shit show and then his mom dying.

I should be nicer to him.

Although, walking on eggshells has never been in my skillset. And I don't think it ever will be. Maybe he needs some time. I'll try tomorrow; see if he wants to go running again. I turn around, my eyes finding a group of kids drinking and smoking. I bite my lip, realizing why Hunter had looked so out of it.

I really am an asshole.

I don't quite understand therapy or triggers, however I know he's still haunted by memories. I should have known. It's not the first time he's had that strange look in his eye, like he's seen a ghost.

I know I should go after him, but at the same time I need to train for the marathon. I shake my head at myself. He will probably be fine. I will talk to him after my run and maybe we can go site seeing later.

With that, I urge my body forward, starting off slow once more to get my muscles adjusted to the speed. The marathon is only four weeks away. I've been training every day for several hours, either by running or weight training, trying to get my muscles ready. Coach warned me not to overdo it and he was the only reason I was able to go on this trip with Rachel.

I try to concentrate on the beauty of France rather than the anxiety burning through me, making my shoulders tense and my heart skittish. The Eiffel Tower is beautiful and massive. The trees are neatly clipped and there's so much greenery for being in the capital of France. Yet, no matter how much I try to concentrate on the beautiful scenery, my thoughts keep being pulled towards the marathon.

If I don't win, I have to pay back all that money. I already know I won't be able to. Coming from a poor family and only being able to go to school due to my track scholarship, makes everything a bit difficult for me. I'm not Lucas. I'm not Hunter. I can't make a phone call and be given money in two seconds.

I have to win. There's no other way.

"Ah, why isn't it the great Seth Garcia," I hear an annoying voice coming up from behind.

The man sidles close to me and I scowl when I meet a familiar green gaze, staring back at me with a mischievous glint in his eyes.

Alex fucking Goode.

My number one rival. We've only met in one or two track meets. However, those short meetings were enough for me to make up my mind. I hate the guy. Absolutely loathe him with my entire heart and soul. Whenever, Alex fucking Goode is around, nothing good is about to happen. He has stolen from me at least two trophies, beating my running score by mere milliseconds and I swear the bastard does it on purpose.

He enjoys toying with me.

And he's doing it now.

He winks at me and ups his pace. I up mine. I'm not going to let him get the best of me. I can run just as fast as him.

"I didn't know you could run outside the states."

My scowl darkens. "I can pretty much run anywhere I want, Goode."

Alex chuckles, tossing back his head easily. His pace quickens and for a brief moment he's ahead of me. Very brief. Super brief. I sidle up next to him, ignoring the burning in my lungs.

"Don't tell me they're letting you run in the Paris marathon," he looks me up and down, his shrewd eyes narrowing on my Walmart shorts and shirt. The most expensive item I'm wearing are my Brooks, which I got discounted from my running store.

"Yes, they're letting me run in the fucking marathon," I gasp, increasing my pace and frowning when Alex easily matches it. "I'm a track star after all."

Alex scoffs and I feel my blood boil, hating the very sound of his voice. My gaze rakes over him, scowling at his strong arms and his long legs. Of course it's easy for him to run ahead of me. He has fucking longer legs.

"Track star?" Alex raises an eyebrow. "You?"

I grit my teeth. I've had enough of this stupid conversation. I pump my arms harder, trying to push myself ahead so I can finally be rid of him. Yet, the bastard still catches up. We both gasp, racing each other around the park, swerving past mothers pushing their baby carriages and people walking idly.

Every time he gets ahead I push harder. Every time I get ahead, it lasts only brief seconds and then he is right there, racing me around the corner. My lungs burn and I feel my muscles shake with the effort, but I'm not going to let this rich bastard beat me.

I'm not going to let anyone beat me.

Sweat drips down my face and into my eyes, blurring my vision. I shake my head. My hair is wet from the effort. The sun is shining higher and brighter. I don't know how long we've been running like this, egging each other on, refusing to give up the fight, but I feel like I'm nearly to my breaking point.

Which pisses me off.

I glance at Alex. His cheeks are reddened. His eyes are focused ahead, his mouth slightly parted, sucking in air desperately. He must be close to giving up, I tell myself. He's going to give up. I know it. I just need to keep-

I gasp, feeling a stitch form in my side and my body immediately slows. My hands fist, watching Alex leaving me behind. I wait for him to glance over his shoulder, wink at me, and maybe stick out his tongue. Instead, he turns back around, smiling wickedly while running back to me. His pace slows to a jog.

"I guess I should wish you good luck, Garcia," he says.

My jaw clenches. My whole body shakes to keep myself from punching him in the nose.

"Break a leg," he says, winking at me before quickly turning around and racing down the pavement.

I stifle the need to shout and scream. I don't think I can run any longer. My whole body feels like I've been run over by a semi-truck. I stumble back towards the apartment, trying to contain my rage, trying to keep calm.

But I can't.

Knowing Alex Goode is here, means that he will be racing in the marathon, as well. And the bastard is good. Too good, which is ironic given his last name. I knew this was going to be hard when I first signed up and promised coach the trophy.

I didn't think it was going to be this hard.

I trudge into the apartment complex, my eyes glancing at the elevator for a moment. I'm so tired, but I know I need to work harder; get my body into the best shape it's ever going to be. So, I take the stairs, dreading each and every step as I pull myself up by using the banister. I groan, feeling my muscles quiver and shake with the movement. I definitely pushed myself too hard.

No, I think as I make the landing, looking down the hall in the direction of Lucas's apartment. It's not that I pushed myself too hard. I'm under prepared. If runners like Alex are going to be in the race, then I need to be pushing myself even harder.

I stumble down the hallway, already thinking of what I need to do. I'll have to stay away from beer for a while. Alcohol will put on weight, which will make me slower. I'll need to eat leaner meat, stick to vegetables, possibly run twice a day.

I lean against the door while I search for my keys. Site seeing with Hunter is definitely out. The only thing I can think of is sinking my swollen muscles into Rachel's tub and taking a very long nap in my bed.

Possibly her bed.

She won't mind.

I groan when I finally get the keys into the door, dropping them onto the floor while kicking the doors closed. "Hunter," I rasp, grimacing at the pain in my throat while I strip off my clothes.

No one answers.

My hands slide against the walls, trying to keep myself upright as I walk into Rachel's room and start the tub. "Hunter?" I call again, wondering if he's alright.

Once again no one answers. Not even Lucas.

I ease my body into the hot water, hissing in both pain in joy as I feel my muscles relax. I lean my head back against the headrest and decide my talk with Hunter will just have to wait. My eyes shut, and I imagine myself crossing the finish line, my body slamming into the banner with Alex just a few feet behind me. I imagine his face, a mixture of anger and horror and a small smile graces my lips.

5

RACHEL

I tug at my pencil skirt, trying to pull it down after I finish walking towards the museum. I take a moment to gaze up at the pyramid made from glass. Architecturally speaking, the building is extraordinary. I could gaze at it for hours. The palace surrounding it makes me want to return to my art history books, peak inside and reread all the facts about the paintings and the artists residing within its premises.

Entering the pyramid, I flash a badge I received in a packet about a week ago, which had also contained information on the French culture and some tips and tricks on how to travel around the city. The guard nods at me, allowing me to walk past the long line of tourists already forming outside the museum.

I guess it's good to get here early.

Thankfully, I'll be working amongst the beautiful paintings for the rest of the summer and won't need to worry about lines. At least for the Louvre. I'm sure there were plenty of other lines waiting for me.

I frown while I stride through the museum, my heels clacking on the polished floor. I really wish I would have gotten at least some site seeing out of the way. I feel like I completely wasted my time, and I'm worried what my boss will think since I missed out on the yesterday's meeting. I'm sure my manager already thinks the worst of me. I know I would.

I inwardly groan and stare down at my attire. Maybe I should have worn flats. I'm probably going to be on my feet all day. I scowl at my skirt, wishing it was a bit longer. In my attempts to look like a stylish Parisian, I ended up looking like an awkward American girl, who has no clue what she's doing in a place like this.

My gaze lifts as I hear the clacking of heels heading towards me. In front of me, I see a petite older woman, looking to be in her late thirties or early forties, with blond hair in a neat bun at the top of her head. Her dark eyes zero in on me. Her dark-rimmed glasses hang low on her nose. I smile brightly, happy to see she's also wearing a pencil skirt and blazer combination just like me. I guess I chose correctly. A small red scarf is tied pristinely around her neck, making me want to go shopping later.

The woman stops a foot from me, looking me up and down for a moment before saying, "You must be Rachel Miller."

I nod and hold out my hand, excitement making my movements jerky. Her English is absolutely perfect with only a slight French accent. "Yes, I am. It's a pleasure to meet you Mrs. Arnaud."

"Dr. Arnaud," the woman corrects me, taking my hand gently and shaking it so quickly I hardly felt her touch at all. "I didn't go to school all those years to be called Mrs."

"Oh." My hand lowers and I instantly want to crawl under one of those paintings hanging on the wall and hide from embarrassment. "I'm so sorry. I didn't mean-"

"You didn't come to the meeting yesterday," Dr. Arnaud says while turning round. I rush after her, not knowing how she is able to walk so briskly and gracefully with heels on.

"Yes, I was having some problems with jet lag. Unfortunately, I fell asleep and woke up 22 hours later." I chuckle awkwardly, hoping she will understand. Given her job, I'm sure she travels all the time and knows how it can affect the body.

"Excuses won't get you anywhere," she says, making me feel even more mortified and angry with myself.

She's right. They won't. My gaze lowers to the floor as I follow her while worry eats at me, making my stomach churn and my fingers pick at one another. I mentally kick myself, knowing I should have just busted my butt and gone to the meeting. Then I wouldn't feel so guilty now.

"Unfortunately, I won't have time to give you a tour of the museum now," says Dr. Arnaud while she turns around. I watch her hand gesture towards a grey door. "You'll just have to make do. This is where you can put your things." Her gaze lowers to my feet as I keep shifting my weight back and forth. "Heels aren't a requirement. You'll be doing a lot of walking here."

Crap. I should have known.

Dr. Arnaud smiles thinly. "Just try not to wear tennis shoes."

I nod quickly. "Of course. I will come better prepared tomorrow."

Dr. Arnaud doesn't say anything, yet I can see the doubt glimmer in her gaze. She opens her mouth, about to say something, when I see a familiar figure enter from behind. A girl about my age, with long brown hair, still wet most likely from her shower, wearing a simple black dress and black flats.

"I'm here!" She gasps while running towards us, her eyes widening on me for a moment. "What are you doing here?"

I inwardly groan, wanting to smack my face, wanting to look up at the ceiling and ask God, why? Why is Lauren of all people here, in Paris, attending the same internship program? Instead, I force a smile, my hand on my purse tightening while I say, "I could ask you the same thing."

"You're late," Dr. Arnaud says, irritation laced in her tone. She purses her lips while she stares at Lauren sternly.

If I was still friends with Lauren, I would feel bad for her. I wouldn't want that look set on me in a million years. I would probably melt to the floor and never be whole again. Lauren visibly shrivels in front of Dr. Arnaud and she lowers her gaze, a slight blush setting into her cheeks. "I'm sorry, my alarm clock didn't go off."

Dr. Arnaud clucks her tongue. Her gaze lifts to the ceiling for a moment before shaking her head. "Excuses, excuses, excuses," she sighs and pinches the bridge of her nose. "Whatever am I going to do with the both of you?"

Lauren and I glance at each other for a moment before Dr. Arnaud continues, "Just put your things in the closet and meet me in the main lobby. Maybe I can find something useful for the both of you to do."

I grimace, watching Dr. Arnaud stride down the hall, feeling like this whole thing was a bad idea from the start. Sure, Mr. Brown believes in me, which is great, but maybe his perception is a bit off. Maybe I'm not cut out for this kind of work.

I mean, I've already made a mess of things.

And Lauren, of all people, is here.

"Seriously, what are you doing here?" Lauren whispers harshly while brushing past me. She uses her badge to open the door and tosses her backpack onto the small table in the middle of the room, which is pretty much the size of a closet with space only for two chairs. Papers are scattered on the table, and I wonder if anyone could possibly use this place as a small office.

If they do, they must never see the sunlight.

I really hope Dr. Arnaud doesn't expect me and Lauren to use this space. We'll probably end up killing each other within the hour.

"I applied," I say simply, setting my bag down next to hers before closing the door. "What are you doing here? I didn't think you were interesting in drawing."

Lauren scoffs while crossing her arms. "Because I'm an art student and this," she gestures towards the whole museum around us, "is an art position, available for all artists." She smiles bitterly and tilts her head to the side. "Or did you forget that there are other creators besides you?"

"What is that supposed to-"

Lauren groans. "Ugh, I'm done talking to you." She raises a hand in front of her, as if she's suddenly the speaking police holding up a giant stop sign. "Stay away from me, Rachel."

"Fine," I say while crossing my arms, watching her leave before quickly realizing that we are going in the same direction. If she doesn't want to talk to me, that's perfectly fine. I don't want to talk to her. I can avoid her. It's not like we'll be spending our entire time together.

And I'm not going to let Lauren ruin my time in Paris.

***

I sit near the edge of the water near the Louvre Pyramid, hearing the splashing of the fountain behind me. Grimacing, I stuff my face with the small baguette sandwich I had prepared for myself in the morning. I sniff, trying to keep my tears for myself. This is my one chance in a lifetime. This is an amazing opportunity.

And here I am, sitting outside the museum, close to bawling my eyes out because of an ex-friend who I should ignore.

Although, ignoring Lauren is easier said than done.

Once again, I mentally kick myself for not going to the meeting yesterday. I had no clue where anything was, or what to do, and of course, Dr. Arnaud was irritated with me for asking so many questions. Questions, which would have easily been answered yesterday. Lauren, of course, was smirking here and there, being rude whenever she had the chance.

"The Mona Lisa is the other way," I remember her saying when I was running down the hall in my heels, trying to fix the display of the paintings before the tourists were permitted inside. It's not like I hated her giving me directions. I hated that she gave me the wrong set of directions. I had actually been going the right way towards the Mona Lisa, but Lauren sent me on a wild goose chase, which left me absolutely lost. When I finally found the painting, Dr. Arnaud had been standing in front of it, tapping her shoe so ferociously I thought it was going to fly off and kick me in the face.

"Miss. Miller, I would really appreciate it if you would tend to your duties rather than gallivanting off," Dr. Arnaud had said. "I run a tight schedule and I can't be waiting around for you to finally show your face."

So much for making a good first impression, I think with a sniff, quickly wiping my eyes.

Just thinking about all the running makes me groan and I turn my attentions to my swollen feet. I point them, trying to stretch the tops and release the tension in my soles before wiggling my red and bruised toes. Angry welts have formed on the tops of my toes while my little one has a large blister threatening to burst. I'm definitely not wearing these shoes tomorrow.

I check the time on my watch, seeing that it's nearly four. I was sent out for a fifteen minute break after working all the way through lunch. Hopefully, not every day would be like this. I would get very skinny pretty quickly. Maybe I should start eating bigger breakfasts?

I sigh and shove on my shoes, hissing and grimacing when I put weight on my feet. I hold my head high, trying to remain calm and collected as I reenter the pyramid, flashing my badge towards the guard. Lauren and Dr. Arnaud are standing near the closet with our bags. Arnaud's hands are crossed, and she looks irritated as she stares down at Lauren.

"Ah, Miss Miller, you're finally here."

I want to tell her I was finally taking my lunch break, but I bite my tongue, knowing the only way to win bees is with honey. Forcing a smile, I murmur, "Sorry," and wait for her to give us her final farewells. Seeing how work is supposed to end at four, I assume she has nothing more for us to attend to.

"I was just telling Lauren, we need to attend to the records, but apparently she has other plans."

Lauren winces, glancing at me before sliding her gaze back to Dr. Arnaud. "I'm so sorry. I thought the internship ended at four every day."

My brows furrow and I turn toward the doctor. "I thought the same."

Dr. Arnaud sighs and shakes her head. "I swear, every year they sound more and more bratty little kids," she mutters.

I swallow, trying to fight the nerve to either cry or scream. I have been working my bottom off all day, running from one side to the museum to the other; helping with the documents, cleaning the portraits, rewriting the descriptions, helping tourists find their way around when I had no clue what I was talking about.

Now, now, Rachel, I admonish myself, *you are in Paris. You have a freaking internship in Paris. Stop acting like a spoiled little girl.*

"Well, I suppose I can let you go early today, if you have plans," says Dr. Arnaud while placing her hands behind her. "But tomorrow, know that you are here until five. And," she turns to Lauren, her gaze narrowing, "try to be on time."

Lauren nods so sharply, I expect her neck to snap. "Yes, of course, Dr. Arnaud."

Dr. Arnaud gives us one more hard look before turning down the hall, leaving Lauren and I alone, in the lobby. Well, I guess, not alone, since there are so many tourists, but more alone that we've been since the morning.

Lauren scowls in my direction before huffing and turning on her heel. "I can't believe I have to spend my whole summer with you," she calls while she strides briskly away.

I glare at her back, stalking towards her since it's the only way out of this building. "I thought we weren't talking to each other."

Lauren rolls her eyes.

"And what was with giving me the wrong directions to the Mona Lisa?" I stumble in my heels, finding any brief movement in my shoes excruciatingly painful. "That was complete bullshit."

Lauren laughs bitterly and shoves open the door. "You would've known if you were here yesterday."

She does have a point, but there's no way I'm going to tell her that. "Like you're any better than me," I say while trudging out into the sun, holding a hand up to my face to protect my eyes from the rays. "You were late today."

Lauren spins around, her face contorted into a mixture of frustration and rage. "By like five minutes. At least I didn't skip a whole meeting, because I was dilly-dallying around."

"I was not dilly-dallying around!" I shout while throwing my hands into the air. I feel the stairs of several tourists watching us and quickly lower my hands, my face either heating due to the summer's rays or embarrassment. Perhaps both.

"Oh, really," says Lauren while placing her hands on her hips and giving me a knowing look. "Then what were you doing, Rachel?"

I open my mouth, not knowing exactly what to tell her. I can't tell her I brought the bros, knowing what she would think; that I'm a whore, that I spread my legs for anyone. I know she thinks those things about me. It's the reason why our friendship fell apart. The reason why she is taking Josh's side in the whole sexual harassment case I reported to the police several months ago. I can tell her it was jet lag, that I took a nap and didn't wake up until the next day.

It could happen to anyone.

Just when I'm about to say that very thing, I see a familiar face appear behind Lauren, looking around aimlessly before settling his blue eyes on me. His lips twitch upwards into a bright smile and he raises his hand, waving at me while walking forward.

"Rachel!" Hunter shouts. The wind whips his hair around and he quickly pushes the locks back.

I grimace, watching Lauren turn around and give a curt nod. She turns back to me, smiling bitterly before saying, "I see." She looks me up and down with a sneer. "So that's who you were doing yesterday."

My shoulders slump and I feel myself deflate, unable to fight her any longer. I know I shouldn't apologize. I haven't done anything wrong. I can date whomever I want. I can be with my guys if I want. We're happy together and who cares what the world thinks.

Yet, somehow, as Lauren continues staring at me, I feel like she wants an apology from me and I don't understand why. I haven't done anything to her. If anything, the only one who is suffering from my actions is Josh, but that's because I have decided I will never let him attack another woman ever again.

Lauren shakes her head and stalks past me. I let her go, not wanting to continue whatever it is we were doing. She can be upset if she wants. Right now, all I want is a bear hug from my Hunter and a very large coffee.

Or ice cream.

Actually, both would really be great.

"Who was that?" Hunter asks while watching Lauren swerve around a group of people. "I know her from somewhere."

I nod. "That's Lauren. You know her."

Hunter shrugs and faces me, taking my hand and lacing his fingers with mine. He leads me through the courtyard, towards a street filled with shops and cafes. "How was your first day of work?" He asks while taking me towards a cafe with several chairs sitting outside. My nose wrinkles when we pass several men smoking cigarettes while drinking their espresso and I'm happy when we're able to find a small table with two seats near the back of the outdoor seating.

"Absolutely terrible," I say while dumping my body into the metal chair. I take off my shoes, not caring if it's sanitary or if it will offend anyone. I can't have these heels on my feet any longer. Not when I know I will have to walk in them towards the metro.

Hunter leans towards me, brushing my hair behind my ear and staring back at me with such adoration in his eyes. I lean into his touch, placing my hand against his. "Tell me all about it," he says softly.

I groan and pull away. "I don't want to obsess about it." I sigh and look around, wondering where the waiter is. "Also, I don't want to complain. I'm sure it will get better after some time. I'm just… adjusting."

A waiter comes out of the main restaurant and I stare at him, willing him to meet my gaze and come over to deliver me the sumptuous goodness of coffee. I watch his eyes lift and when they meet mine, he immediately returns inside the cafe. My hands fist and I breathe in deeply, telling myself to be patient. All good things will come in time.

"How was your day?" I ask while staring at the cafe's doors unblinkingly, silently begging the waiter to return and take my order.

Hunter shrugs. "I didn't really do much. Met with Dr. Forrester this morning, went on a run with Seth."

My brows furrow and I glance at Hunter, wondering why he would ever want to join Seth on a run. "Why did you do that?" I ask, unable to hold myself back. "Were you wanting to be tortured?"

Hunter laughs and I find my foul mood drifting away. I watch him run his fingers through his hair. He looks better than before; clean, with more color in his face. His arms and chest are thicker than before, but not as thick as he used to be. I can tell he's improving, and it makes me feel like things are going back to what they once were.

Of course, things will always be different, but I like this new Hunter.

"Dr. Forrester told me to try new things, get new hobbies so I can find a routine here."

I clap my hands together, excitement making me giddy. "You should try an art class."

I watch Hunter's nose scrunch upwards and he shakes his head. "Nah, I don't think that's for me."

I roll my eyes. "Because you haven't tried it, yet."

"Why try it when I know I'm going to suck?"

I grab his hand and pull him towards me. "Just try it. So what if you suck? It will give you something to do. You can learn about the artists. Check out the museums."

Hunter nods, yet I can tell he isn't interested.

"It will give you something to do and something for us to talk about."

A light glimmers in Hunter's eye and I can see that there is some intrigue. Perhaps he likes knowing we will have something in common if he takes an art class.

"I don't know," Hunter says awkwardly while rubbing the back of his. "I still think I'll be terrible. I'm not good at… much. I'm not good with my hands."

I waggle my eyebrows. "I completely disagree."

Hunter tosses back his head and laughs, covering his mouth with one hand. I turn, catching the gaze of the waiter and raise my hand while Hunter tries to control his giggles.

"Yes, what can I get you?" The waiter says in a thick accent.

"Two very large coffees," I say. The waiter doesn't write down my order, but I figure it's just coffee. What's the point in wasting paper?

"Anyway," I continue, "I think it would be good for you. It's something new, like your therapist wants. And, art can help you convey your feelings."

Hunter makes a face. "I don't like feelings."

"I know." I pat his hand. "But you can't keep everything bottled up inside forever. Or else it will explode into a huge, goopy mess neither of us want to clean up."

Hunter waggles his eyebrows and I laugh, knowing exactly what kind of "goopy mess" he's thinking of.

The waiter returns, placing two tiny cups in front of us. I open my mouth, holding up a finger, yet he is already gone, serving another customer. My bottom lip sticks out as I turn my gaze down at the tiniest cup of coffee I've ever seen.

I'm in Paris, I remind myself. One of the most amazing cities in Europe.

I need to stop comparing things to back home and be happy with what I have.

I take a sip and grimace at the strong bitterness that assaults my tongue.

6

LUCAS

I sit in the blue velvet chair, watching men and women walk by, dressed in black and navy suits. I'm not quite dressed to impress with my dark denim jeans and my button-down shirt, but I don't want to seem desperate in front of Samuel. I don't need him thinking that he has the upper hand. The guy could be manipulative. That's one thing I remembered about Samuel Allen. It's also the one thing that made him an exceptional lawyer. He's adept at manipulating the law to get what he wants.

I don't want to be on his bad side.

The receptionist catches my gaze and offers me a small smile. Her eyelashes flutter and I inhale deeply, feeling both frustrated and worried while I look away. The old Lucas would have been leaning against her desk, wondering how to get her out of her skirt, probably inviting her for some mid-afternoon cocktails. Yet, all I can think about is Rachel and my ruined summer plans with her.

I frown, staring at the blue seat in front of me. I should have planned this better, found some internship that would have made them happy and then bailed half way through it. Now, I'm going to have to readjust everything.

I lean back in the chair, gazing up at the chandelier hanging above me, scowling at how gaudy this office is. The only thing I ask for, I pray to the chandelier, the only thing I must do, is take Rachel to the top of the Eiffel Tower. It's one of the most romantic things any couple could do together, and I want that with Rachel.

My heart beats in my chest and I feel my face heat at the thought of her in that tight, black pencil skirt. I don't know what's wrong with me. I've never felt this way about any girl in my life. Ever. But, I feel like I am really falling for her.

I don't want my family ruining this for me.

"Ah, Lucas Brent," I inhale deeply at the familiar sound of Samuel's voice. "I'm so glad you came."

Showtime, I tell myself, quickly rising and pasting on my most charming smile. I take his offered hand, giving it a firm shake while looking him in the eye. "Likewise."

Samuel Allen hasn't changed much since my prep school days, when I often found him drinking martinis with my parents while watching his daughters playing tennis. Thinking of them now, I wonder how they are doing. I know the twins, Danielle and Lucy Allen, were accepted into a fancy school abroad, but I didn't know which. Like Tom, they have appeared to be gone without a trace. I'm tempted to ask Samuel, yet I don't know if it's a sore subject.

The twins had looked more like Samuel, than their mother with thick, curly red hair and freckles. However, rather than blue eyes, Samuel's are green and his red hair is graying at the sides as well as in his beard. His family has a Scottish background. I have no clue where they obtained their money or why Samuel decided to set up his law firm in Paris rather than New York, where he grew up. In fact, I don't know much about the man other than he's my father's friend; meaning I don't trust him whatsoever.

"Come," says Samuel while gesturing towards a hall. "Let's meet in my office. I should have a pretty good brandy we can share. Do you like brandy? Your father likes brandy."

"I like it well enough," I say while following him through the hall.

Samuel chuckles, the sound grating on my nerves. "I suppose kids your age like any sort of alcohol. One of these days, you'll only be able to drink the good stuff."

We turn a corner and Samuel grabs a door, throwing it open. "Please," he says, motioning for me to enter before him.

I take the two steps into his office, halting in the middle and gazing out at the beautiful view of Paris. A large oak desk sits in front of the window with a thick blue cushioned chair. There are several neatly stacked papers on his desk and to the right is a golden plated cabinet, stocked with a variety of high quality liquor.

Samuel strides past me, grabbing a key from his desk and unlocking the cabinet. "Please, sit." He unlocks the door and takes out a bottle nearly filled to the brim. "Don't wait on my account."

I'm already getting an ill feeling as I sit in the chair behind me. The cushion is low, much lower than his and once again I feel like a child in my father's study, getting scolded for dirtying my pants after a day playing in the garden. My hands grip the armrests, keeping myself there and ignoring the need to run out of the room.

I try to focus on something other than the impending doom twisting my stomach. My gaze lands on a photo of his twins in their cap and gown. The picture must have been taken after they graduated high school. Another photo sits next to it, displaying his new wife, who is nearly the same age as his daughters. Samuel divorced several years ago after his wife finally got sick of him messing round with other, much younger women when she wasn't looking.

Apparently, she didn't get much in the settlement.

At least, that's what Father tells me.

"Here you are," says Samuel while handing me a glass. He clinks his own against mine before taking a seat in his chair, looking more like an evil king sitting on his throne rather than a wealthy lawyer. He sips at his brandy, his eyes narrowing on me for a moment, trying to size me up and probably see what I'm worth. At least, that's my assumption.

"So, Lucas," he starts, setting his glass on the desk. "What can I do for you?"

I take a small sip of brandy, trying to fight the need to grimace against the burn ravaging my throat. I take another small sip, hoping for a little liquid courage. Clearing my throat, I tap my fingers against the glass before saying, "I was hoping you had a position open at your firm." I wince at the shaking in my voice, not understanding what has come over me. I'm not a child anymore. I'm a strong, confident man.

Samuel raises an eyebrow and I feel my heart leap into my throat. My fingers tap faster against the glass and my gaze slides once more to his daughters. "A position?" He asks, confusion laced in his tone.

I nod like my life depends on it. "Yeah, an internship. I was hoping something might be open."

Samuel chuckles and leans back in his chair. "Isn't it a bit late to be asking about internship programs?

I blink, knowing he's right, but hoping I come off us the stereotypical rich kid, asking and demanding for what he wants. "Is it?" I tap my chin. "I had no clue. I figured, I'm here. You've offered before. I might as well try."

Samuel purses his lips. "Yeah, I have offered, Lucas." He strokes his beard and I see something mischievous glint in his eyes. My heart races, knowing something is off, something bad is going to happen. "I've offered many times before. It's interesting that after all these years of offering you a position in my firm, Lucas, you're finally here, demanding for it."

I feel my brows tent and I straighten in my chair, wanting to appear taller, but it's difficult in this seat. "I'm not demanding for anything."

"Yes, you are." Samuel tilts his head to the side. "You call me out of the blue, show up here and ask for a job. A job, I'm assuming, will get your father off your back so you can do God knows what."

I open my mouth, about to disagree with him, but Samuel lifts a finger, wagging it between us. "I'm not finished, boy."

I bristle. Boy? I haven't been called boy since I was ten.

"What's even more interesting is that you seem to think I wouldn't see right through this little ruse of yours." His brow furrows. "Do you really think I'm that gullible, Lucas?"

My mouth hangs open. I can't breathe. I can't speak. I should have known this wouldn't work, yet in my desperation, I didn't really think things through.

"Well?" Samuel asks, looking at me expectantly.

I shake my head. "No, I don't think you're gullible."

Samuel smirks and rises from his seat. I copy his movement, not quite understanding what's going on. He smacks my back and leads me to the door. "Our interns have already been chosen," he says while opening it. "Whatever is going on between you and your father, leave me out of it."

"There's not… it's not…" I sputter, trying to come up with words, but all vocabulary has evacuated my head, leaving me standing in front of Samuel, feeling both shocked and worried. If my father comes tomorrow, if he so much as speaks with Samuel about what I'm doing with my summer… I'm so totally fucked.

"You can show yourself out," Samuel says with a polite smile before closing the door in my face.

I stand there, staring at the door for a moment, wanting to knock on it. My hands fist at my side, as if readying myself to do it. I clench my jaw, not wanting to beg for a position I will hate, not wanting to beg a man in league with my father. There has to be another way. I turn around and trudge back down the hall, ignoring the receptionist's pretty smile and her sultry, "Have a nice day."

I shove open the doors and grab my phone, calling for a taxi through one of my apps and pacing back and forth while I wait for it. I will just have to tell my father the truth. That I want to try out writing this summer. That I want a bit of freedom before I sell my soul to the LSATs and grad school.

That I want one summer with my girlfriend before my father makes me break up with her.

I swallow the lump in my throat, turning my face up to the sun and closing my eyes. Deep down, I know it'll eventually happen. Eventually, I will have to say goodbye to my life with Rachel. It pains me. Every time I think about it, I feel like I can't breathe. I don't know if it's because of my impending loss of freedom, or the fact Rachel makes it easier for me to breathe, for me to pretend on front of my father, or when I'm on the phone with him.

Because at the end of the day, I know she'll be there for me with her bright smile, and her emerald green eyes; with the sprinkle of freckles on her nose and her plump red lips.

The taxi arrives and I throw myself inside, leaning against the window and watching the buildings go by. I wonder if there's another law firm I can join at this rate. Father won't like it, but at least it will be something. He'll probably snub his nose at any firm he hasn't decided is good enough for someone with the Brent family name to be working at, but at least he can't say anything about me dawdling my time away. I'll have to look into it. I grimace, wondering about the whole visa situation. With Samuel, it wouldn't have mattered, but with another firm, I will have to spend the next several weeks applying for a study visa… or a work visa. Whatever it is I need, I'll have to figure out how to get it, which could be used as an excuse for my father.

The taxi stops outside the apartment complex and I tip the driver, rushing out of it and into the elevator. I look at the time, seeing it's already six o'clock. A day completely wasted. How wonderful. I could've been looking at places to go site seeing with Rachel over the weekend. I could have been planning our romantic date at the tower.

I throw open the door, feeling angry and anxious about what's to come. I'm about to kick off my shoes, but I stop, hearing giggling and soft jazz playing in the background, coming from the kitchen. The whole place smells like spaghetti bolognese and burnt toast.

I frown.

"When is Lucas getting home?" I hear Rachel ask.

"I don't know, I haven't seen him all day," I hear Seth.

"Well, more for me," comes Hunter's voice, making me smile.

I kick off my shoes and stride inside, stopping when I see Seth sitting on the island and Hunter leaning against it. The doors to the terrace are open and I can see plates for four set out along with a bucket filled with ice and wine. Rachel twirls around. The apron tied around her waist swings with her movement and she takes a bite from her wooden spoon, her gaze meeting mine and widening in surprise.

"Oh, you're back," she says, her voice filled with excitement. "I was just wondering where you were."

I take in her flushed cheeks, the red tomato sauce staining her mouth, her golden, curly hair tied into a messy bun. Striding towards her, I grab her chin and place a chaste kiss on her lips, unable to stop myself from tasting her. I lick my lips. "Delicious," I murmur.

Rachel's face flushes a deeper red. Her gaze lowers to my mouth while her eyes glaze over in want. "I'm glad you like it."

My cock twitches and I don't care if Hunter and Seth are watching us. After the terrible day I've had, all I want is her lips on me, her body writhing under me as I pound her into the bed. She looks so delectable, so beautiful, I just want to eat her up and never let her go. I want to hold her. I want her to hold me.

"Didn't you mention something about tonight," I murmur, closing the little distance between us. My hand rests on her hip, pulling her flush against me.

Rachel chuckles. "I need to finish cooking dinner." She turns away, setting the spoon down on the counter. "Aren't you hungry?"

"Very," I say, my voice harsher this time as my hand slips from her hip to her ass, pulling her flush against me. I grind my hardening cock against her, biting back a moan.

Rachel gasps, her gaze flying to mine as I continue rocking against her. I feel someone move to my side. I hear Seth jumping down from his place on the island. Hunter pushes her hair to the side, kissing the crook of her shoulder.

"But, my dinner," Rachel breathes.

"It can wait." I capture her lips, kissing her fiercely, pouring all my anxiety and pain into that one kiss. My tongue strokes her lips, asking for entrance. She grants it to me. Her gasps spur me on as my tongue entwines with hers. Her teeth graze against my bottom lip and I moan, wanting and needing her more. My hands reach for her hair, burying themselves in her thick locks. I pull her head back, deepening the kiss until all I can do is breathe her in and I desperately wish for this moment to never end.

Rachel moans. Her leg lifts and I grab it, resting it against my hip while I grind harder against her. I feel Hunter's fingers slipping between us, playing with the button of her skirt. With one quick movement, her skirt is undone, slipping down her waist while Seth kneels in front of her.

Rachel breaks our kiss and my mouth follows her, wanting more. I kiss her neck, sucking tenderly at the sensitive flesh. Her leg slips from my hip and Seth grabs her skirt, pulling it down to the floor while placing sloppy kisses against her thigh and knee. Hunter's fingers dip into her panties and she gasps, her hands searching for me. I grab them, wrapping them around my neck while Hunter continues to press against her womanhood. She gazes up at me and I love the desperation in her gaze; the yearning.

I want and need more of it; more of her.

Her hands meet mine while she continues stroking my tongue with hers. My whole body tingles with need. I feel twisted and tied so tight, my muscles are shaking in expectation as she undoes the button to my pants, her fingers pulling the zipper down. I shudder when she dips her hand inside, pressing agonizingly against my underwear. My cock leaks and I thrust myself into her hand, desperate to be out of these clothes and inside her.

The bell rings faintly in the background. She stills against me, her eyes fluttering open, filled with alarm and worry. She breaks away from the kiss, but I'm not ready for her to leave. My hand strokes her hair, while I press a tender kiss against her jaw.

"Ignore it," I breathe into her ear.

For a moment, I wonder if she will leave me like this; so hard I'm about to rip out of my boxers. Then, she turns her attentions back to me, a small smile on her lips. She arches against me, going up on her tiptoes, her mouth slightly parted-

The bell rings again, and then again, as if the person standing on the other side of the door is being hunted down in some suspenseful action movie. At least, that's what it better be.

I'm tempted to tell Rachel to ignore it, but Hunter is already pulling away from her and Rachel is grabbing her skirt from Seth. She quickly pulls her skirt up, buttoning herself back inside while Seth rises from the floor. Thankfully, I'm not the only one looking flustered as I look around at the bros, finding Hunter trying to fix his cock in his jeans while Seth strides towards the sink, splashing water on his face.

"Who the fuck is it?" Seth mutters while turning off the faucet.

"It better be fucking Liam Neeson," Hunter grumbles while dumping his body onto the couch.

I push myself back into my pants and zip myself up while I listen to Rachel open the door and say, "Hello?"

I cross my arms, scowling at the counter, knowing as soon as that door closes I'm going to grab Rachel, toss her over my shoulder, and punish her very sweetly for allowing someone so stupid to disrupt our fucking.

"Oh, why, hello," I hear a familiar voice, making my nose scrunch up in distaste. That better not be who I think it is.

"I apologize if I'm disrupting your dinner time, but I'm looking for a Lucas Brent."

I still. All desire leaves me in one swift motion as I hear Rachel say kindly, "Oh, yes. He's here. Come on in."

I slowly turn around. A chill creeps across my skin as a bearded red head appears from the small foyer. He stops as soon as he catches my gaze, giving me a knowing smirk.

"Lucas," says Samuel while holding out his hand, waiting for me to shake it.

I stare at the hand as if he's the devil offering me anything my heart desires for my soul. I hate the slight shake in my hand as I go to grasp his, shaking it firmly as I ask, sounding too bewildered for my own ears, "What are you doing here?"

7

RACHEL

I look between Lucas and this older gentleman, Samuel. I can't quite call him a man. He really does seem the gentleman type with his short clipped hair and his immaculate looking suit. Only his beard is off-putting, reminding me of a lumberjack but lacking all the flannel. Something in his aura seems off, and when I turn my attentions to Lucas, I can't help but wonder why he appears so boyish; like a terrified little boy caught with his hand in the cookie jar.

"What are you doing here?" Lucas asks while shaking Samuel's hand.

Samuel chuckles, tossing his head back and shaking his head slightly. "Is that anyway to greet your new boss?"

Lucas's face pales. "So, you're actually giving me the position?"

Samuel flashes another bright smile while looking around the room. He settles his gaze on me, the smile widening and reminding me of a shark. A shark who uses teeth whitening strips. "Aren't you going to introduce me to your friends?" He asks.

I hear Hunter rise from the couch. His fingers brush against mine and I grind my teeth, containing the need to strip down and straddle him. I feel so sensitive. Just five minutes ago, we were going to have sex, and I had to up and ruin it by answering the door. Of course, at the time I thought it was going to be some silly kids needing a scolding. I didn't know it was going to be an actual guest… or colleague for Lucas.

Otherwise, I would've taken my time; perhaps left him out there until we were all satisfied.

My gaze slides to Lucas, and I see him leaning against the island, his arms crossed while he scowls down at the floor. I suppose the whole getting offered a job thing isn't to his liking. I wonder why, but I can't ask him now in front of his employer. That would be… rude, right?

"I'm Hunter. Lucas's friend from school."

"And I'm Seth." Samuel turns around, finding Seth guzzling down a glass of water while he gives a slight wave of his hand. "Also a friend from school."

Samuel's attentions return to me and he tilts his head to the side while crossing his arms. "And let me guess. Girlfriend?"

My face heats, not knowing how I should answer since we aren't totally public. I glance at Lucas, but he isn't looking at me. His eyes seem fixated to the floor. I push my hair away from my face while I say shakily, "My- my name is Rachel."

"And I suppose you are all here with Lucas for the summer? Bumming about?" Samuel raises an eyebrow at me and for some reason I think his question is pointed at me.

"I think I'm the only bum here," Hunter says with a bright smile while patting my shoulder. "Rachel here actually got an internship at some hoity-toity museum." I smile shyly while fiddling with ends of my hair. "Have you ever heard of the Loover?"

I grimace at his pronunciation of the Louvre and chance a glance at Samuel, who smiles politely yet there's a menacing glimmer in his eye. "No, I can't say I have," he says. "But I have heard of the Louvre."

I nod, feeling embarrassed for Hunter. Glancing at the football player now, he seems absolutely ignorant to the mispronunciation and absolutely bored with the conversation. He gives Samuel one last glance before striding away and sidling up close to Seth, whispering something behind a hand.

"Yes," I say quickly, hoping to be over and done with this conversation soon. Something about Samuel doesn't quite sit right with me. "That's where I'm working right now. The Louvre." I chuckle awkwardly and give a shrug. "I work with Dr. Arnaud. She's a museum curator and art historian at the Louvre."

Samuel scoffs. "Can you really call an art historian a doctor?"

I make a face, feeling queasy and wanting desperately for Lucas to come in and save me. By the looks of it, though, he seems more interested in having a stare down with the floor. "Well, she did put in the work to get her doctorate. So, I guess, she deserves to be called a doctor in her field."

Samuel strokes his beard. "I suppose you're right in that sense. But I find art such an impractical degree. What can one really do with it?"

My eyes widen and I cross my arms, tilting my hip to one side as I prepare the ongoing debates I've had with others in the past. "How can you say that and live in Paris?" I find myself asking, which is not what I wanted to begin with at all. I fight the need to wince, deciding holding my head high and straightening my back is better than allowing this old man snub his nose to the most beautiful skill known to man. "Art can be used in many ways. It's not only aesthetically pleasing to the eye."

Samuel smirks. "Oh, really?"

"It's used in marketing everywhere. Photography for instance, has had a huge surge in recent years with not only selfies, but with influencers photographing products, writing reviews, and pretty much becoming the next ad campaign. Take Nstagram, for instance," I say while holding up one finger. "It can be used to document one's life, but it can also be used to market authors, makeup, fashion." I throw up my hands, feeling passion taking over and forgetting this man is Lucas's new boss. "You name it, it can be marketed. Take the running store I used to work for with Seth." I stab my finger into his chest. Samuel's gaze lowers to it, looking amused rather than irritated. "I used to take products from the store and photograph college athletes using them in order to get more customers. It was great, wasn't it Seth?"

Seth nods vigorously. "Definitely was, until you were fired."

I cringed.

"I wonder how they'll ever be able to sell GU without you there. We'll be drowning in GU next year."

I frown. "Not really helping, Seth."

Seth shrugs and goes back to whispering to Hunter. My eyes narrow, wondering what they are discussing so secretly.

I sigh and shake my head. "Anyway-"

"Enough, I get it," says Samuel quickly, holding up his hands in defense. "Art is great." He chuckles while stroking his beard. "I like your enthusiasm. Maybe I could use you for some marketing, since you're so passionate about it. I assume you are a photographer?"

I nod. I don't quite understand what is happening here as I watch Samuel taking out his wallet. He pulls out a small card and hands it to me. I look down at the simply black script, reading: Samuel Allen. Law Office Allen. Phone Number 71 5046 1972.

"You should give me a call. I've been wanting to do some more advertising for my firm."

"Oh," is the only thing I can say while I stare down at his card. "I guess I could…"

"Everything is online these days. And like you said, everyone is looking at that Nstagram stuff. It would be good to have an online presence."

I nod again, unable to take my eyes off his card. Is this really happening? Am I getting another job offer? I purse my lips as I think of photographing people in their office rather than running around like a chicken with its head cut off at the Louvre. If I dump my internship and work with Samuel, then I wouldn't have to see Lauren's glare day after day. Or deal with her sabotaging me.

But, I wouldn't be working in the Louvre. And I'm sure dropping an internship program looks pretty bad. I should just stick it out with Dr. Arnaud.

However, working with a fancy law firm in Paris would look good on my resume.

"Thank you," I say while shoving the card into my very tiny skirt pocket. "I'll consider it."

"Please do." Samuel turns around, his gaze on Lucas as he says, "I expect you at the office no later than eight." He looks Lucas up and down for a moment. "And wear a suit. I can't have my clients thinking I hire just anyone off the street."

Lucas's head bobs up and down. "Yes, sir," he says faintly.

"Well, then, I wish you all a good evening. Rachel, it was a pleasure," Samuel adds while taking my hand and giving it a firm shake.

"Likewise," I say with a smile, not knowing if I'm telling the truth or just being polite. I watch him show himself out, the door clicking close behind him.

The door closing must have snapped Lucas out of his hypnotism with the floor, because he strides towards me, taking my arm and pulling me towards him. I expect a kiss, my body already leaning into him, ready to continue what we had been up to before. But instead, Lucas says harshly, "Don't call him."

My brows furrow and I blink, wondering if I heard him correctly. "What?"

Lucas sighs, sounding frustrated while he rakes a hand through his hair. "Don't call him. Throw his card away. He's a manipulative asshole."

I yank my arm away from Lucas. "Then why are you working for him?"

Lucas groans, pinching the bridge of his nose while turning around. "Because I have to," he says with his back facing me.

I reach for him, placing a hand lightly on his shoulder, but he pulls away from me. "Not now, Rachel. I'm not in the mood."

My hand lowers and I bite my bottom lip as I feel my eyes prickling with unshed tears. I try to ignore Hunter and Seth glancing at each other. Hunter pushes away from the counter, his eyes filled with worry, but I quickly shake my head, making him stop mid-step.

"Do you want to talk about it?" I ask tentatively, flinching when Lucas releases an exasperated sigh.

"No," he says harshly while facing me, his gaze now glued to the floor. I want to ask him what's so special about the God damn tiles, but I bite my tongue, not really in the mood to start a fight. "Just tell me you won't work for him. He'll work you to the bone. And he's a jerk." Lucas closes his eyes and grabs my hand, giving it a quick squeeze before releasing me. I have no clue why he is acting this way, and it's alarming to say the least.

What's going on?

Why did Samuel suddenly show up at our door?

Why is Lucas acting so strange?

"Ok. I trust you," I say, grimacing as the words escape my lips. I do trust Lucas, but I don't like throwing away opportunities. Not to mention, this is my choice to make. Maybe working for Samuel wouldn't be so bad, compared to Dr. Arnaud. Maybe Samuel isn't as bad as Lucas thinks. I don't think taking a few pictures here and there is that big of a deal.

Lucas visibly relaxes. His shoulders slump forward and I watch him straighten. He seems a bit better, yet the color in his face hasn't returned. I watch him stalk towards the foyer, following after him like some lovesick fool.

"Where are you going?" I ask while he puts on his shoes.

"Out," he says simply. "I need a suit… and a walk."

"I can go with you," I say, forcing a smile, but Lucas is already shaking his head.

"No. I need to be alone, Rachel."

"Ok." I try to sound understanding, but my heart still cracks and I feel like at any minute I'm going to burst into a million pieces. I watch the door close, nibbling on my bottom lip while waiting for it to reopen; waiting for Lucas to come back to me and explain everything.

I wait several minutes until I realize that's not going to happen.

I trudge back to the kitchen, finding Hunter and Seth both leaning against the island, looking at me with pity and worry in their gazes.

"Everything ok?" Seth asks.

I nod, turning towards the stove. "Everything is fine," I say with a sniff. "Let's just-"

I'm about to say let's have dinner, but I gasp, staring down at the burnt Bolognese sauce. Quickly, I turn off the stove, but it's already too late. "No," I moan, grabbing the wooden spoon on the counter and stabbing the blackened beef.

Dinner has been officially ruined.

"What is it?" Hunter asks from behind and I grind my teeth as I hear him gasp. "What the-"

I groan, tossing my head back and clamping my eyes shut. Inhaling deeply, I try to calm my pounding heart, wanting to grab the pot and throw it across the room. So much for a nice night.

"Well, we could always order pizza." I hear Seth say.

I whirl around, my hair smacking me in the face from the force and I scowl at Hunter and Seth. "But I didn't want to eat pizza," I say while stamping my feet, probably looking like a spoiled brat. "I wanted to make a nice dinner for us all to share outside." I throw a hand at the terrace, where the plates and bottle of wine are still resting.

Hunter shrugs. "Well, you can always make it tomorrow."

I grind my teeth to keep myself from screaming, knowing none of this is Hunter nor Seth's fault. It's my fault for getting so distracted.

"Come on," says Seth while grabbing my hand and pulling me towards him. "It's not a big deal."

"Yeah," says Hunter while stroking my hair. He nuzzles my air and I shiver when he nibbles on my lobe. "We can still have some fun out on the terrace."

I raise an eyebrow. "Oh, really?"

"Yeah," says Seth while taking a step towards the glass doors.

I giggle as he tugs me towards him, allowing him to guide me outside, onto the terrace and towards the table and sofas. I gaze at the setting sun in the distance. The Eiffel Tower is beginning to glow and I can't take my eyes off it as I sit down. Seth pours me a glass of wine while Hunter sits next to me, pulling me into his lap while stroking my hair.

"It's beautiful," I breathe while leaning into Hunter's touch.

"Very."

I giggle, remembering what he said to Samuel. "You do realize I work at the Louvre and not the Loover?"

Hunter nips my ear. "I do now."

I take a sip of my wine while Seth sits down next to me. He grabs my legs, putting them onto his lap and I moan while he massages my feet. "Now, where were we?" Seth says with a mischievous gleam in his eye.

A warm pit gathers in my stomach and I feel my insides tighten in desire while he runs his hands up and down my leg. Hunter's arms wrap around me, his fingers inching towards my skirt. I wiggle against him, enjoying his breath hitching at the small movement.

"Somewhere good," I say while watching Seth climb towards me.

He plucks my glass from my hands and rests it on the ground before dipping his head down. His teeth fondle with my button and my face heats, feeling him undo it easily. I watch him grab the zipper with his mouth, pulling it down while his hands slide up my legs. I feel Hunter's hands move under my shirt, his fingers stroking the wiring of my bra.

Seth grabs my panties, pulling them down and over my feet before grabbing my skirt, leaving me completely bare from the waist down. I look around, feeling extremely embarrassed that we are outside doing this, despite the fact this is Lucas's terrace and there's no one around.

"What if someone hears me?" I whisper harshly while Seth breathes against my womanhood.

"I hope they do," he says before lowering his mouth, flicking his tongue against my clit and making me arch my back against Hunter.

I bite back my moans, knowing someone will definitely hear me. Hunter pulls down my bra, his fingers pinching and pilling my nipples while he kisses my neck up and down, over the hickeys I covered in makeup. I hiss, trying to control myself, not wanting to let my voice out. Seth pushes a finger inside me and I gasp, my head lulling against Hunter's shoulder. Hunter grabs my chin and nudges me towards him, claiming my lips with his. I moan as Seth continues to suck and thrust inside me, letting myself go now that Hunter is silencing my voice. My hands search for something anything to cling to.

Seth grabs a hand, lacing his fingers with mine while Hunter grabs the other. I squeeze them tightly, feeling my body soaring higher and higher. My legs tighten around Seth and I can feel myself nearing climax. Hunter pulls at my bra with his other hand, his lower body thrusting against my bottom. I arch against him, feeling his hard cock through the fabric of his pants.

Hunter breaks away from me, releasing my hand while sliding his between us. I hear him fumbling with his zipper, cursing under his breath. Gasping, I stroke Seth's hair with my free hand, thrusting against his mouth and finger. He inserts another and I shout, tossing back my head while I ride him, needing sweet release. Hunter's cock, now free from its prison, pushes into my backside and I need to have it inside me. I want to be filled to the brink.

I want to have both of them thrusting their hard, big cocks deep inside me.

Pushing Seth away from me, I grab his shirt, pulling it over his surprised face while keeping him at bay with one foot pressing against his sexy abs. I move onto my knees, my hands grabbing his belt and undoing his pants quickly. His cock springs out of his underwear and Seth chuckles, quickly kicking away the fabric while I move to straddle him. I hear jingling behind me, finding Hunter pushing down his pants before grabbing my ass, smacking a hand against it.

Hissing, I lean into him while my lower body toys with Seth, stroking the tip of his cock against my clit.

"I guess someone doesn't care about being loud anymore," Seth says, a smile splayed across his face while I continue my ministrations. His hands grasp my hips, quickening my movements against his dick.

Hunter's cock pushes against my ass cheek while he smacks me once more. I shudder, my hand reaching up and grabbing him by his hair, tugging him towards me. "Now," I moan. "I want you now."

Hunter's hands cup my ass while his teeth nibble on my shoulder. "No prep?" He whispers into my ear and I moan, shaking my head while wiggling my bottom against his cock. He growls low in my ear and his hands move to my hips, grasping Seth's hands. He moves me slightly, until my wet, slick entrance is hovering above Seth's dick. I shudder with anticipation. He moves my hips slowly down, until Seth's tip is pressing against me. Hunter's fingers slide to my front, stroking up and down my clit.

I bite my bottom lip to keep from crying, begging. All I want to do is sink onto Seth's dripping cock. I look around frantically, wondering where the condom is. Seth is doing the same, reaching for his pants. His eyes are glazed over in want. My eyes turn to his twitching cock, leaking precum down his pulsing length.

"For fuck's sake," Seth mutters while grabbing his pants, frantically digging into his pockets. His hips are moving and I can tell he's trying very hard not to thrust up into me.

Hunter strokes his thumb against my little pleasure nub and I gasp, tossing my head back against Hunter's shoulder. He moans in my ear, his teeth grazing against it once more and I move my bottom against him, loving and hating this torture he is putting me through.

"Finally," Seth says shakily and I hear something ripping while I nuzzle my forehead against Hunter's jaw.

Hunter grabs my chin, claiming my lips with his. He runs his tongue along my bottom lip, his teeth tugging for a brief moment. "I want to be inside you," Hunter says between kisses.

I thrust my bottom against him. "I want you," I whimper.

"I want you more," Seth mutters and my eyes fly to him, watching as he snakes an arm around my waist and pulls me forward. I nearly topple over him, but Hunter steadies me. His hands grab my hips and he sinks me slowly down onto Seth's cock.

Seth bucks underneath me, moaning while his head lulls from side to side. I shiver as his thick length fills me to the brink. Biting my bottom lip, Hunter continues pressing me down onto Seth until the hilt. I try not to cry out; try not scream in absolute bliss. My body fights against Hunter's hands while Seth continues to thrust, trying to speed things up, but Hunter is control, moving me slowly up and down with his hands on his hips.

Seth whimpers below me. His hands smack against Hunter, trying to get him to release his hips. "Fuck, Hunter," he grunts. "Lemme… fuck." Seth gasps, his hands flailing to grab something. I grab them, squeezing them tight while Seth's eyes meet mine, looking like he's experiencing both pain and pleasure all at once.

Hunter slides against his cock against my ass while he continues moving my hips slowly up and down. The pace is slow. Too slow for Seth, he wiggles underneath me as if he's desperate for release. I feel Seth's dick twitch inside me, his cries for more and faster going unheard. Even I try to speed it up, but Hunter's too strong and I'm too weak to what he's doing to me to fight all that heard.

"Are you ready?" he whispers in my ear and I feel his cock nudging against the entrance to my ass.

I give a weak nod, unable to do more as I try to bite back my desires, knowing whomever lived in this apartment complex would hear me. With one thrust, I cry out, feeling Hunter fill me completely. I fall forward, my hands on either side of Seth while pain explodes through me. Pain and pleasure mixing into one entity I cannot possibly separate.

Seth's mouth reaches for me and I take him, kissing him deeply and harshly while Hunter thrusts hard and deep into me. My pace quickens as Hunter loses control; unable to keep the slow torturous pace from before. My mouth wrenches away from Seth and I grab his hands, gasping and whimpering against his shoulder in a vain attempt to silence myself.

"Rachel," Seth whispers in my ear. He places sloppy kisses against my shoulder. "Let me hear you. I want to hear you."

I shake my head, too worried what the neighbors will say tomorrow.

"Rachel," Seth whimpers, sounding as if he's begging. He thrusts deep into me at the same time as Hunter and I'm unable to stop myself from moaning.

"Yes, Rachel, let us hear you," Hunter gasps, thrusting harder into me, this time matching Seth's rhythm.

I'm unable to stop myself. I push myself up and Hunter's hands circle around my waist, helping me balance as both Seth and Hunter thrust deep inside me. Hunter's hands cup my breasts while Seth's fingers play with my clit. My moans turn to cries. My cries turn to screams until finally I'm reaching my peak, unable to stop myself from shrieking my release while Hunter and Seth continue thrusting into me at the exact same time.

I continue screaming as my orgasm takes over me, making me feel light as if I'm free falling through a cloud of nothingness.

"Rachel," Seth cries while he thrusts into me, his cock twitching while my walls around him tighten.

"Yes, yes, oh fuck yes," Hunter mumbles into my ear, digging his dick inside me until I feel him still, filling me with his cum while his forehead presses against my shoulder.

Seth's body slowness under me and looking down I watch his teeth grind. With one last thrust, he whimpers, coming deep inside me. Hunter releases my waist and I fall forward, not even bothering to brace for impact as I topple over Seth.

I'm still high on my orgasm. My mouth can't stop kissing Seth. I kiss his chest, his shoulders, my head nuzzling into his body while Hunter's hands stroke my bottom and my back.

"I want to do it again," Hunter murmurs. I feel his body leaning forward and my whole body shudders in need as he kisses my back.

"Bro, I don't think I can do it again," Seth says between breaths while pushing back his head.

"Not with you, idiot."

I giggle and push myself up. My gaze meets Hunter and I brush his hair away from his forehead. He takes my hand, placing a chaste kiss on my palm. I lean towards him, nuzzling my head against his arm. "I want pizza," I whisper while closing my eyes.

Hunter chuckles softly. "I knew eventually you would give in."

"You're ordering it this time," Seth mutters and I feel him get up from the couch.

I open my eyes, watching Seth pick up his clothes, taking in his thin, muscled shape, which is so different from Hunter's. My gaze travels up the length of him, taking in his sexy build and feeling the fires restart within me.

But Lucas isn't here.

I frown, wondering if he's alright and if he is already back from his walk. Probably not, or else he would have joined us.

I glance at the kitchen, finding it empty.

I can't help but wish Lucas is here, with us. Worry seeps into my heart and I hope everything is okay.

***

I sit in front of my computer, tapping my fingers against the vanity while I wait for Charlie to pick up on the other line. Lucas still hasn't come home and I need something to take away the worry. Seth and Hunter have already gone to sleep and I don't want to bother them, seeing how during all dinner I was obsessing about Lucas.

Seth seemed irritated about the whole thing while Hunter seemed worried.

"Don't worry about it," I remember Hunter saying while patting my hand. "It's nothing."

"Yeah, listen to Hunter," I recall Seth saying while yawning and stretching his arms, looking absolutely unconcerned.

I straighten in my chair as the black screen morphs into Charlie's image. I lean into my computer, my gaze widening at the disarray her room is in. Clothes are everywhere while her table is littered in makeup, powder, brushes, and an assortment of hair accessories.

"Don't look at the mess," says Charlie while moving her body closer to the screen. Probably in the hopes of blocking the scenery behind her. She tilts the camera upwards, away from her desk and smiles brightly at me. "I know I need to clean."

I narrow my eyes, finding her bed just behind her, covered in clothes. "You're worse than me."

Charlie rolls her eyes. "Yeah, yeah. I know I need to clean. It's hard moving in and out of my parents place."

"Why don't you just stay at your apartment during the summer?"

Charlie scrunches up her face. "Because it's expensive and I don't feel like getting a summer job."

I purse my lips. "Then, how do you afford your-"

Charlie sighs in exasperation. "Enough about me. Tell me about Paris." She twiddles her fingers in front of her while raising her eyebrows. "Anything interesting happen? Have you met any cute Parisian boys to pass my number off to?"

I giggle and shake my head. "I've been way too busy for any of that."

Charlie pouts. "You couldn't have been that busy."

"Trust me. I have been." I slump in my chair. "I haven't even been able to go site seeing."

Charlie smirks mischievously. "Why not?" She waggles her eyebrows. "Too busy in the bedroom? Have you even been going to your internship?"

I roll my eyes. "Yes."

"Really?" Charlie leans forward and the screen. "Are those hickeys?"

My hand flies to my neck, and she chuckles while I move my hair forward, trying to cover the offensive bruises. "No," I sputter.

"Don't lie," Charlie laughs. "So you've been busy."

I shake my head. "Yes, I've been busy." I pick at my fingernails. "I met Lauren today. She's in the same internship program as me."

"No," Charlie gasps, slamming her hands onto her desk.

I nod. "Yes."

"I thought only one intern is chosen for the summer program."

I shake my head. "I guess not."

"Have you even talked to her?"

I groan. "Oh, yeah. We've totally talked. She still hates my guts. She sent me on a whole wild goose chase in the museum and made me look like a freaking idiot to my boss."

Charlie purses her lips. "Oooh. That's not so good. So what are you going to do? I guess you can't quit."

I sigh. "Yeah, quitting isn't really an option." I'm tempted to tell her about the opportunity with Samuel Allen. Yet, seeing how I already told Lucas I wouldn't call him, I decide to hold my tongue. I would much rather figure out what to do about Lauren, seeing how I already made a decision to work at the Louvre.

I might as well make the best of it.

"Well, I think it would help if you ladies just talked it out. Like, maybe if you explained to her in great detail what happened with Josh, she'll understand. I don't think she's absolutely evil. She's gotta empathize with you on the whole thing."

I tap my chin. "I don't know, Charlie. She really hates me for what I did to Josh."

Charlie scoffs. "You did nothing to Josh. If he didn't want to be expelled from school, then he shouldn't have been a shitty person and attacked you."

I smile while tears come to my eyes. That's exactly what I needed to hear. It isn't my fault Josh ended up getting kicked out of school. It's his own. And I'm so lucky to have a friend like Charlie on my side.

"Thank you," I sniff, quickly wiping my eyes before the tears fall.

"But I still think you should talk to Lauren," Charlie says while pointing her long, neatly manicured finger at me. "I think it will be good to clear the air."

I sigh. "Fine."

Charlie smiles brightly, clapping her hands together. "Good. Now that we have that settled, tell me how you got those hickeys. I'm dying to know what kinky things you've discovered in France."

I raise an eyebrow and shake my head at Charlie. "We've been here barely three days."

Charlie shrugs. "So. I'm sure you could've picked up some new tricks by now."

I shake my head at Charlie, unable to stop myself from laughing and wishing she were here with me instead of Lauren.

However, Charlie is right. The sooner I settle things with Lauren, the better my trip will be in France. I just don't know where to start, or if she will even listen to me.

8

LUCAS

I stride into the office and ignore the receptionist twiddling her fingers at me. Looking around, I don't see Samuel anywhere, which I should've expected. The man is probably already in his office, hard at work, making all the money. Most likely he'll tell me later today that I need to come in even earlier.

I look down at my suit, smoothing out the wrinkles. Apparently, the Brent name can get me into any shop. I was able to find a store about to close last night, but once I flashed my father's name and my ID as proof, I was in and trying on suits in no time. It's both irritating and wonderful the way I can use my father like this.

Irritating that I need him and wonderful I can get pretty much anything I want.

I just have to pay for that kind of power with my freedom.

I check the time on my Rolex. 7:59. I'm right on time.

"Mr. Allen is in his office," says the receptionist brightly. "If you want, you can wait here or-"

I force a smile and jam a thumb at the hallway. "I will just wait outside his office. Can't let him think I'm late on my first day."

The receptionist nods enthusiastically and I walk down the corridor towards his office, pausing when I discover his door open. I frown, hearing him speak, wondering if he's firing the intern he hired before, or if he already has a client in there.

"Well, Frank, I would love to have dinner with you and Christina later."

I still at the sound of my father's name on Samuel's lips. Is he really talking with my father? Is he actually here in Paris? I peak around the door and slowly step forward. Samuel turns in his chair, his smile brightening when he sees me. Something horrifying twinkles in his eyes and I know just by that look, Samuel has something terrible up his sleeve.

He's going to use me and spit me out just like my father.

"Yeah, we can definitely be there around seven. I'll let Lucas know. I'm sure he'll be excited to see you after all this time."

I scowl at the floor. It's the only thing I can do. I don't know why Samuel suddenly agreed to do this. Obviously, he's hoping to get something out if it. Last night was definitely making a deal with the devil. I spent the next several hours trying to figure out a way to get out of working for Samuel Allen, but it didn't matter. There was no other way around it.

And the bastard met Rachel. Meaning he would probably tell my parents about her.

Just thinking about last night has me grinding my teeth, wishing I would have stayed; wishing I would have seduced Rachel into not answering the door. If I had only tugged her back to me, kissed her, then maybe I wouldn't be in this mess.

No. That makes no sense.

If I only told my parents the truth before, I wouldn't be in this mess. Samuel is the only way out and I'm going to have to work for him until the end of summer if I want to continue being sponsored by my parents.

That's the reason for all this.

I'm a coward. I can't stand the thought of getting by on my own. I want my freedom, but I want someone else to pay for it. I'm weak.

And I'm a fucking asshole for trying to pin the blame on others.

"Lucas."

My gaze rises and they land on Samuel, now rising from his throne. He motions to the chair in front of him and I stride towards it, sitting on the edge and trying not to bounce my leg up and down frantically.

"Thanks for coming on time. I apologize for making you wait. Your parents arrived in Paris last night and wanted to invite me to dinner. It's quite interesting though," he adds while stroking his beard. "They think you've been working for me since the beginning of the week. Apparently, they thought that was the plan from the beginning."

My heart drops to my stomach and my hands clench the armrests. My face heats, feeling like I'm sitting on the beach under the sun rather than in an air-conditioned room. My whole body sweats as I wonder what Samuel said to my father. Is the ruse up? Am I in the deepest shit of my life? I imagine my father's face, staring down at me with a dark scowl. In my mind, I can see my father's body elongating while I shrivel into a childlike form, unable to escape his wrath.

Samuel smiles, tilting his head to the side. "Don't worry. I didn't say anything to them. Your secret is safe with me." He winks and I watch him come around the desk, knowing he's planning something in order to keep me under his thumb.

Samuel Allen doesn't do favors.

"Come along," he says while nodding towards the door. "Let me get you acquainted to the staff. I wouldn't want you spoiling anything when your father grills you at the restaurant later." His dark smile makes my stomach twist. Suddenly, all I want to do is heave my breakfast all over the carpeted floor and run very far away.

Instead, my body rises and I find myself following him out of his office and deeper into his law firm.

***

I stare out the window in the taxi. Every cell in my body demands I open the door and throw myself out, knowing exactly what awaits me at the restaurant. I clench my jaw, remembering the morning working under Samuel; learning his staff, the way around the office, being sent around like a gofer.

Honestly, it's not hard work.

I just don't see myself becoming a lawyer. Just listening to Samuel on the phone with his clients made me want to take a sharpened pencil and stuff it into my ears. I could have been at home, working on my latest writing, applying to the next contest, getting my name out there.

Instead, I was copying papers, taking notes, and answering phones.

"Stop sighing. You sound like some lovesick girl."

I glare at Samuel sitting next to me, too busy with his cellphone to notice me.

I could have been waiting outside the Louvre for Rachel with a bouquet of flowers and an apology. I didn't even get a chance to see her last night when I got home. Her light was off. I had wanted to have breakfast with her in the morning, but unfortunately she had just run out of the apartment right when I finished with my shower.

It would've been nice to have some shower sex; continue with our fun from last night.

I tilt my head back, closing my eyes briefly while imagining her leg wrapped around my hip; my cock grinding against her front while she gasps against my ear.

"We're here," Samuel says in a sing-song tune and my eyes snap open, finding him already standing outside the taxi, waiting for me while staring at his watch. "Don't make me light a fire under your ass. You know how much your father likes punctuality."

I don't say anything while sliding my body out of the taxi. Checking the time, I see we're only five minutes late. Although, five minutes late in my father's world is pretty much like being an hour late. He's the most impatient asshole I've ever had to deal with in my entire life.

I trudge up the stairs while Samuel bounds up the steps. He holds his phone up to his ear and I already suspect it's my father when I hear, "Yes, yes. We're here. Traffic was terrible."

I fight the need to roll my eyes. If I start now, I will never stop. A man dressed in a tux opens the doors for us, and as soon as we enter, we are greeted by staff waiting at the reception, giving a slight bow of their heads while they carry pristine, white napkins in their hands. I frown at the green carpet beneath my feet decorated in gold and black swirls. The walls are white while a chandelier hangs from above decorated in gold and what appears to be white pearls.

"Good day, sir," says the man in the front with a slight tilt of his head. "Do you have a reservation?"

"I'm meeting with the Brent family."

"Ah yes, of course. Right this way." The man gestures towards the main entrance and I follow Samuel. I frown at the emerald sofas and the row of chandeliers lighting the room. Large windows display green gardens while a woman in the back of the room plays a violin. My stomach churns when I see my mother and father sitting next to a window. My father is busy with his phone. He's tall and reed like. The only way he stays in shape is by golfing, playing tennis, and screwing women behind my mother's back.

Not like she really cares, I think while turning my gaze to my mother, who sips on her glass of champagne. She still looks quite young, due to Botox and whatever other plastic surgery she's done to her body and her face in order to stay beautiful. Her blonde hair is neatly done, hanging over her shoulders while her white suit clings to her well-endowed figure.

I look nothing like her; rather I look more like a younger, less scary version of my father. If it wasn't for the birth certificate as proof, I would've thought I was born from a completely different woman. But, either my parent's paid someone off, or Mom actually did give birth to me. I guess it doesn't really matter. She turns and her blue gaze lands on me, making me wish I could disappear.

I force a smile and straighten my back, wanting to get this done and over with as quick as possible. My smile falters when I see Alex sitting with my parents, slumped over in his chair and dressed in all white Puma gear. He looks bored, but perks up when he sees me approach.

"Lucas," he says with a forced smile. "Long time no see." He holds out his hand and I take it, giving him a firm shake.

I guess we are pretending he didn't force his way into my apartment the other day. I'm fine with that. "What are you doing in Paris?" I ask, hoping I sound excited.

"Alex is here for a marathon, Lukey," says Mom. "Isn't that great?" She takes another sip of her champagne, downing it quickly. A server approaches, refilling her glass before she has time to reach for the bottle.

"Wonderful," I say with too much enthusiasm.

"It better be done tomorrow," I hear father say to the poor person on the other line. He scowls at his plate as if the person is right in front of him. "It was supposed to be done yesterday." Father's scowl darkens. "I don't want to hear your excuses. Either get it done, or you're fired." Father hangs up the phone and shakes his head at Samuel. "I swear, kids these days are getting dumber and lazier."

Samuel chuckles. "Not all of them," he says while nodding towards me and taking a seat next to my father.

I hold back a sigh, sitting next to Mom and grabbing a glass. I need alcohol if I'm going to get through this meeting. And lots of it. The server steps forward, grabbing my glass and pouring me a hefty amount. I try not to down it in one go. Over the brim of my glass, I see Alex raise an eyebrow at me.

"I hope you don't mind us showing up like this," says Mom sweetly while taking my hand and giving me a gentle squeeze. I don't know who she's talking to.

"It's no problem at all," Samuel answers. "It's been too long. I was actually surprised you didn't make plans earlier since Lucas is interning with my firm and all." Samuel smacks my back and I bite back a grunt.

Father's gaze slides to me and a shiver ripples through me, making my skin want to crawl away under that dark gaze. I take another sip of champagne, waiting for the interrogation to begin. His head tilts to the side while he scrutinizes me. I wonder what he will decide is wrong this time. My suit? My haircut?

"I hope Samuel isn't giving you a hard time, son," he says instead, making me blink in surprise. "I would have liked if you worked with me in New York instead, but it's great you have Samuel to teach you the ropes."

I force a smile and nod. "I thought it would be best to learn under someone different. Someone who won't give me preferential treatment."

Father nods and I know I've said the correct words. *Yeah, just say what he wants and then he will leave me alone.*

"Well, we are just so proud of you," Mom says while tapping my hand. "And of you, Alex. Can you believe these boys are growing up so fast?"

Father scoffs and gestures towards Mom. "Typical," he says flippantly. "Mothers never wanting their children to grow up. If Christina had her way, she would insist Lucas would live with us for the rest of his life. If it weren't for me, he would probably still be in his diapers, being spoon fed."

I clench my jaw, fighting that need to scoff or roll my eyes. Mom was never there when I was a kid. She didn't change my diapers, or feed me. That was all Nanna. If anything, Mom would like to have me around so she could introduce me to all her friend's daughters; make a proper match with me and some wealthy, cocaine addicted girl who probably ate two almonds a day and enjoyed talking about the latest Gucci line.

I don't know why, but my mind goes to Rachel, wondering if she's cooking dinner right now; wondering if she's done any site seeing with Seth and Hunter. They're probably busy having fun without me. All I want to do is rush through this dinner and run back to them.

Maybe I can call in sick tomorrow.

"Oh, please," says Mom while swaying in her seat. "You're the one who didn't want him going to that school." She points her glass at my father, nearly spilling champagne all over the table, but with a practiced wrist, she tips the glass up again and brings it to her lips. I cringe, tempted to take away the alcohol. She's obviously had way too much to drink.

"Ah, yes, how is Colorado?" Alex asks with mock intrigue.

"Wonderful," I say, flinching at the bitterness in my tone.

I glance at Father, wondering if he caught it, but his gaze is glued to Mom and her swaying. The server steps forward, reaching for the bottle, but my father shakes his head. "Water," he mouths to the server, who darts off to the kitchen.

"I hear you will be working at your father's hospital next semester," says father, turning his attentions away from Mom.

Alex nods, sitting upright now that he's on display for the adults to grill. "Yes. I will probably have to put running on the side. We're still working it out. Dad doesn't want to sideline the running since I've been winning so many medals recently."

If Seth were here, he would probably throw his body across the table and tackle Alex to the ground. Imagining it brings a smile to my face.

"I can't believe we know a track star," slurs Mom.

I open my mouth, wanting to say she knows Seth, but I promptly close it. She probably doesn't even remember Seth, and if she does, she most likely doesn't think much of him, given he's a nobody. Definitely an amazing runner, but he doesn't come from money like Alex.

I slump in my chair while my parents continue on. I'm ready to be done with this meal, but our orders haven't been taken yet. At this rate, I'll be here for hours. I glance over my shoulders, blinking when I see several servers heading our way, carrying tiny plates.

They set them in front of us and I stare down at the tiny grilled eggplant in front of me.

"I hope you don't mind," says Father with what looks to be a polite smile. "I ordered the ten courses degustation menu."

I fight the need to groan.

"Oh, wonderful," says Samuel while neatly cutting into his eggplant.

"Thank you," Alex says politely.

"Great," I murmur, stabbing my eggplant with my fork.

***

"You really don't have to come up," I say in the elevator.

My hands can't stop fidgeting in front of me. My parents are standing behind me, practically escorting me home. It's like they want to know every single little thing going on in my life. I swear, Samuel must have told them something, otherwise why would they seem this nosey?

"Well, I just want to see you have everything," says Mom.

"Your Mom does worry about you, son."

My frown deepens.

They want to know who I have over. They want to see what kind of people I've been surrounding myself with recently. Although, trying to get out of dinner around the eighth course was probably a bad move. Even Alex gave me a look like I had completely lost my mind.

I check the time on watch: 10:30. Maybe everyone is asleep?

I push my key into the door, unlocking it and pushing it open. My heart deflates when I hear alternative rock music playing in the background followed by Rachel's giggling.

Please, let them be clothed, I think while kicking off my shoes. "Hey!" I call. "I'm home."

"Finally!" Rachel shouts, running out of the living room and into the narrow hall leading towards the entrance. She stops when she sees me and my parents, surprise all over her face.

I can't help the smile coming to my lips as I gaze upon her, finding her in fluffy bunny slippers and matching pink bunny shorts and tank.

"Oh," she breathes while peeking over me. "I didn't know you were bring back guests." She scowls at me and swats my arm. "You should have called and told me. I could have changed."

"Dude, who's here?" Seth shouts from the other room. "Do I need to change?"

I want to ask if he's wearing clothes, but I grimace, knowing my parents would have a million more questions. Turning around, I force a smile, trying not to grimace at Mom's alarmed face or Father's quizzical look.

"This is Rachel," I say while gesturing towards my girlfriend. "She's a… friend." I want to tell them that she's mine. That I care for her more than I've ever cared for any other person, but my tongue doesn't work. It never works around them.

And once again, I don't want them interrogating me.

"Oh, well it's nice to meet you Rachel," says father with a forced smile while holding out his hand. "I'm Franklin Brent. Lucas's father."

"Oh, it's so nice to meet you," says Rachel with a bright smile. She turns to mom and holds out her hand. "I'm Rachel."

Mom takes Rachel's hand briefly and gives it a gentle squeeze. "Christina."

"Are there people here?" I hear Hunter ask, making me want to roll my eyes and rub my temples.

When will this day ever end?

"Yes, there are people here," I groan, not able to contain the real me inside any longer. "Please, come say hello to my parents."

"Well, I'll let Hunter and Seth entertain you." Rachel slowly backs away. "It was really nice to meet you."

Mom clucks her tongue and her head tilts to the side. "Let me help you, sweetie," she says, her eyes narrowing on Rachel while she follows my girlfriend into the kitchen.

I watch them go, wondering if I should be nervous at all. But Rachel is good with people. She was able to get me, Hunter, and Seth to like her after being such assholes to her.

She'll be fine with Mom.

9

RACHEL

"How long have you known Lucas?" Christina asks while I scrub the barbecue off the plate.

Lucas's mom had said she would help me in the kitchen, yet all she's done is watch me. It's not like I'm complaining or anything. It just seems a bit… strange. I turn around, finding her leaning against the counter with arms crossed, her gaze scrutinizing my pajamas. Her brows furrow for a moment when her gaze lands on my bunny ears and I feel heat sting my ears, feeling absolutely mortified that I'm finally meeting Lucas's mother and I'm in my PJ's.

And he introduced me as his friend.

I try not to feel so upset about his phrasing of our relationship, but no matter how much I try I can't push the cracks in my heart away; nor can I get rid of the butterflies in my stomach. Christina hasn't stopped staring at me and I'm beginning to wonder if there's something actually wrong with me.

"Um, since the beginning of this year. I'm a freshman at Aurora."

"Oh, a freshman. How… nice."

I purse my lips while turning around. I don't want Christina to see my face, knowing it's probably as red as a tomato right now. I feel embarrassed. Lucas really should have called. Sure, it's his apartment and everything, but his parents are dressed so nice and we're… not.

Although, it doesn't matter for Hunter and Seth.

They're not Lucas's girlfriend.

"And what do you study?"

I scrub against the dishes furiously. I should put them in the dishwasher, but I need something to do with my hands to keep them from picking at my fingers. "Art." I push a stray hair behind my ear. "I'm actually here on an internship. I'm working at the Louvre."

I hear footsteps behind me and feel Christina hovering at my side. My body stills and I turn, eyes widening when I find her mere centimeters from me. She smiles bitterly, a dark look in her eye making me want to crawl into the cupboards and lock the door. "I know exactly what you are," she whispers so softly I barely register she's saying anything. I look back, wondering if the bros are noticing any of this, but they are too busy speaking with Lucas's father about sports at Aurora.

Christina grabs my chin and jerks my face back to her. "Acting all intriguing in order to capture my son's interest. Deep down you are nothing."

I flinch, taking a step away from her. Tears brim my eyes and I quickly blink them away. I need to remain strong. I can't back down. "You're wrong," I whisper, hating the shaking in my voice. I glance over my shoulder, hoping to catch Lucas's eye, but he's too busy staring at the floor, leaning against the wall, as if he wants to be sucked inside the building and hide there for eternity. There's something in his gaze that is incredibly off.

I turn back to Christina, nearly jumping out of my skin when I find her standing right next to me. She strokes my hair away from my face. It's such a tender touch when she's staring at me as if she loathes my very being. "You will never be good enough for my son," she says lowly. "He'll drop you in the next few months. You just wait."

I don't move as she strides past me, knocking her shoulder against mine. I feel like I'm in high school again and the popular girls are picking on me for my fashion sense.

But instead, this time, it's my boyfriend's mother, and she absolutely hates me.

I fidget in the kitchen, watching Christina pat Hunter and Seth's shoulder, not knowing if I should go over there and socialize. I clench my jaw, feeling the tears about to erupt. Turning on my heel, I pad towards the closest bathroom, between Seth and Lucas's rooms and shut the door with more force than intended.

Standing over the sink, I gasp. My hands clenching the marble while I try to quiet my sobs. Tears slip down my face and I'm unable to stop myself from crying. I look at myself in the mirror, scrutinizing the freckles on the bridge of my nose, my curly blonde hair. I know I shouldn't listen to Lucas's mother. I know we come from different worlds and she's trying to look out for her son.

But I can't help the feeling, knowing she's right.

I'm nothing to Lucas.

I'm not a big breasted gymnast. I don't have money.

What can I possibly bring to the table with Lucas?

What does he even see in me?

I hear laughter wafting towards me. It sounds like Hunter. I close my eyes, concentrating on his deep, heady voice and inhale deeply while calming my breath. They will think it's strange if I remain locked in here. I should go back to the kitchen. They'll be gone in the next ten minutes.

My eyes slowly open and I wipe the tears from my bloodshot eyes and blow my nose in the tissue. I grimace at my red nose and the makeup lingering on the paper, but this is the best I can do for now. No point in going to my room and redoing the whole thing, especially since it's late at night and I should be heading to bed.

I sigh and my shoulders slump forward in defeat. Turning away from my reflection, I trudge out the bathroom door and force a bright smile. The bros have made a semi-circle around Lucas's parents and Seth seems to be deep in conversation with Lucas's father.

"We know someone who will be participating in the marathon, as well," Franklin says while crossing his arms, a smug look in his eye. "Do you know an Alex Goode, per chance?"

I watch Seth's hands fist. A dark, roaring rage glimmers within him, his muscles tensing while he holds his ground. "Yes," he says lowly, his fists trembling in a vain attempt to keep his anger hidden. "I know of him."

"He's our little star," says Christina, yet her gaze is glued on me as she speaks. I still under her eyes, watching her look me up and down once more, scrutinizing my clothes before offering a cruel smile. "We've known his family since Lukey was in kindergarten. We'll of course be cheering him on, but still, best of luck." Her gaze slides to Seth, and she wrinkles her nose.

"Thank you." Seth tilts his head to the side, his pitch raised as if he's asking a question. His gaze slides to mine, and he gives me a shrug. "Well, speaking of running." He stretches his arms over his head. "I should go… run. It was a pleasure seeing you again."

Franklin gives a curt nod, holding out his hand. "Likewise."

I watch Seth give Lucas's father a firm shake before turning on his heel and heading back to his room, most likely to change.

"Well, I suppose we should be off then," says Christina while looking at her watch. The crystals, or perhaps, diamonds glisten under the light and I faintly wonder if the woman is flashing it to me on purpose. "It's getting late."

"I'll be stopping by Samuel's office soon," says Franklin while shaking Lucas's hand. I watch Lucas bristle, fear flashing on his face. It's very brief, but it's there. Why am I getting the sense this isn't a normal family visit?

"Yes, of course, sir."

Christina kisses Lucas on the cheek and I nearly jump out of my skin as she turns to me. "It was a pleasure meeting you Rachel." Her smile makes my skin curl. "It would be great to see you again. Maybe at the club? Or for brunch sometime?"

She looks at me expecting an answer and I have no clue what's the correct thing to say. Just ten minutes ago she was telling me I would never be good enough for her son, and now she is inviting me to a country club in Paris for some tea or wine? I feel my head bob up and down, my mouth hanging open, breathing a soft, "Sure."

What else am I going to say, with both Lucas and Franklin staring at me? As if I could say anything else.

Christina tilts her head to the side, placing a hand on my shoulder and squeezing it gently. "Perfect," she says sweetly, the sound of it curdling my insides.

I watch both Lucas's parents walk down the foyer and out the door, Lucas following after them like a lost puppy, probably to make sure they make it to their limo safely. My legs shake, as if supporting me up is no longer their task. I stumble towards the couch, flinging myself down on it while placing a hand against my forehead.

"Alright, I have my therapy session with Dr. Forrester," I hear Hunter say from behind. "No one bother me for the next hour."

I give a slight nod, hearing his steps heading towards his room. I hope Christina was being polite. I don't care if brunch consists of diamond studded cupcakes with champagne consisting of golden flakes. I don't want to go.

I hear stomping behind me and glance over my shoulder, seeing Seth in his running shorts and tank, a runner's belt around his waist. He leans over the sink, guzzling down water before splashing the liquid over his hair and face.

"Are you really going running? At this time?" I ask incredulously.

"Of course I'm running!" Seth shouts while slamming his fist onto the counter, scowling at me as if I'm this Alex Goode that has him all worked up.

I glare back at him, slowly rising from the couch. I have no clue what's going on, or why the mention of Alex Goode has him all riled up, but I'm not going to be treated like a pushover. "I was just asking." I jut my chin out and cross my arms, feeling as if we've suddenly been transported back to the beginning of the year, where the bros and I were consistently at war with each other. "It's getting late. I was just worried."

Seth's gaze lowers and I watch the muscles in his arm and shoulders relax. "I know," he murmurs with a slight shake of his head.

"Who is Alex Goode? How do you know him?"

Seth grimaces and shoves himself away from the sink. "He's a fucking asshole." I watch him stalk towards the door, slamming it behind him.

I release a sigh and look up at the ceiling, wondering if this is a one-time occurrence, or if I am going to have to deal with not only Lucas's parents showing up around dinner, but also Seth's bad attitude. I know he's stressed about the marathon, but I don't quite understand why. Although, Seth hasn't told me how he obtained the money to be able to go with us to Paris, only that his coach knew there's going to be a race and that Seth should join.

Part of me wonders if there's more to it than that. But, knowing Seth, I suspect he's not going to tell me. Simply asking him is bound to set him off and I am in a state where all I want is to come home to a happy, calm house after a hard day dealing with Lauren and my boss.

"They're gone," I hear Lucas call happily from the foyer.

"Did you see Seth?"

Lucas shakes his head while he strides inside, smiling brightly while reaching for me. His arm comes around my waist and he pulls me to him, nuzzling his nose against mine. "He must have taken the stairs. I was lazy and took the elevator."

He goes to kiss me, but I push my hand against his chest. Before any kissing begins and continues, I need to talk to him about the way his mother spoke to me. Otherwise, it'll probably brew within me until it explodes into an ugly mess. I don't want Paris becoming any more tainted with bad experiences than it already has.

"Your mom acted kinda strange towards me," I say, watching a hint of surprise and worry come over Lucas's face.

He stares at me for a moment, before chuckling faintly and pulling me closer to him. "I wouldn't worry about it," he whispers. He places a kiss against my jaw, and I shudder with desire as he grazes his teeth against the sensitive part of my neck.

I grit my teeth, recalling the way Christina held my chin. "She was very aggressive, Lucas." I scowl when he doesn't say anything, his kissing getting sloppier, needier. "Lucas, stop," I say angrily, sliding my hands between us and pushing him away again.

Lucas sighs in frustration, raking his hands through his hair furiously. "What, Rachel? What is it?"

"I'm trying to tell you something." I wish Lucas was looking at me, yet he's staring at the floor. "Your mother was quite rude to me in the kitchen. She said-"

"My parents are just like that."

My mouth lingers open, trying to form the words, trying to tell Lucas that his mother thinks I'm nothing, that he will drop me soon. However, Lucas's gaze silences me. There's something broken in there that I don't quite understand. Something I don't think I will ever understand.

He steps towards me, taking me into his arms again. "Let's not fight," he whispers into my ear. "My parents always stress me out. Let's just pretend they were never here and go back to what we were doing the other night." He pulls away from me, a smile on his lips, yet there's sadness in his gaze. I watch him waggle his eyebrows up and down, and I wonder if this is what he's used to; pretending to be happy, to ignore his parents and the way they treat people. I wonder if he does those things in order to be and feel happy.

And I wonder if he's only with me in order to rebel against his parents. Maybe his mother is right. He will drop me when he gets bored.

Despite my worries, I allow him to claim my lips. I lean into him, wrapping my arms around his neck and hold onto him tight. I don't know why, but I feel like we are doing this for the last time; like his parents coming here are some sort of foreshadowing to the end of our future together.

I kiss him like it's the last time, sliding my tongue against his, lifting my leg onto his hip. He catches it and presses his hardening cock against me. I rub my body against him, moaning each time he hits that sensitive nub. His hand cups my bottom, massaging me threw the pink bunny shorts. I whimper, unable to stop myself no matter how much I try. I'm trapped with this man. There's no escape. All I want is for him to take me, have his way with me.

Lucas moves and I have no clue where we are going, or where he is taking me. His other hand catches my leg and soon my legs are wrapped around his waist, holding him tight while he kisses me.

"Rachel," he murmurs against my lips. "I want you so bad."

I moan. The words making me shudder with desire. We stumble backwards onto the couch. His body presses me into the cushions. I kick my bunny slippers off while running my hands through his dark, silky hair. He groans against my lips while entwine my tongue around his, breathing him in, unable to pull away as if he's the only one making breathing possible.

My hands slide down the front of him, reaching for his belt, deftly undoing them while my lips kiss a path from his mouth down his neck. He pulls down my shorts and I kick them to the side. His hand slides up my leg, before pushing in between my lips.

What a lovely night not to wear any underwear.

I gasp, tossing my head back while he strokes my clit. He slides his fingers up and down, teasing my hole, before sliding back up. I bite my lip, trying to contain myself, knowing Hunter and his therapist might hear if I open my mouth.

"Let me hear your voice," Lucas whispers in my ear, making me shiver and pull at him to get him closer.

He kisses me, drinking me in. His other hand massaging my breast through my bunny shirt. My hands slide down his back, pushing his suit pants down. I cup his bottom through his boxers, wanting him deep inside me. His hand moves quickly, massaging me harder as if he's clinging to me and never wants to let me go.

I don't know why we are so desperate for each other. It's like he's read my mind. I watch him pull away. His shirt is rumpled. I reach for him, wanting to take it off, but he gently bats my hand away. He takes out a condom from his wallet and tears it open. I help with his boxers, tugging them down and watching him slide the condom onto his cock.

Spreading my legs, I reach for him, watching him crawl on top of me. He kisses my forehead lightly, then each of my cheeks before placing his soft lips onto mine, kissing me gently while shoving deep inside me.

I gasp. My hands cling to his shoulders. My fingers dig into his shirt. I need to have it off him. I want to feel him on me, but he's thrusting so deep and hard into me. He's so big, filling up every inch of me. Each thrust sends me over the edge.

His hands slide up my front, toying with my nipples while he continues pounding into me slowly and deeply. Gazing up at him, I don't know what he sees, with my mouth agape, moaning and thrusting against him.

"Lucas," I breathe, trying to tug him closer to me, but he remains rooted above me, watching me as my head lulls from side to side.

His jaw clenches and his hands slide away, grabbing the bottom of my shirt and tugging it over my head. As soon as the garment is off me, his mouth is on my breasts, sucking and tugging tenderly. I grind myself against him, whimpering and near the brink. I want him to move faster. I want him to touch me more. He keeps driving me crazy with that mouth of his. I watch him as he looks up, my whole body trembling with need as I gaze back at him, at the glimmer of adoration and affection in his eye.

I still when Lucas strokes the side of my cheek. The touch is simple, yet it nearly unravels me. He releases my nipple. His tongue swirls around it for a moment before he moves away. I bite my lip as he thrusts faster.

His movements are becoming more erratic. I grab his hand, my nails digging into his skin.

"More," I say, louder than I should. I hear him gasp as my nails rake against his arms. "Lucas, more." I clench my jaw, trying to keep my voice down as Lucas pounds harder and faster into me.

"You want more, Rachel?" Lucas growls.

My head lulls up and down.

Lucas chuckles while his hands grab my hips. He moves swiftly until he's lying with his back on the couch and I'm straddling him. My face flushes and I press my hands against his chest, trying to balance myself on top of him.

Gazing down at Lucas, I see a mischievous gleam take hold of him. His head tilts as he says, "More, Rachel. Give me more."

I lean forward, grabbing hold of his shoulders and slowly lower myself onto him, earning a sharp gasp that sends my whole body tightening with desire. I do it again, watching Lucas toss back his head.

"Like that?" I breathe.

He nods. "Faster."

I quicken my pace, taking several moments with each thrust to grind my clit against him. My whole body feels like it's tightening around him. I can't stop. All I want is that sweet release. Lucas grabs my breasts, pulling and pinching my nipples as I continue moving against him. I feel myself slowly rising, as if I am having an out-of-body experience.

"Fuck, Lucas," I murmur as he grabs my hips, setting the rhythm and not letting me stop. I feel him hardening within me, his cock twitching. My lips part, and I feel myself losing all sense of reality around me. I grab his hands, holding them close to my chest while I toss back my head. My soft whimpers turn into loud moans as the pleasure I'm experiencing turning into my peaking climax exploding through me.

"Lucas!" I scream. I continue screaming, my mouth gaping open. I don't care if Hunter and his therapist can hear me. I can't stop. My whole body shudders and tightens around Lucas while my mind becomes slush; only focused on Lucas and his thick cock stuffed deep inside me.

Lucas moans, thrusting into me even harder, once, then twice. He bites his lip while stilling inside me. I watch as he empties inside me, his body becoming lax on the couch. He pulls me down on top of him. His mouth is on my brow, kissing me while he gathers his breath. Hands run up and down my arms and I nuzzle into his shirt, wondering why I didn't bother to pull it off him before.

"Don't worry," he whispers against my hair. "Everything will be fine now."

I don't know if he's talking to me or himself, and I feel something dark claw at the back of my mind; once again taunting me on whether this is the last time Lucas and I are going to be together. I still want to talk to him about what his mother said. Just because we had sex doesn't mean that everything is fixed.

I lift my head, looking up at his half-opened eyes and the calm on his face. Maybe I should bring it up later. I don't want to worry the mood. I can do it tomorrow when I get back from work. Thinking about work makes me grimace and I purse my lips, not knowing what I should do about Lauren and my boss tomorrow.

I honestly don't want to go.

10

LUCAS

Fuck. Fuck. Fuck. Fuck.

I'm fucking late for work.

I slam open the door to the office, ignoring the receptionist who gives me a grim look while she talks to whomever on the phone. I have no clue how I'm going to explain this to Samuel. He's so much like my father. I look at the time on my watch, grimacing when I see it's ten minutes past eight. Sure, I'm ten minutes late, but for men like Samuel and my dad, that's like an eternity. Most likely blaming the traffic isn't going to cut it. It's not my fault that someone got into an accident. These things happen.

I knock at Samuel's door, waiting for him to answer while I shift nervously from foot to foot. I am so screwed. I should have left earlier, but I was so drained from spending most the evening with my parents. I needed that extra fifteen minutes of sleep.

"That better be Lucas," I hear Samuel say on the other side.

I grimace while opening the door, peaking inside and seeing Samuel's dark scowl from where he sat at his desk. His chin is in his hands, elbows pressed into the dark wood while he leans over, his glare darkening on my form.

Open the door further, I bow my head, keeping my gaze fixed on the floor. "I'm sorry," I say, cringing at the slight tremble in my voice. "It was the traffic. I'll-"

"I don't care if you stopped to help a little old lady cross the street. What's so hard about being on time?"

I grimace at the bitterness in his tone. Lifting my head, I swallow the lump in my throat and hold myself deathly still, knowing no amount of fidgeting will help me get through the terribleness that this morning is becoming.

"I'm really sorry. It will never happen-"

"When I decided to take you on, I thought I was taking on a member of the Brent family," says Samuel while slowly rising from his chair, reminding me of a tiger on the hunt. "I was irritated that you could just waltz in hear and ask for a job, but I thought: hmmm, it might be good for the firm." I watch him stroke his beard mockingly. "He's Franklin's kid after all. I'm sure Franklin raised him to uphold company values." His hand drops, smacking his pants and I cringe at the sharp sound it makes. "But, no, seems like you're just like all the other blockheads who come in here, wanting an internship." He stalks towards me and my eyes widen as I watch him shove a finger into my face. "Do you know who I had to let go to make space for you? Do you know all the time and energy that went into finding the perfect candidate?" I watch him turn on his heel, throwing his hands into the air in frustration.

"No, sir, I don't-"

"Of course you don't!" Samuel shouts while slamming his hands on the desk. "All that was pretty much a waste of my fucking time now that I had to let him go and replace him with you." I grimace as he turns around and waves a hand in my direction. "I should tell your father about how much of a freaking asshole you've been."

My eyes widen. "No," I say, taking a step towards him.

"Demanding a job from me, then half assing it. Now coming in late."

"I'm sorry," I say, my voice cracking. I feel like a little boy again. My legs tremble and my stomach twists. I feel like I might throw up, or go to my knees and beg. I root my feet into the floor, demanding my body remain upright. "Really, I won't-"

"I should tell him that you weren't planning on interning with me."

My skin goes cold and I watch him grab his cell phone from his pocket.

"What is it you wanted to do, Lucas?" Samuel asks while tapping something onto his phone. My breath stills. I can hear my heart pounding in my ears. I pray to God he isn't texting my dad. Samuel chuckles bitterly. "Did you want to be a writer? Was that it? Was that how you were going to spend your summer?"

I take another step towards him. "Please, I'm very sorry. It won't happen again. I swear." I press my hands together. It's the closest I will get to begging. "Please, don't call my dad. Just give me another chance."

Samuel stares at me. His phone lingers in his hand. He's going to do it. I can't believe he's going to call my dad. Then all my plans will be foiled. What will I do then? I stare at him, wondering what more I can say to get him to listen to reason. I'll wash his dirty underwear? Clean the dishes? Mop the kitchen floors? Although, these are all tactics that would work on the bros, not on a grown man. Not to mention, my bros would never rat me out to my parents, no matter how pissed off they are with me.

The office phone on the desk rings and I flinch. For a moment, I think it's my dad as I watch Samuel reach for it. Part of me wants to lunge for it, smack it away from Samuel's freckled hands, grab it and throw it out of the window. However, I don't, knowing nothing would help. Samuel still has his cellphone. He probably already has plans to meet them for cocktails later. Sooner or later, he'll find some way to tell them.

"What," Samuel says bitingly to the receptionist.

I watch him nod, watch him slide his cell back into his pocket. "Alright, I'll be there in a minute. Bring them some espresso and sparkling water." He slams the phone down before turning towards me. His gaze rakes over me, as if he's sizing me up, while he strides my way.

"Well, lucky for you, I have a meeting." He smiles brightly at me, as if he hadn't been yelling at me for being late. "Make yourself useful and take notes."

"Ye-yes," I stutter, running after him as he strides briskly down the hall and further into the firm.

I follow him into a bright meeting room with large windows displaying a clear view of Paris. My gaze lingers on the Louvre for a moment, wondering if Rachel is enjoying her time working at the museum. I silently wish I was with her.

"Lucas," I hear Samuel mutter and I flinch, turning towards the men seated in front of the smart board. My eyes widen as I see red hair and an annoying face. One I genuinely hate with a loathing passion.

"Marcus," I say as cheerfully as possible, holding out my hand while watching Marcus take it. He's dressed in his finest with a pin-striped suit and a gold Rolex hanging off his wrist. I turn towards his manager, a grey old man with a thick gut and flabby cheeks. "It's nice to meet you, sir," I say politely while shaking his hand and taking a seat next to Samuel.

"What are you doing here?" Marcus asks while waving a hand at me. "I thought you were still in Colorado or something."

"Mr. Brent is my intern," Samuel says distantly while taking out several files. I have no clue what is going on, or why we are meeting with Marcus and his boss. Are we suing their client? Is one of Samuel's clients suing one of theirs? Maybe Samuel has a point. I obviously don't care about this job. He probably briefed me about this yesterday and I wasn't paying attention.

Samuel clears his throat and I turn to him. His frown alerts me to the fact that I should be doing something, yet I have no clue what. "Notes," he says while nodding to the pen and notebook on the desk in front of me.

I grab the pen and nod, waiting for Marcus's boss to say anything of interest, yet all I can think about is Rachel last night and the way her body had felt against mine. I should have listened to her about my mom. I honestly just wanted to forget about the whole situation. I wanted to bury myself in her, have her soothe all the aches and pains of having to deal with my parents. Both my parents could be cruel when they wanted to be. They snubbed their noses at anyone without money, not trusting anyone, not letting anyone in.

It's sad, when I think about it. The only thing they really care about is looks, and which of their friends they can use. My brows furrow and I frown while gazing out the window. Am I going to end up like them? Is that what is in store for me after I graduate college? Am I going to wind up with friends who only care what I can offer them?

I turn to Samuel, watching him speak, realizing I haven't written anything down. This is ridiculous. I should just quit and have Samuel hire back his intern. There's no point in continuing with this ruse. I obviously am not made for this kind of job.

"Alright," says Samuel while standing and holding out his hand to the man. "Thank you so much for coming."

I jump up. I haven't written anything down. I don't even recall Marcus's boss's name. What is wrong with me? I quickly grab the notebook, jerking it towards me so Samuel can't see that I've done absolutely zero work. All I've done is worry about my future and about Rachel.

"I hope to hear from you soon," says Marcus's boss, Mr. Grey Haired Guy.

Samuel chuckles. "Oh, you most definitely will."

I follow them out. The moment Samuel is alone I'm going to tell him it's better we let bygones be bygones. I'll come up with some excuse for my dad. I'm sure I can make up something on the fly.

"Hey, Lucas," I hear Marcus's grating voice, feeling his hand tapping on my shoulder.

I slowly turn around, cradling the notebook even closer to my chest. "What's up, Marcus?"

"There's a party going on in about two weeks. It's a black-tie event. Nice wine. Lots of opportunity to meet potential clients and partners."

I smile, fighting the need to grimace. "Oh, I don't know. I might be busy with the Rachel and the-"

"He'll attend."

I turn around, finding Samuel behind me, looking smug. "Well, I don't know-" I start.

Samuel smacks my back. "It'll be good for you to get my and your name out there. We could always use more clients. Not to mention, Mr. Blake will be there. I need you to talk to him; get him interested in our firm."

"Sounds great," says Marcus and I instantly want to punch him in the face for bringing this up in front of Samuel. I need to get out of this. I'm already in way to deep. "I'll have my assistant send you the invite."

How does he have an assistant? I want to ask, but I clamp my mouth close and nod dumbly. I watch him follow Mr. Grey Haired Guy out the door, wishing I could walk out those doors, as well.

"Hey, we need to talk," I say while turning around, finding Samuel already walking back to his office. I chase after him. "I think you should hire the guy you let go. I don't think I'm a great fit."

"I agree," Samuel says without looking at me, striding into his office and throwing the files down on his desk. "You suck. My other intern was much better."

"Ok," I start, feeling uneasy at how he's agreeing with me. "So, we agree. I should go. I'll give my dad some sort of excuse. And we can-"

"No."

My brows furrow and I cross my arms. "No?" What does he mean no?

Samuel nods. "That's right, no." He sighs and turns around, leaning against his desk. "Knowing you, you're going to give your dad some sort of lame excuse he'll likely buy so long as he doesn't know that you are dawdling your time."

"That's not true."

"Oh?" Samuel grabs his cell and hands it to me. "Prove it. Tell your father right now that you didn't come here to work for me. You came to write and enjoy Paris."

I don't dare touch that phone, knowing the moment I do I will have to tell Dad the truth. And he can't handle the truth.

Samuel smirks. "I thought so." He returns the cell to his pocket. "Therefore, you are going to work for me and you are going to get me Mr. Blake. If you don't, I will tell your father everything."

My eyes widen. "You can't," I whisper.

Samuel's smile widens while he crosses his arms. "I most definitely can."

11

RACHEL

My stomach grumbles angrily at me while I slowly unwrap my sandwich, which I bought from a small, mom and pop store on my way to work today. My shoulders feel tense from running around the entire morning. Who knew so much happened behind the scenes at a museum? Originally, I thought I would be lounging around, drinking espresso while providing help to any lost tourists. Recent events have proved that is definitely not the case, and I'm kinda an idiot for thinking so.

I have a feeling Dr. Arnaud would agree with me on that. I grimace thinking about my boss. She has yet to grace me with a smile and I'm beginning to think I will also be a stain on her good day.

I should have gone to the first meeting, I tell myself, mentally kicking myself for being, once again, a freaking idiot. I lift my gaze, watching the tourists take pictures in front of the palace. I haven't even attempted site seeing. Maybe this weekend, when Lucas isn't at work. Seth could use a break from thinking about the marathon.

I'm really beginning to worry about him. This morning he only had a banana and a table spoon of peanut butter for breakfast before his run, and I know he's shooting for at least 15k. He's pushing himself way too hard. At this rate, he's going to get hurt.

I shake my thoughts of Seth and look at the time, groaning when I see I've already wasted 10 minutes of my precious lunch obsessing about things out of my control. Thankfully, I haven't had to deal with Lauren too much today. Only a curt hello from me and a dark scowl from her.

I'd call that a good day.

My feet dangle while I sit on the wall, listening to the rushing water from the fountain. I shove my sandwich into my mouth, moaning as the meat and cheese practically melt into my mouth. My phone vibrates in my dress pants and as I munch on my single bite, I frown at the unknown number on the caller ID.

"Hello?" I ask into the receiver in-between mouthfuls of food.

"Did I catch you at a busy time?"

My brows scrunch at the familiar voice, trying to place it, yet no-one is coming to mind. Definitely not my mom, nor is it any of the bros. "Who is this?" I say hoarsely after swallowing my lump of food.

"It's Samuel Allen." I hear him chuckle, my eyes widening. How does he have my phone number? I look around, wondering if he's going to say he's standing across from me, but there are too many people and I can't find him in the crowd.

"How did you get my number?" I ask while standing.

"I got it from Lucas, of course."

My brows pinch together. Lucas told me he didn't want me working for Samuel. So, why did he give him my number? "Ok," I say hesitantly. I stuff my sandwich back into my bag, eyeing it sadly, but my lunch is nearly over and I don't want Dr. Arnaud chewing me out for my tardiness.

"I was wondering if you gave any thought to the job I offered."

I grimace. I was hoping I could just let that whole thing silently die. I wasn't expecting him to call me and demand for an answer. "Well, I don't know," I say while walking briskly inside the Louvre. "I'm already busy at the museum. I don't think I would have the time."

"Really?" He sounds astounded, as if I told him I won a million dollars, which makes me even more nervous and curious. "It would be great experience for you, given that you are a photographer. Of course, I understand. If you don't have time, what else can I do?"

I nod along, smiling awkwardly at Dr. Arnaud staring at me from the other side of the hall. Her eyes narrow on my cellphone and I know I should hang up in the next two seconds or else she's going to take my phone and squash it in her tiny hands.

"But, I took you for the type of person to seize what you want."

I grimace, not liking here this conversation is going.

"Is the museum really giving you everything you hoped and dreamed of?"

No, I think while Dr. Arnaud turns towards me. Each step she takes in my direction makes my hard pound louder and faster in my ears.

"Are you able to use your skills to your full potential?"

No, I'm pretty much a doormat and a delivery person, I think, my grasp tightening on my phone as Dr. Arnaud draws closer.

I turn away from Dr. Arnaud, my voice lowering as I say, "No, but I made a commitment."

"And how is that going?"

Absolutely terribly.

"Miss Miller," I hear Dr. Arnaud calling bitterly.

"Alright, fine," I whisper harshly into the phone. "When and where should I meet you?"

"I'll text you the address. Be here within the hour."

My eyes widen. "Within the hour?" I ask way too loudly.

"Miss Miller!"

"See you soon," I hear Samuel say before the line ends.

I quickly straighten, nearly jumping out of my skin when I see Dr. Arnaud standing directly behind me. I smile brightly while shoving my phone back into my bag. "Why, hello Dr. Arnaud," I say awkwardly. "How are you?"

She raises an eyebrow. "Did you not hear me call you?"

I point to myself, feigning disbelief. "You were calling me? I had no idea."

I can tell she's trying desperately not to roll her eyes. Instead, her head raises, and she clucks her tongue. "Your lunch time is over. I'll need you in the basement for this afternoon."

I nod vigorously. "Of course."

I watch her slowly turning around, walking down the stairs. My thumbs twiddle around each other, not knowing what to do. The basement is boring. Doing some photography for Samuel's firm sounds way more interesting. I feel myself slowly inching towards the exit. A twinge of guilt stabs through my heart and I feel like I'm being pulled back and forth.

I came to Paris to work at the Louvre; the most beautiful museum in all of Paris. Possibly the world, although I can't say for sure since I've travelled pretty much nowhere. I worked so hard to get here. I shouldn't be changing gears at the drop of a hat. I should be working hard to fulfill my dream.

But I don't want to work in a museum when I graduate school. I want to be out there, in the world, taking pictures of people and places. Not cooped up here where Dr. Arnaud can cluck her tongue at me while Lauren mutters some snide comment under her breath.

I turn around and walk as quickly as possible towards the door. I can't believe I am actually doing this. I am actually bailing on my internship. A smile comes to my lips and I have no clue why I'm suddenly feeling so giddy. I've barely started this program. I'm only a few days in, and already I'm leaving to pursue something I enjoy more.

My heart drops to my knees as I run into Lauren.

"Where are you going?" she asks, looking me up and down, before scowling at me.

I ignore her while I quickly brush past, knowing if I stop to talk to her I will change my mind.

"Hey!" Lauren shouts and I groan as I hear her footsteps chasing after me. "Where the hell are you going?"

I turn on my heel, watching her stop mere inches from me. "It doesn't concern you."

She crosses her arms and smirks. "Don't tell me you're actually leaving?"

I roll my eyes and turn around.

"Wait?" I hear her shout. "You're actually leaving?"

"Yes! Lauren!" I shake my head. I don't know why I am bothering to say anything to her. "I'm leaving. Why do you even care?"

I hear her scoff. Why is she still following me? "I don't care."

"Then go away."

"I just can't believe you are willing to throw everything away to go fuck around with your boy toys."

I grind my teeth to keep from screaming. I turn on my heel, my hands fisting. I'm so tempted to punch her in the face. "You must be kidding me. That's not what's going on here."

Lauren scoffs and I watch her flick her hair over her shoulder, reminding me of some mean high school chick picking on one of her underlings. "Oh, really? That's not what's going on here?"

"I got a job. That's where I'm going."

Her brows furrow and she stares back at me with a mixture confusion, curiosity, and anger. "A job? What about your job here?" She gestures towards the Louvre.

I shake my head. "I-" I groan. "I don't even know why I'm telling you. Just leave me alone."

"You can't tell me you are actually dropping your internship program for some other job. You do realize this was a pain in the butt to get into."

I cross my arms. "Of course, I know it was a pain in the butt to get into. It's a pain in the butt to do, too."

Lauren laughs bitterly. "You must be kidding me. It's a pain in the butt because they only accept the best. You should know that. I can't believe you are just going to up and leave something just because it gets a little hard for you. Life is hard, Rachel. Eventually you're going to learn that."

"Yeah, I know Lauren!" I shout. "Now, leave me alone!"

I turn around and run, dodging the crowd of tourists. I run all the way to the crossing, where I stop to catch my breath. When I turn around, I'm happy to see Lauren hasn't followed me.

***

"Very nice," Samuel says from behind.

I feel him come up from behind, looking over my shoulder at my camera while I snap another shot of his assistant in his office, holding a phone. The scenery of Paris's European architecture is so beautiful and the lighting in the room is magnificent.

"I knew you were right for the job."

I smile and snap another shot. "I think that should do it," I say while looking at the photo. "I think this one is the best yet."

"Great, that's all for now Jacklyn."

The receptionist nods while standing from the desk. I try not to stare at her white stilettos or how tight her white pencil skirt is. The woman could actually be a model. I'm shocked she chose to work at a place like this with legs as long as hers.

"I can email the photos to you, if you want," I say while returning my camera back to my bag. I'm actually lucky I brought it with me today. I wanted to get some photos in this morning, but unfortunately I had been running late, like usual.

"That sounds perfect. And you'll also do that Nstagram thing?"

I swallow my giggles, knowing it would be rude. Him not understanding the whole advertising on social media is why he brought me in. I shouldn't laugh in his face. Still, Nstagram thing?

"Yes, I will upload them tonight."

I linger by the door, waiting for him to excuse me, but instead he leans against his desk with his arms crossed in front of his chest.

"I like you, you know," he says sweetly.

That stomach curdling feeling is coming back. Why is he saying this so suddenly? Especially since I was just photographing for him for the past hour. God, I hope this isn't some weird sexual harassment thing. Maybe that's why Lucas didn't want me working with him.

"Thank you," I say hesitantly, taking a step towards the door.

Samuel doesn't move and I'm left wondering what else I should be doing for him. Should I give him a card or anything? Tell him how much he owes me for my services?

"How have you and Lucas been since you've arrived in Paris?"

My heart stops. Not this again. Why are we talking about Lucas when I came here to work? "I really don't want to talk about that," I say, my voice a little too soft. It's like my tongue doesn't want to work. "Is there anything else you would like for me to do? Should I leave my contact information with your receptionist?"

Samuel sighs and I watch him push away from his desk and step towards me. "I'm just worried about you getting too close to him. I've known that boy since he was a kid. Frankly, I know everything about him."

He's getting a little too close for my tastes. I'm suddenly reminded of Josh coming after me, pushing me down on the couch, grabbing my leg. I take another step back, my hand seizing the door. I'm ready to run and scream if I have to.

However, Samuel stops a foot from me. He tilts his head to the side, a bright smile on his face which doesn't match the dark glimmer in his gaze. "I have a feeling Lucas will drop you eventually. Better sooner rather than later. I wouldn't want you getting too attached only to wind up hurt in the end."

I blink. My eyes prickle with unshed tears.

"I know how the boy works with women. I just don't think you're well matched. You have," I watch him tap his chin while I try to remain calm. Don't cry, I tell myself. Please, don't cry. "Well, you're too driven for the likes of him. Do you understand what I'm trying to tell you?"

First Christina, now him?

Why do I get the feeling that everyone close to Lucas hates me?

I give him a curt nod. "Of course," I breathe, my tongue loose. "Is that all?" I open the door, ready to go whether he wanted me to or not.

Samuel nods his head. "Yes, that's all Rachel."

I don't wait. I don't say goodbye. I turn on my heel and run down the hall towards the doors. As soon as I'm out of the building, standing near the corner of the street I burst into tears. I cover my face, trying to swallow down my sobs, but I can't stop. It's like the floodgates have opened and there's no hope in turning them off.

"Rachel?"

I turn around, expecting to see Samuel behind me, wanting to say more cruel things. Instead I see Lucas, staring at me with surprise and worry.

"Are you alright?"

I shake my head and run to him. "No," I sob, wrapping my arms around his waist and burying my face into his chest.

12

LUCAS

I stroke her hair and breathe in her floral scent, holding her to me and not wanting to ever let go. "What's wrong?" I whisper while I continue caressing her, unable to stop. "What happened?"

She inhales deeply, trying to calm her sobs. I take her chin with one hand and lift her gaze to mine. Makeup runs from her eyes, giving her a bit of a raccoon look. But she's my raccoon and I don't think I can ever find her anything, but beautiful. She wipes her eyes under her ears, cleaning the smudges before taking a step away from me.

"I just-" She pauses, inhaling deeply and running a hand through her hair. "I just feel like I'm not doing anything right. I feel like your mother, Samuel, everyone looks down on me."

I raise an eyebrow. "Samuel? What does he have to do with any of this?"

She sighs and her shoulders slump in defeat. "He called me today, asking if I would take his offer."

My eyes widen. "I thought-"

"I know, I know," she says quickly. "I wasn't going to take it, but things at the Louvre suck and I thought it would be nice to do something I actually enjoy." She sighs. "I messed up."

I turn around, staring up at the building and feeling rage brim within me. "So, that guy made you cry?" I turn towards her as I feel the fire take over. I want to go inside that building and smash his precious chair over the top of his head. How dare he make Rachel cry.

Rachel shakes her head. "It's nothing. Forget it." She grabs my hand and tugs me toward her.

I'm tempted to go inside and have a word with Samuel, but at the same time, what's that going to do. Lacing my fingers with Rachel I smile brightly. "Why don't we do something fun? I have a big party I have to go to in about two weeks. Why don't you be my date and we get you a fancy dress for the occasion?"

I watch her smile and nod. "That sounds great."

I tug her towards me, already knowing the perfect place to go where we could try on clothes and have some champagne. It's the kind of store my mother loved going to and thankfully it's close by. Rachel giggles while she holds me close as we walk and I feel like her mood is already lifting.

We pause in front of the store to Jean Vouigh Jean. Rachel's gasp has me smiling. The shop can't be found anywhere outside Paris. This is the only location and the way they treat their customers is absolutely brilliant. I nudge Rachel forward, my smile widening as I watch her slowly step beyond the golden doors, held open by butlers dressed in all black. I nod at their bowed heads in acknowledgement.

Rachel pauses once more inside the store. There are several steps in front of us, yet her gaze lingers on the extravagant chandelier, the shop clerks dressed in short red dresses waiting at attention, and the mannequins donned in silk and jewels.

"What is this place?" Rachel breathes.

I chuckle and tug her towards the steps. "Heaven," I say, finding her reactions absolutely adorable.

"Excuse me," says a shop clerk while she strides towards us in her red stiletto shoes. She smiles politely, yet there's a scrutinizing gleam in her eye as she stares at Rachel. "Do you have an appointment?"

"No, but I'm Lucas Brent from the Brent family in New York," I say.

"This place is absolutely beautiful," says Rachel, still looking around in wonder. "How is this even real?"

"The Brent family?" The woman says in shock. "You're Christina Brent's son?"

I nod. "Christina and Franklin Brent."

The shop clerk claps her hands happily. "Of course," her smile widens and I stop myself from rolling my eyes, knowing the only reason why she is being nice to me is because of my family's money. I hate it, yet I love it. Having the Brent name definitely comes with some perks.

"I am Alice and I will be helping you for today." She snaps her fingers, and a butler appears with a platter of champagne. I grab two, handing one to Rachel.

"Oh my God, pinch me," she whispers.

I reach over and pinch her bottom.

"Ow!" Rachel shouts before smacking my shoulder.

I chuckle and grab her hand, guiding her over to mannequins dressed in glittering blue garments. "We're looking for a dress."

"The occasion?" Alice asks, her gaze sliding over to Rachel.

"Black-tie event."

"Ah, yes, so you would need a gown." We follow her to the other side of the shop, drinking our champagne while I watch Rachel's wide eyes and agape mouth. Her eyes are still a little swollen and her makeup is still a little messy, but that doesn't matter.

I feel like I've completely and utterly fallen for this woman.

"We have dresses in every size and occasion. Would you like something sleeveless or something more conservative?"

Rachel looks at me. "I have no clue."

"Sleeveless," I say to Alice before downing the rest of my champagne. I snap my fingers at the butler hovering near us and he offers me another.

Alice holds out a sleeveless grey dress and I can't hide my distaste even if I wanted to. Rachel shakes her head. "Grey isn't really my color. I like black, green, red-"

"Oh! Try the red!" I say, watching Alice quickly look through the dresses hanging on the wall behind her.

She finds several red dresses and I follow her towards the backroom, where several white lounge chairs are resting in front of changing rooms. Alice places the dresses inside while I take my seat, excited to see Rachel in something nice for once.

"I don't know about this," says Rachel from the other side of the curtain after several minutes waiting for her to undress.

"Let's see it. Don't be shy," I say with a chuckle.

The curtains open and I watch in awe as Rachel steps forward. The dress is completely sleeveless and shaped in a heart in the front. I have no clue what that neckline is called. I'm sure my mother would know if she was here. It's simple with a high slit ending a bit higher than necessary.

I want to tear it from her body and make love to her.

I want her wearing that to the party.

"Yes," I say while Rachel turns around.

Rachel laughs. "Yes? What does that mean?"

I down my drink and rise from the couch, stalking towards Rachel. The butler holds out the platter and I place my glass on it, not bother for another as I reach for Rachel and wrap my arms around her waist. "It means," I say while nuzzling my nose against hers. "That we're getting this dress."

Rachel chuckles. "Oh, really? But I have three others to-"

"You're getting this dress," I growl, loving the way Rachel tosses her head back in laughter and smacks my shoulder.

"Fine, I will wear this dress. This is probably the fanciest thing I've ever tried on."

"What about shoes?" Alice pipes up.

"Well, a princess has to have shoes."

Rachel shakes her head. "It's too much. This dress is already way too much."

I shrug. "Don't worry about it."

I see something flash over Rachel's face, as if she wants to tell me it does matter. She looks uncomfortable. I've never seen anyone be so concerned about money, given that I'm the one paying.

I don't know how to feel about it.

It definitely feels different than what I'm used to.

Alice brings over a pair of open toe black stilettos with crystals embroidered into the front. Or perhaps they're diamonds? Doesn't matter. Mom and Dad are paying anyway.

"These would look amazing," says Alice while she kneels in front of Rachel, sliding the shoes onto her feet.

Rachel wobbles in front of me before gathering her balance. She smiles while placing her hands neatly in front of me. Now, all we need is a tiara, and she looks exactly like a princess. "Beautiful," I say while taking her hands and kissing them. "We'll get everything."

"Perfect. Would you like more champagne? Perhaps some canapés while we package everything nicely for you?"

Rachel shakes her head. "Oh, no. That's quite alright. We'll just-"

"Yes," I say quickly, in a commanding voice that reminds me of my father.

Rachel flashes me a look. "Really, it's alright. We can celebrate with McDonalds. I don't need-"

"Where will the canapés be served?" I asked, already turning around and following Alice towards a staircase.

I don't know what's come over me. It's like I want to flash my money in front of Rachel. I want her to know I will always be there to take care of anything and everything for her. Yet, somehow I feel like I'm doing it wrong. I don't understand how though. Usually women like having money spent on them. They like going on fancy trips, sleeping in my family's fancy houses, buying $5000 dollar dresses, decorating themselves in diamonds and sapphires.

But Rachel is different.

I can always be myself around Rachel. Somehow, my parents being here and working under Samuel has unlocked something disgusting within me. It's like I've suddenly become Marcus, wanting to flash my wealth.

Why can't I stop?

Maybe it's because it's the one thing I'm good at. It's the one thing proven to work on the ladies. And I so desperately want it to work with Rachel.

Seriously, I must be falling in love with her.

Alice seats us on the third floor of the shop's building near a window displaying a small beautiful garden and a fountain with two mermaid statues, their mouths open as if they are singing. The butler places two glasses of champagne in front of us while several other servers appear out of nowhere, placing small plates of cucumber and smoked salmon mousse, roast beef with black truffle and brie, as well as an assortment of chilled meets and a variety of cheeses.

Rachel blinks at the food, a look of shock marring her face. "Wow," she whispers. "I've never been treated like this before."

I smirk. "Like what?"

She turns her wide eyes onto me. "Like a princess."

I chuckle and shake my head, grabbing one of the roast beef canapés and stuffing it into my mouth. "Just an average day in the Brent household." I don't know why I said that. I feel like I'm acting like a complete asshole.

"Really?" Rachel asks with wide eyes. "I never had days like today." She frowns, her gaze lowering in the food. "Sometimes I feel like we're living in two completely different worlds."

I shrug. "It's not always shits and giggles. Actually, most of the time it can be a real royal pain?"

Rachel purses her lips. "How?"

I lean in close, grabbing my glass and taking a sip. "I'm not free. My parents pretty much make every decision in my life. I have to study what they want. Work where they want. Pretty much take a shit where they want."

"But you got to attend Aurora."

I chuckle and shake my head, recalling that huge argument. "That's because I didn't apply to any schools until the last second, so Aurora was the only one that accepted me. The only reason why Dad went along with it, is because Aurora has a good rowing program and he didn't want me embarrassing him by attending college a year later."

I'm probably being too open about my family, but I don't care.

"Oh," Rachel says simply. "But your family cares about you. They take an interest in what you're doing."

I scoff. "Of course they do. It's because they don't want me ruining the Brent name." I lean back into my chair and stare out the window, scowling at the couples walking together. "Once college life ends, I can't choose where I work. I can't choose what I do. If I want the money and the name, I have to go along with everything my dad wants from me."

"But, at least you have a family and the money to pay for school and your life style."

I turn my scowl to Rachel. "What?" I can't believe my ears. Why is she taking their side?

"There are so many people in the world who don't have the money to attend college, go to Paris. Many don't have families and come from broken homes. At least you have connections."

I shake my head, wondering if I'm hearing her wrong. "Wait, what?"

"You're actually pretty privileged. Sure, your parents have a lot of control, but if you were to leave them or go against them, you would still be better off than many."

"I'm not better off." I cringe at the anger in my tone. I don't want to yell at Rachel, but somehow she's not understanding me and the hell I've had to put up with my entire life. "I don't have anything if I go against my parents."

"That's not true-"

"I don't have the freedom to do what I want. I definitely don't receive any love from my family."

"But-"

"I thought you of all people would get that. You met my parents. You've seen how crazy they are."

Rachel sighs. "Ok."

Ok? That's all I get is a measly ok?

I see Alice out of the corner of my eye coming towards us. It's probably a good thing, because I don't like where this conversation is going. "Mr. Brent," she says sweetly, "everything is packaged and ready for you downstairs."

I force a smile. "Perfect, we'll head down there now."

Rachel keeps her head down as we follow Alice down the stairs. I don't want to be angry with her. We were having a blast until just now. But why can't she understand my situation? Why can't she understand that I can't live my life like a normal person?

Maybe she's right.

We are from two completely different worlds.

13

SETH

I gasp for air as my arms continue pumping and my legs surge forward. My lungs burn. There's a stitch in my side I don't know if I can continue to ignore. But I must. I need to break my running record if I want to win this race. I need to beat that bastard Alex Goode. I scowl as I remember racing him. That asshole had been toying with me. I can still remember the stupid back of his head as he passed me by. He had done it so easily, as if I was moving at the pace of an elderly turtle.

I shake my head and focus on the scenery around me, however it's difficult. A group of high schoolers are smoking in the corner of the park. The sun is beginning to set, and I can only look at the Eiffel Tower for so long. Not to mention this view is getting rather boring.

It's my fault.

I should find a new place to run. This park is too convenient, given that it's only about five minutes away from the apartment. Also, it wouldn't be so boring if I wasn't so intent on running in it three times a day.

I slow my pace, taking it easy so my heart doesn't slam to a stop. I need to be careful. I can already hear Coach in my head, scolding me for not practicing as safely as I should. A two-hour run in the morning, and hour after lunch, and another before dinner plus stretching and weightlifting throughout the day.

My whole life has become running.

I come to stop, bracing my hands on my knees while regaining my breath. I should be happy. This is what I wanted. Running is my life, the one thing I'm actually good at, but I feel like all the fun has been zapped from it. I can't drink, for fear my weight will go up and slow my pace. I haven't been eating the dinners Rachel has been painstakingly making. Just thinking about the pasta she made the other night has me salivating.

But no. I've stuck to pretty much high protein and low carbs since I met fucking Alex Goode in the park. I grit my teeth just thinking of the asshole. This whole thing would be much easier if he hadn't shown his stupid face. I wouldn't need to push myself to the breaking point. If he wasn't here, I could be spending most my afternoons with Rachel.

She is the reason why I came to Paris in the first place, but now I hardly ever see her.

I straighten and tilt my head back, sucking in the cool air into my lungs while I stare up at the stars beginning to twinkly above me. As soon as this race is done, I'll make it up to her. We'll go site-seeing, get something French to eat, and have some much needed couple time.

I trudge through the park in the direction of the apartment. My feet move slowly, and my muscles complain with each movement. I stretch my arms over my head, knowing I will need to take an ice bath later tonight to soothe the muscles. I grimace when I step on my right foot feeling something twinge in my heel. Hissing, I lift my leg, having a look at the bottom of my foot, moving the ankle around. I didn't step on anything. There aren't any needles or rocks poking out of my shoe.

Strange.

I step on my foot again and frown when I feel pain once more in my heel. Interesting. I guess I should try not to run on it. I groan and press my palms into my eyes. Easier said than done. I'll ice it and wrap it. That should do the trick. It's all I can do until after the race, and then I'll have a doctor take a look at it.

I take the elevator this time to be safe. Probably walking up the stairs won't do me any good. When I open the door, I pause in the foyer, leaning against the door while I listen to someone humming in the background. The whole place smells absolutely delicious, like sweet apple pie. My stomach grumbles, and I grimace, feeling myself want to kick my new diet to the curb so I can beast down a slice or four.

"Rachel, is that you?" I ask while kicking off my shoes and closing the door. I groan when I step on my right, clenching my jaw to keep myself from crying out in pain.

It's nothing. Ignore it. I will be fine. Nothing is wrong with my foot.

"Yeah, I'm making pie."

I force a smile and round the corner, my eyes widening on Rachel wearing a short black dress and an apron. Her bunny slippers are nestled around her feet. She looks absolutely adorable. How can I possibly leave this woman alone all by herself?

I step toward her, ignoring the pain in my heel and trying not to limp as I say, "Smells like it."

"It should be done in a few minutes," says Rachel with her back to me. "Want a slice?"

My stomach growls and I wince. "No, I probably shouldn't. I need to keep my weight down so I can beat my score."

Rachel turns around, crossing her arms while frowning at me. "Is everything ok?" She tilts her head to the side, which I find both cute and unnerving. "You're acting a bit strange these days."

I scoff and walk towards the sink. "I'm fine," I say before turning on the faucet and guzzling down some water.

"Are you sure? Is it the race? If you're stressed about it, you know you can talk to me."

I roll my eyes and wipe the water from my mouth. "I'm fine," I say again while straightening. Yet even as the words escape my lips, I don't quite believe them. I feel quite the opposite of fine. In fact, I feel like complete utter shit. The race is only a week away, and I barely have time to get into the shape I need to be in to beat that fuck-face Alex Goode.

Rachel moves in front of me, pressing a hand against my forehead before caressing my cheek. "You don't look fine." Her frown deepens. "You look exhausted. Have you been getting any sleep?"

No.

"Yeah, I've been getting sleep," I say while pushing her away, stepping away from her and the sink. I keep my back to her, not able to see the worry in her eyes. My gaze slides to the clock on the wall. It's nearly eight. I need to be up at six tomorrow since I will be pushing for a three-hour run. I should probably eat a protein bar and start the bath.

"Why don't you meet me tomorrow after work? We can go get some coffee. Do something fun."

I grind my teeth, feeling annoyed. I don't know why. She wants to spend time with me. I should be happy. I should want to spend that time with her. "I can't. I have to train."

"Can't you take at least an hour off? It's not like-"

"No," I snap while whirling around, scowling down at her. "I can't take an hour off. I have to train, Rachel."

She rests her hands on her hips. "I don't understand why. It's just a race."

I chuckle bitterly. "Just a race? You think this is just a race?" I throw my hands in the air. "I have to win this race in order to keep the money Coach gave me. Did you ever think what would happen if I don't win?"

"No," Rachel says, her voice hesitant. I see the hint of tears gleaming in her eyes, and I know I'm being too cruel. I know I should stop while I'm ahead.

But of course, I don't.

"I have to win, Rachel. That's why I can't eat pie," I say while counting on my fingers. "I can't take an hour off to go get coffee. I can't sleep in or do whatever I want. I have to run. I have to train. I have to win this race so I can be here with you."

Rachel shakes her head. "But you're not with me." Her bottom lip trembles, and I know she's going to cry.

"Well, what do you want me to do, Rachel? If I lose, I'm fucked. Absolutely, royally fucked!"

Rachel steps towards me, but stops, her gaze dropping to the floor. "You didn't have to come. I didn't want you to… to spend your days stressing over some stupid race."

I scoff. "You must be kidding me!" I shout. "How could I not come?" I shove a finger in her direction. "I wanted to be with you, because I love you, and I can't stand the idea of not being with you; of you gallivanting off with the others and leaving me behind."

"We weren't leaving you behind, Seth."

My hands fist at my sides. "Yes, you were. If I had stayed, would you even be thinking of me? Would you even care?"

Her mouth parts. She looks absolutely horrified as she stares at me and I know I've gone too far, but I can't take back my words now that they're already out. "Of course, Seth."

I shake my head. "You don't know that."

"I do know that."

I stare back at her, not knowing what else to say. I should take her into my arms. I should hug her and apologize, but for some reason I can't move. I'm too angry. I can't believe she thinks this race is stupid; that she thinks everything I'm doing to remain in Paris with her is stupid.

"Seth," she says, reaching for me.

I turn on my heel, ignoring the pain twinging in my right while I stalk towards the foyer and shove on my shoes.

"Seth, where are you going?"

"For a run," I say while throwing open the door, hearing it slam shut behind me.

14

HUNTER

I stare at the basket of fruit in front of me. The room is small with no windows. Drawings hang on the pristine white walls, watching me as I press my pencil against the paper. I bite my tongue, trying to concentrate as I make a line, frowning when the line isn't what I intended. I glance to the elderly woman sitting on my right. Her wrinkle veiny hands move precisely as if she's done this before. One strand of her grey hair hangs over her face.

My frown deepens when I see that her basket of fruit is pretty much an exact copy of the objects before us. The woman's eyes lift, and she frowns at me, moving her drawing away from my prying gaze. I sigh and turn back to my own drawing, scowling at the shaky line. I have no clue where to start. Looking around, I see the others are drawing easily while the instructor walks around, nodding approvingly. She points randomly at someone's paper, smiling as if the guy has drawn the most extravagant thing in the world and not a basket of fruit.

I press my pencil against the sheet once more, knowing I need to have at least something for her to look at. I get to work, starting with the apple. I draw a circle, but realize that's all wrong. The apple isn't necessarily a complete circle. More like tooth shaped. I try to erase my lines, but they're still there, just faded, staring back at me. I try again, but my lines aren't right.

Fuck it. Apple done. What's next?

I move onto the banana, which is, unfortunately, positioned in front of the apple. My lines cross as I draw the curved oval. I'm not in the mood to start all over and the instructor is about three people down. I move onto the grapes, drawing several weird little circles that look nothing like the green fruit before me.

How the hell does anyone draw this shit?

Isn't this supposed to be one of the easiest things in the world?

"Mr. Smith."

I still when I hear my name, slowly peering up and offering a nervous smile. "Umm, I'm not done," I say, not even wanting to look at my shitty drawing.

She smiles brightly and nods. "It looks good."

She's a fucking liar.

"Umm, thank you," I say while turning back to my paper, staring down at the dark lines that remind me of a kindergartener's work.

"Keep up the good work," she says while patting my shoulder.

I scowl at my drawing. That's it, I give up. There's no way I can ever be an artist. I will have to find something different to occupy my time.

After drawing class ends, I file out of the small room and into the museum. I look around, wondering if I will be able to see Rachel, or of she's nearly done with work. The Louvre is amazing. I can't believe Rachel was able to score me a class here. I'm almost sorry I have to give it up.

Almost.

I sigh and push my hair away from my face. I hate that Rachel went through all the effort in finding a class for me to join, but if it doesn't work, then why try forcing it? I'm not an artist. Never have and never will be.

I grab my phone while following the people out of the museum, looking at the time and noticing its five. Another great thing about the class: it ends around the same time as Rachel's work. I stop just outside the museum, moving to the side so I won't be in the way.

There are still a tone of tourists hanging around, taking pictures of the palace surrounding the glass pyramid.

My eyes linger on someone standing about two feet away. I recognize her from somewhere, but I can't quite remember her name. She looks like one of Rachel's artsy friends, but I'm probably wrong.

"Hey!" I shout, smiling and walking towards her. Maybe she knows where Rachel is. Perhaps she works with Rachel at the museum. "Are you one of Rachel's friends?"

The brunette turns around, her eyes widening on me. She holds her bag closer and seems to shrink as I tower over her. "Oh, hi, Hunter."

My smile brightens and I hold out my hand, taking hers and shaking it. "Sorry, I don't remember your name," I say while releasing it. "Are you Lucy?"

"Lauren," she says softly, her gaze sliding to the ground.

"Do you know where Rachel is?" I look around once more, yet I don't seem my blond anywhere. "Is she still inside?"

Lauren nods vigorously. "Yeah. Dr. Arnaud needed to have her finish something."

"Do you want to join us for coffee?"

Lauren shakes her head. Something about her is strange. She refuses to look at me. Her shoulders are all hunched together as if she's worried I'm going to yell at her. I don't quite get it. Sure, I'm tall and well-muscled, but I don't think I look that scary. I used to think I looked pretty appealing.

"Are you sure? Are you busy?"

"I'm positive," Lauren rushes out. "Besides, I'm waiting for someone."

"Oh, ok. Well, you should come over sometime."

Lauren makes a face. "I don't think that's such a good idea."

I shrug. "Why not? It'll be fun. Rachel will probably enjoy having some female energy around I bet. I'm sure dealing with all us guys can be a little annoying from time to time. We also have loads of room."

"Hunter!"

I turn around, my heart swelling when I see Rachel rushing towards me, carrying several bags on her shoulders. She nearly trips on her way towards me. I gasp, reaching for her, but she quickly rights herself.

"I'm coming!" she shouts, several people turning towards her and watching as she fumbles to keep the bags on her shoulders.

She's so beautiful.

"You know what, I'm going to go wait over there," says Lauren.

Before I have the time to stop her, I find Lauren already marching towards the other side of the square. I frown. "That's weird," I mutter under my breath, not quite understanding why she's being so awkward.

"Sorry I'm late," Rachel huffs. "Dr. Arnaud had me running all over the place. I swear to God, I think she's punishing me for leaving early."

"That's fine. I was talking to your friend, Lauren."

Rachel makes a face while dropping her bags onto the ground. "Lauren?" Her nose wrinkles in distaste. "Why were you talking with her?"

"Well," I start, not knowing where to begin. I feel like I've done something wrong. "Should I not be talking to her?"

Rachel sighs and crosses her arms.

"I thought she was your friend."

Rachel grimaces. "She was my friend. She's not anymore." Rachel runs a hand through her hair and shakes her head. "You know what, let's not ruin the afternoon. I want to hear all about your new art class." She waggles her eyebrows while bending over to retrieve her bags.

I groan while grabbing a few. "Let's not. I don't want to ruin the afternoon either."

15

RACHEL

I sip at the delicious coffee while I look at Hunter's drawing. It's supposed to be of a bowl filled with fruit. Unfortunately, for Hunter, it looks more like a circle, a curved oval, and three smaller circles barely attached together hovering over what's supposed to be a bowl, yet looks like another curved oval. The lines are very shaky, as if Hunter had been too nervous to even drawn.

I sigh and shake my head. I really wish beginner art classes would begin with something else, but I guess each teacher has their own method.

"It's terrible," says Hunter mournfully, leaning over the table with his elbows pressing against the wood. His coffee sits in front of him, untouched, and he stares at me with such a puppy-dog expression, I have no clue what to say.

"It's not terrible." I set down the paper and grimace while watching him snatch it away, stuffing it into his backpack. "It's your first time."

Hunter groans. "I don't know why I even try."

"Were you good at football the first time you played?"

Hunter shrugs. "I was good at running. I was pretty skinny when I was a kid. And small."

"But obviously you didn't know the rules."

Hunter nods. "And I sucked at catching."

I smile and reach for his hand, giving it a gentle squeeze. "See, but then you got better, right?"

Hunter sighs. "Sure. I got better, but I still think I should drop the class. I'm too old to be any good at drawing or art."

I shake my head, lacing my fingers with his and not letting him go. "I think you are being too hard on yourself."

Hunter pulls away from me and I feel something hard piercing through me. My eyes prickle and I'm suddenly reminded of Seth pulling away from me. "Maybe it was stupid coming to Paris."

No.

I blink away the tears, sniffing while I watch him look away from me. Not him, too.

"I feel like I'm dragging down the group. I have no clue what to do with my life, with this summer."

"Don't say that," I whisper, wiping my eyes to keep from crying. "Please, don't say that. I'm happy you're here. You're not dragging us down at all."

Hunter groans and shakes his head. "You have your internship, Lucas has his crazy family to deal with, and Seth has his marathon."

I try very hard not to roll my eyes, finding myself brimming with anger as I think of both Seth and Lucas. Out of the whole group, Hunter has been the only one spending time with me, catching up over coffee dates, walking with me to and from work. And, although he isn't as busy as the other two, I feel like he actually cares.

He's like a big sensitive teddy-bear that I never want to let go of.

"Please, don't think that about yourself, Hunter. I like that you're here."

Hunter perks up, offering me a sad smile. "Really?"

I nod. "I also think you should continue with the drawing class."

Hunter groans.

"Just listen to me for one moment." I raise a finger and wag it in front of him. "Art can't be learned in one day. This was your first class. Of course you're not going to be amazing after one day."

"Yeah, but-"

"And didn't your therapist say that you should stick to a routine? Won't this help you have a routine? Doesn't this give you something to do with your time?"

Hunter frowns, but his head bobs up and down. "I did try running with Seth." He pauses, his face grimacing and I wonder if Seth snapped at Hunter, as well. "The guy has become a bit crazy."

"I know," I say, lowering my gaze to my coffee cup. "He needs to win the marathon."

Hunter scoffs. "Yeah. It's all he ever talks about. Every time I see him, he's leaving for a run. I'm worried he's going to injure himself."

I nod while taking my spoon, dipping it into the coffee and swirling the liquid. "Well, I guess we have to just trust him to know his limits."

Hunter rolls his eyes. "Yeah, he knows his limits alright. He'll run right past them and next thing you know we'll find him cursing and grumbling about a torn muscle."

I grimace. I don't want to think about Seth getting hurt. It's bad enough he looks like he's lost too much weight. He was already thin before, from running hours every day and training, but at least then I had nothing to worry about. Now he looked like he was wasting away, trying to get his weight down in order to improve his running time. This morning I woke up, wondering if I was going to find him passed out on the side of the road on my way to the metro.

Thankfully, I didn't.

But it still is a concern.

"I'm sorry, Rachel." My thoughts are drawn back to Hunter as I feel his hand on mine. Worry fills his gaze and I force a smile. "I don't want to worry you. Let's talk about something else."

I sigh. "I don't know what else to really talk about. My internship sucks. Lucas isn't really talking to me right now."

"Lucas isn't talking to you?" The shock in Hunter's tone makes my heart squeeze. The whole thing had been a shock to me, as well. All I wanted to do was point out that there were people out there that had it much worse than him. I guess, when it comes to Lucas, I'm not really supposed to have my own opinion.

"Since when?" Hunter asks.

"Since we got back from our date a couple days ago. We went shopping. I'm supposed to go to some work thing with him." I sigh and run my hand through my hair, feeling agitated all over again. "He was complaining about his family and I upset him by telling him he's quite privileged compared to the majority."

Hunter shrugs. "Well, it's true. The asshole is privileged. Who owns a giant apartment in Paris and a cottage," he uses air quotes for 'cottage' since the house is actually a giant mansion in the mountains, "in Colorado."

I nod. "I know. I think he's just a little touchy when it comes to his family."

Hunter rolls his eyes. "And who isn't? You think I have it all sunshine and flowers with my dad?" Hunter makes a face, and I chuckle at his pursed lips and wide eyes. "I can tell you, we fight at least once a week. Even when I'm in Paris, he video chats me in order for us to get our weekly fight in. Families are always frustrating."

I giggle and shake my head. "I hardly think your dad and Lucas's parents are alike." Thinking of Lucas's mom makes my smile drop. Christina had been so cold. She was nothing like Hunter's dad, who seemed intent on getting to know Hunter's friends, including me. Hunter's dad was so warm compared to Lucas's parents.

"Honestly, I would just let it go," says Hunter. "There's no point in bringing it up with him. His snooty ass will get over it."

I make a face. "I'm not so sure about that."

"Oh, he will." Hunter waggles his eyebrows. "I see the way he looks at you. Give him a day or two and the whole thing will blow over."

I watch Hunter take a drink from his coffee, wondering when this big hunk of meat had become such a wise man. I think therapy has really been helping him learn how to express himself, teaching him that he doesn't need to be the strong guy all the time. It's taken a lot of hard work, yet I like the man he is becoming.

"Now, on to more important things. What's going on with that Lauren chick?"

I groan and hang my head. Nevermind. Definitely not liking the new and improved Hunter. "I told you I didn't want to ruin the afternoon."

"Too late, I already brought it up. My curiosity has gotten the best of me. Is she doing the internship with you?"

I purse my lips and nod. "Unfortunately."

"Well, what happened? I thought you two were friends."

"We were until she turned into a huge bitch."

Hunter's eyes widen and I chuckle at the surprise on his face. "Sorry, I've never heard you use that language before to describe anyone. It's a bit of a shock."

"Well, it's true. She is a bitch."

"Care to explain why?"

I groan and tilt my head back, asking God, 'Why now? Why can't I just enjoy a cup of coffee with my boyfriend without discussing all the problems in my life?' "It's the whole Josh thing."

Hunter's brows furrow in confusion. "What Josh thing? I thought that was taken care of."

I point my spoon at him. "Exactly. It was."

"Then what's the problem."

I rest the spoon next to my cup and lean forward. "The problem is that Lauren is taking Josh's side."

Hunter stares back at me, his expression horrified. "Wha-"

I nod. "She thinks that I'm a whore that tried to seduce Josh."

Hunter's mouth gapes open. His lips move, yet nothing escapes except for a confused, "Huh?"

"Yep."

"But why would she think that? You're not a slut."

I gesture between him and I. "It's because I'm dating you, Lucas, and Seth. She seems to think I spread my legs for just anyone."

"That's disgusting. And that's not true. Not to mention, even if it was, it doesn't take away the meaning of 'no'. She's a fucking idiot."

I shrug, wiping at my eyes. I feel tears beginning to surface, and I don't know why. I've already gotten over my loss of friendship with Lauren. I shouldn't be feeling sad, but I do. The whole thing just sucks. I still don't understand why she's taking Josh's side in all this.

Why doesn't she believe me?

I sniff and quickly stand, needing to find some place to hide. I'm about to burst into tears just thinking about the whole thing. I don't understand why I'm so upset about Lauren. It must be much more than that. Part of me thinks I should have never come here. It's just been one struggle after another. I feel stupid for thinking I could ever do something like this; travel somewhere, get a job at a museum, carry on my relationships with the bros.

It's getting to be too much.

"Rachel," I hear Hunter say while I turn around, finding myself walking towards the back of the cafe.

A sign hovers above a door with a picture of a woman and I quickly open it, rushing inside and pushing the door close. Hunter rushes inside before I can slam it in his face. He leans against the door, watching me with eyes filled with worry.

"Are you okay?"

I shake my head, tears streaming down my face. "No," I sob.

He locks the door before reaching for me. I wrap my arms around his waist, burying my face into his chest while his hands stroke my back. "Sssh," he whispers in my ear. "It's going to be fine. Everything is alright. Just ignore that stupid girl."

I shake my head. "It's not just her."

"Then what is it?" Hunter asks while pushing my hair away from my face. He presses a gentle kiss against my forehead and for a moment I let my eyes flutter close, enjoying his warmth and proximity.

I don't know what I would do without Hunter. I don't know how I got through last semester without him. I don't think I could do it now.

"I just feel so stupid. I feel like it was stupid of me to come here."

Hunter chuckles. "You are not stupid."

I sniff and wipe my eyes. "Yes, I am."

Hunter strokes my hair away from my face. "No, you are not. Things are just a bit more difficult than you thought they were going to be. And maybe you're going through some culture shock or homesickness. It's difficult working abroad and dealing with friendships and boyfriends while being abroad. Everything is new and different."

I nod. "Maybe you're right."

Hunter pulls me closer, wrapping his arms around my waist. "Of course I'm right."

I chuckle and lean into him, not wanting to ever let go. "I just wish Lauren believed me."

Hunter sighs. "I can't promise you anything with that, but I can promise you that worrying about it won't do any good."

My bottom lip trembles and I inhale deeply to keep myself from crying. "And what am I going to do about Seth and Lucas? I hate that they're mad at me."

"They're not mad at you. They're fucking idiots, that's what they are, but they're not mad at you."

I push away from him, wanting to see his face. As I meet his gaze, I see the love and support. I feel it wash over me and take hold, pushing away my dark thoughts. "You promise?"

Hunter laughs while he nods. "I promise."

I lean onto my tiptoes, meeting his lips. He kisses me gently, his tongue stroking against mine, igniting fires within my core. I lean into his touch, my leg lifting. He grabs it and holds it close to his hip. I gasp, feeling himself grind against my center. Leaning into him more, we stumble backwards, his back thumping against the door. Hunter groans low in his voice, pulling away from me. His eyes linger on my lips, which feel swollen from his touch. He caresses my cheek while his hand slides down my thigh to cup my bottom.

"We should probably get going," he whispers, his voice filled with desire.

I press against him, feeling his hard cock through the fabric of his jeans. "So soon?"

Hunter chuckles lowly, leaning towards me. I watch his tongue lick his bottom lip, my stomach twisting with need. "Here?" he asks, nodding to the bathroom around us.

I wrap my arms around his neck. My mouth is centimeters from his. I can taste the coffee on his breath. "Why not?"

Hunter growls low in his throat. His mouth lowers, seizing my lips while his hold on me tightens. He kisses me deep and hard, his tongue stroking mine while his teeth grazes my bottom lip. I gasp as I feel his hand slide down my front, pressing against me.

I need to get rid of these clothes.

I end the kiss, my hands deftly undoing his belt while he tugs up my skirt. The fabric bunches at my waist. I undo the button of his jeans, pulling down the zipper before pressing my palm against his hard cock. Hunter groans and thrusts himself against me. His underwear tenting. My insides tighten as I gaze down at the tent in his underwear, wanting his large girth deep inside me, pounding away all my worries.

Hunter turns me around, guiding me towards the sink. I blush as I meet my gaze in the mirror. "Wait," I say, not knowing if I really want to look at myself while we do this.

My whole body shudders as I feel the hard press of his clothed cock against my ass. His hands circle around me. His fingers press into the front of my panties. My mouth hangs open as they circle around my nub. My whole body feels pulled taut. My hands tighten on the sink in front of me, trying to keep myself upright despite the wobble in my knees.

"What? You don't like this?" Hunter breathes in my ear before nipping my lobe.

I moan and wiggle myself against his hard shaft. I feel so wet. I love and I hate this. I don't know what to think anymore. His fingers find their way inside my panties and I clench my jaw as I feel them enter inside me, pushing as deep as they can go. His thumb flicks against my clit and my whole body spasms. I toss back my head, my hands trembling as they hold tight. I fear at any point the sink my break from how tightly I'm gripping it.

"Hunter," I whimper as he continues to finger me.

He chuckles in my ear. I hear rustling behind me and quiver as I feel the warmth of his hard, leaking dick on my ass. My thighs spread apart, desperate to have him deep inside me. He kisses my ear, slowly traveling down to my neck where he sucks tenderly.

"I need you inside me," I whisper harshly, bucking against him.

Hunter groans, his teeth sinking harder into my neck, making me twitch and writhe against him. "I don't have a condom," he says and my whole body stills, not knowing what to do. I'm so primed and ready to go. I feel like my juices are leaking all over him. I know he's been tested. He and the bros are safe, but what about the other uncertainties?

I look at myself in the mirror, watching Hunter kiss up and down my throat, one hand coming up to cup my breast while the other continues playing with me. I want him so bad. I thrust myself against him, feeling his cock slide against me.

"Come in my ass?" I rush out, my voice trembling with desire.

Hunter lifts his head, a wicked smile on his lips. "I thought you'd never ask."

His hand moves from my breast down to my panties. I feel him tugging them down and I quick them away, not caring where the land. His fingers continue pumping in and out of my front. His thumb moves faster over my clit, strumming me to the breaking point. In the mirror my face looks flushed, my eyes glossed over as if I'm high; high on desire and need. I feel Hunter's cock at my back entrance and my whole body twitches, waiting for him to enter me.

He rubs his dick against my ass. His hands grip my hips, holding me steady while I lean over the sink, panting like a dog in heat. I groan while sliding my ass against him, wanting him to thrust as hard as possible into me. I watch him shiver in the mirror, watch him bite his lip.

My mouth gapes open as he slowly enters me. At the same time another finger pushes into my front. Three fingers thrust into me while he continues pushing himself into my back until he's full wedged inside. I feel so full. It's not the same as having Lucas or Seth here, but it still feels so good. My whole body shakes while I adjust to his girth.

"Fuck, that's good," Hunter gasps while tossing back his head.

There's a knock at the door and both our heads jerk towards the sound, watching as the handle jiggles. The lock keeps the door in place, but my heart is still racing, wondering if the person on the other side can hear us.

My clit twitches with desire at the thought.

Hunter thrusts into me, hard and as deep as he can go. My nails scratch at the sink. I bite my lip to silence myself, but a small cry still escapes. He thrusts again, at the same time as his fingers. His thumb circles around me. I gaze at myself in the mirror, watching my teeth sink into my bottom lip. Hunter looks at me through the mirror, his mouth hanging open in a silent moan.

"I want to hear your voice," he rasps before thrusting into me again.

I buck against him, gasping as he thrusts harder, deeper. I'm unable to hold back any longer. I don't care who stands on the other side of that door. They no longer matter. All that matters now is Hunter and his big cock going in and out of me. Hunter moans as he thrusts into me and I meet each and every one. My whole body quivers, and I whimper as his thumb slows its movements on my clit, leaving me wanting.

Hunter pulls out of me. Before I can complain he spins me around, picking me up easily until I'm sitting on the sink. I gasp, looking around and worry that we are going to break this thing by the time we're done. However, all complaints and worries die as he captures my lips and thrusts deep into my ass.

I wrap my arms and legs around him, moving with him, feeling myself soaring so high I may never come down. His hand reaches between me, stroking my clit while I continue grinding my ass against him. He gasps, but I seize his bottom lip before he can pull away from me. Hunter chuckles, kissing me back and thrusting hard into me. I cry out, my fingers digging into his shoulders, my legs tightening around him.

"I'm going to come," he says in between kisses. His cock twitches in me, his thumb moving faster on my clit taking me even higher. My whole body feels so tight, pulled taut and ready to shatter into a million pieces.

"Me too," I say against his lips. He moves and I gasp, grinding against him and wanting to take him all as deep as possible. "I'm going to come."

Hunter moans, his pace quickening. He leans into me until my head thumps against the mirror. His hand tangles itself in my hair, pulling on it tight and making me moan. I love the way he touches me, the way he makes me feel, the desires he stirs within me. I thrust against him hard. There's knocking at the door, but I don't care. I'm so close to release, I can see it right in front of me.

"Fuck!" Hunter shouts and I feel his semen pour into me as he continues thrusting.

He stares down at me, his lips parted as he moans. With one final thrust and flick of his thumb I gasp, feeling myself taken to the other side, crying out my orgasm while my whole body tightens around him. His eyes widen in alarm and he gasps, leaning forward and pressing his forehead against my shoulder.

"Oh, fuck, Rachel," he moans. He kisses my collarbone. His hands stroking up and down the length of my body.

There's another knock at the door followed by, "Bonjour?"

We scramble into a standing position. I push down my skirt, glancing over my shoulder to see if we broke the mirror or sink, but everything seems alright. My face flushes with embarrassment. My whole body wobbles as I try to regain feeling in my legs. My gaze meets Hunter's, and I nearly burst into a fit of giggles at how wild his hair has become. I push down the locks, yet I'm unable to straighten them. I don't even check to see how my hair is as I quickly unlock the door, finding a man on the other side, scowling at the both of us with his arms crossed.

I force a smile and rush out, not even bothering to explain why I have a man inside there with me. "Sorry," I murmur while passing by him, sharing a sheepish look with Hunter.

I catch the man's eye roll and watch the door shut.

"Well, I guess we should get going," says Hunter while taking out his wallet.

I look around, happy to see that no one has moved our bags from the table. "I'll go get our things," I say cheerfully, ignoring the stares. I guess I should have fixed my hair.

As I reach the table, there's a tap on my shoulder. Turning around I find the man standing behind me, looking even more irritated than he did before.

"Yes? Can I help you?" I ask uneasily.

The man scowls and with two fingers, holds up my bright pink panties. "I believe these are yours."

My face flushes. I must look like a freaking tomato. I snatch them from his hands. "Thank you," I squeak while stuffing them into my bag, feeling absolutely mortified.

The man rolls his eyes and walks away. I should probably feel worse than I do. I shouldn't be screwing anyone in the bathroom.

I should feel guilty.

But I don't.

16

LUCAS

I stare at myself in the mirror while tying my bowtie. The suit has been impeccably made, and it fits me like a glove. I look like I'm a 007 wannabe. If I was in a better mood, I'd be checking out my ass in the mirror, but I've already attempted tying this bowtie five times. My hands won't stop trembling.

I scowl when I pull at the ribbon, watching it completely unravel.

Well, I guess I will try again. For the sixth fucking time.

I shouldn't be nervous. I'm around these kinds of assholes more often than not. If it wasn't for my freaking life being on the line, it wouldn't matter at all. Yet Samuel's threats have me acting like a complete idiot. Part of me really thinks I should just tell father the truth. Just let the cat out of the freaking bag. What is he going to do?

Sure, he can take the money away. He can demand I move back home. He can tell me either I work for him after I graduate or I'm out on my own. Will that be so bad?

I swallow the lump in my throat. My fingers pause, allowing the ribbon to lie around my neck as I imagine my future without my parents' backing. Me, in a tiny studio, writing at a desk while wearing torn jeans and mismatching slippers, empty cups of ramen surrounding me. That doesn't sound so bad. Yet, I imagine what my life will be with Rachel, her frustrated with her four jobs, the bros coming home late, passing out on the one tiny bed we all have to share.

I wrinkle my nose.

Yeah, I need my father's money. Maybe I should just give in, become a lawyer like him. I can always write on the side. I grab the ribbon tying it quickly and smiling at the neat bow I make. I'll just have to convince everyone to move to New York with me, which won't be so bad for Rachel, since she's from the area. Seth can still work at a running store there and Hunter can visit whenever he can between games. That's if he gets into the NFL.

I will just need to keep all this secret from my parents.

And when I get married-

I pause, frowning in the mirror, wondering what they would say if I decided to marry Rachel. I could see them both saying no, bringing over a different girl; someone who is a family friend with tons of money.

Then what?

I shake my head. I'm getting in way over my head. Rachel and I have only been dating for not even a year. There are a million things that can happen between now and then. I shouldn't be fussing over it.

But still, it's my freedom on the line.

And tonight could decide everything for me.

I should just tell Father the truth.

My phone buzzes, and I sigh in frustration. I pick it up and scowl when I see Samuel's name. Another text message, most likely about the stupid event. Samuel has been texting me all day with little reminders of what to say and how to act. It's like he thinks this is my first time at a black-tie event. Doesn't he know I'm a Brent? Mother hosts these stupid little things all the time.

I open the message and shake my head. *Don't forget to speak with Mr. Blake.*

I roll my eyes. Like I could possibly forget to speak to him. Does Samuel think I'm a complete idiot? Honestly, I have no clue what I'm going to say about Samuel's firm to score a meeting with the man. I don't even know what Blake looks like or why he could use

Samuel. The more I think about it, the more frustrated and worried I get.

I turn away from the mirror and slide my cell back into my pocket. I will just have to put on the charm. I'm good at faking it. I can bullshit my way through tonight just like I bullshit my way through my job with Samuel.

I stride out of my room, inhaling deeply to calm my racing heart. "Rachel?" I shout, hoping she's already dressed and ready to go. As much as I don't want to go, I know I can't be late. "Ra-"

I stop, pausing in the threshold, staring at Rachel standing in the middle of the kitchen. She's wearing the red dress and the black open-toed shoes. Her curly hair is up in a simple bun with a few strands framing her face. Crystal earrings glitter from her ears, matching the crystals on the shoes, yet I have a feeling they are fake. She slowly turns to me, offering a hesitant smile.

"Wow," I breathe, slowly stepping towards her. "You look absolutely beautiful."

A blush settles on Rachel's face, making her look even more radiant and she nods her head, her gaze dipping to the floor. "Thank you."

"Have the others seen you?"

Rachel chuckles. "Seth went for a run two hours ago and Hunter has been busy drawing."

"So, no," I say, unable to hide my joy. This is all for me for tonight. No bros taking her attentions away. All mine. I take her hand, lacing my fingers with hers and tug her towards the door. "Well, let's get going. If we stay any longer, I'm going to try to get you out of that dress."

Rachel laughs, tossing back her head while following me towards the door. "Oh, no. We can't have that."

I lead her down the hall, walking briskly. I know that if I don't, I'll grab her and carry her all the way back to the apartment. I can't take my eyes off her. She's like a goddess. I have never seen her done up before. She always looks beautiful. Even in her bunny pajamas or after an all-nighter; even with her hair in disarray and her mascara sheered all over her face, she looks beautiful. I don't think I can ever love another woman the way I love Rachel.

The limo is waiting for us in front of the apartment, and Rachel stops, her mouth gaping open as she watches the chauffeur open the door for us. I hold out a hand, chuckling at Rachel's surprise.

"Well, come along. We don't want to be late."

Rachel takes my hand, and I tug her inside, helping her slide over. As soon as I'm inside, I reach for the champagne, knowing I'm going to need some liquid courage to get me through tonight.

"I thought we were going to be taking the taxi," says Rachel as she watches me pour a glass.

I hand it to her while shaking my head, pouring an even larger glass for myself. "Nah, it's better to arrive in style at events like this."

Rachel chuckles, taking a sip before asking, "What exactly am I getting myself into tonight?"

I shrug. "Who knows? Hopefully it won't be lame. No promises," I add while clinking my glass against hers, downing it quickly before pouring another.

She places a hand on mine, taking the bottle away from me and setting it back in the mini fridge. "Actually, I was hoping we could talk."

I lean back in my seat, my brow furrowing as I look down, watching her nibble on her bottom lip. "What about?"

Her gaze slides to the chauffeur before returning to me. I straighten in my seat, leaning over and saying to the man, "Do you think you can give us a little privacy."

"Of course, Mr. Brent," says the chauffeur in his thick French accent

I watch the black window go down, waiting until it's locked into place before turn back to Rachel, taking her hand into mine. "What is it?" I press my lips against her knuckles. "Are you nervous?"

Rachel shakes her head. "No, it's not that. I just want to know if we're okay?"

I frown, not really understanding the question. "What do you mean?"

"Well, last week when we were having canapés after you bought me this beautiful dress, you seemed upset."

I clench my jaw, remembering the way she had talked about my privilege; how she didn't understand where I was coming from at all. I nod. "Yeah, I remember."

I wish I could block the memory. It's not my favorite. Honestly, I want to forget the whole thing happened. However, it happened and the conversation only proved that we came from two completely different worlds. Originally, I didn't think that would be a problem. Now, I'm not so sure. My parents won't approve of her. I already know that. It wouldn't matter if I didn't need their money and their name to get by.

I also didn't like the fact she called me privileged. It's the truth, but it doesn't mean I have to like it.

"Are you still mad at me?"

I don't quite know how to answer that question. Yes? No? It's still too soon. I'd rather shove it under a rug and talk about it later, especially since I have to focus all my attentions on wooing Mr. Blake tonight.

I force a smile. The worry in her eyes seizes my heart, clenching it tight as if it will never let me go. My hand slides up to her face, cupping it gently while I nuzzle my forehead against hers.

"You have nothing to worry about," I breathe, knowing it's not quite the truth.

She doesn't need to worry, but this is a discussion we'll have to have at a later time. My thoughts are elsewhere, and my gaze dips to her lips. I stroke her chin, pushing it upwards. I kiss her gently, putting all my love and affection into that one touch. She opens for me, moaning softly when my tongue flicks against hers.

I pull her closer to me, wanting and needing more. My hand slides up her leg, pushing her skirt up. She gasps when my fingers slide against her panties, her legs opening for me. I'm so very glad I had the chauffeur close the window. I don't know when I will have another opportunity like this.

My mouth travels from her lips down to her throat as my fingers slip inside her underwear, pushing inside her. I moan as I feel her wet insides tighten around me, as if she's already primed and ready for me. I kiss the tops of her breasts, grazing my teeth against the flesh lightly. My other hand tugs at the red fabric until her nipple is exposed. I nibble on it lightly, enjoy her gasps, the way she grabs my hair and digs her nails into my scalp. I suck on it gently before grazing my teeth against it again. I decide I don't ever want to leave this car. I just want to stay in here with Rachel, block out the rest of the world, and forget my family troubles. Forget about Samuel and his stupid firm.

Rachel pushes me away, her hands reaching for my pants. She deftly unbuttons and unzips them. I moan as she pushes the fabric apart, exposing my tenting underwear. She leans forward, a mischievous smile on her lips as she pushes my underwear away, exposing my hard cock. I gasp as she licks my sensitive tip, already twitching and leaking with precum. Licking my bottom lip, I watch her lick my shaft, running that sweet, velvety tongue up along the side before teasing the slit.

I lean back in my seat, trying to keep my hands off her so she can work her magic. It's hard though. She's so beautiful. Her mouth is amazing. All I want to do is grab her head and shove myself deep inside her; use her like she's a sex toy. I want to hit the back of her throat, make her gag, make her swallow all of my cum.

I hiss when she takes my tip into her mouth. She suckles gentle before swallowing me whole. I shudder as I hit the back of her throat, grinding my teeth to keep from moaning too loudly. Her hand grabs the base of my cock, tightening and loosening while she takes me, sucking me. Her teeth grazes against my sensitive flesh and I twitch, knowing I'm getting close.

I push her away, claiming her lips with mine and pushing her against the window. I grab her leg, tossing it over my shoulder. I rip her panties down, desperate to be deep inside her. She gasps and I see the longing in her eyes. I know she wants it as much as I do. I tease her clit with my cock, enjoying her shudders as her fingers dig into my shoulders. My mouth seizes her nipples once more, and she cries out as I suck on it. My hands tug at her underwear, pulling them down around her knees while I position myself at her entrance.

"Mr. Brent, we should be there shortly."

I still, my whole body trembling to keep myself from shoving deep inside her. "How much longer?" I ask, hating the desperation in my voice.

"Precisely three minutes."

I swallow. That's definitely not enough time for what I want to do to Rachel. She stares at me, a smile on her lips, her gaze daring me to finish what I started. I try to do the math in my head, but it still won't be enough to get us both off. Slowly, I push away from her, my whole body screaming at me to stop, to demand the chauffeur to pull over in a side street.

But I can't be late.

Rachel's leg slides off my shoulder and she tucks her breasts back inside before pulling up her underwear, giggling softly to herself. I tuck myself back into my underwear, clenching my jaw at the strength it takes not to rip Rachel's clothes off her.

"Are you going to be alright, Lucas?" she asks me, her gaze sliding to my hard cock tenting my pants.

I try to think of my grandmother, but my mind is filled with Rachel tossing back her head, moaning in my ear as her leg is on my shoulder. I clamp my eyes close, demanding I think of something else; of Samuel scolding me, of my parents demanding I attend a university in New York.

That seems to do the trick.

"Fine," I breathe, my voice shaking.

Rachel leans into me, her breasts pressing against my arm and I feel my cock reawaken. "Rain check in the cloakroom?"

I practically growl as I grab her, pulling her close to me, imagining her pressed up against the wall as I fucked her hard and deep. "Naughty girl," I whisper in her ear.

The car pulls to a stop, and I am instantly straightening, pulling my arms off her while she makes space between us. The door opens, and I step out first, offering my hand to Rachel. Her eyes widen on the photographers standing around us, taking photos of everyone arriving at the event. She takes my hand, looking starstruck while staring at the restaurant in front of us, one of the oldest places in Paris with a Michelin star chef.

Tonight will definitely be interesting, I decide while guiding her inside, not knowing how I'm going to keep the wolves from attacking my date. The wolves being the elite and the wealthy, who will probably treat Rachel with disdain since she doesn't come from money.

The man at the front takes my jacket while Rachel waits for me, gazing up at the chandelier as if she's never seen one before. She probably hasn't. Maybe in movies, but not in real life. I stride towards her, taking her hand and leading her deeper into the restaurant, finding familiar faces I wish I could hide from. Everyone is dressed in their finest and I'm happy to see the women are wearing something similar to Rachel's dress. At least she won't look like a complete fish out of water.

"Lucas!"

I groan inwardly, recognizing that voice while I slowly turn around, finding Marcus walking briskly towards us with his arms spread wide. "So happy you could make it."

"Happy to be here," I say while taking his hand, giving it a firm shake.

Marcus frowns at Rachel, looking her up and down with confusion written all over her face. "Do I know you from somewhere?"

I'm about to answer 'no,' but Rachel speaks before I can answer for her.

"Yes, I met you in Colorado at your cottage."

Marcus taps his chin, shaking his head. "I'm sorry. I can't seem to place you."

Rachel chuckles and waves her hand. "It's fine. It was our first time meeting each other. I don't think you want to remember it anyway."

Marcus's frown deepens, looking as if someone just insulted his designer suit. "Why? What happened?"

I grimace, recalling the time Hunter made a complete ass of himself. He ended up breaking one of Marcus's expensive vases and we had to leave.

"Umm, well-"

"It doesn't matter," I say quickly while tugging Rachel in the opposite direction. "Anyway, Marcus, thanks for the invite. Hope to see you around here again. Do you think you can point us in the direction of the cloakroom?"

Marcus's brow furrows while Rachel gives me a knowing look. I give her a shrug. She can't blame me for wanting to finish what we started.

"Cloakroom? Why do you need a cloakroom?"

Rachel sighs and shakes her head.

"Well, would you like to tell him, honey?" I ask while looking at Rachel.

I chuckle as she scoffs, giving me a dark look while smacking my shoulder lightly. "You are terrible."

"I have no clue what's going on," says Marcus, sounding absolutely bored. "Anyway, enjoy the party. It was a pleasure, Raven," he adds while walking briskly past us.

Rachel turns to me, leaning in close and whispering, "Raven? Where did he get that?"

I roll my eyes. "Welcome to my world. Where people just don't care unless you are loaded with gold and cash."

Rachel frowns, turning her gaze back to Marcus, who's currently boring another victim with his haughty charm. I roll my eyes as I watch him tilt his head back, his fake laugh making my ears twitch in irritation.

"God, I hate that guy," I hear a familiar voice behind me.

Glancing over my shoulder, I find Alex there with a glass of champagne in his hand and a bored expression on his face. "You and me both," I mutter. "Why are you here?"

Alex rolls his eyes while taking a very large swig from his glass. "Couldn't get out of it. Mother insisted I show my face."

My arm slides around Rachel's waist. While gesturing to Alex, I say, "Rachel, I'd like for you to meet-"

"Alex Goode," Rachel finishes, taking Alex's outstretched hand and giving it a firm shake. I can't help, but notice the cheerful smile on her lips, as if she's been dying to meet the man all night. I also can't stop the little twinge of jealousy tugging at me, wanting to jerk Rachel far away from this track star and have my way with her in the cloakroom.

"It's a pleasure to meet you," Rachel continues. "Seth has been cursing your name pretty much since we arrived."

Alex chuckles, a mischievous gleam glinting in his eye. I'm surprised by the genuine smile he gives her, which only makes my body pull taut as I want to place myself between my friend and my girlfriend. My arm around her tightens, pulling her closer to me, yet neither seem to notice.

"Ah, so you know the great Garcia."

Rachel flicks her hair over her shoulder and my gaze narrows, wondering if this is some sort of flirty strategy. "Well, I kinda have to. We live together." She turns that smile towards me, and I feel all jealousy within me melt in that moment. "Me, Seth, Lucas, and Hunter."

Alex's attentions return to me, raising his eyebrows in intrigue. "That's quite a full house."

I wrinkle my nose, not knowing what exactly he is getting at. "Quite," I say simply. His eyes narrow, but that's all I offer. He doesn't need to know what goes on in my private affairs.

"Oh, it's quite alright," says Rachel with a soft chuckle. "We live in a house near campus anyway. I was lucky enough to snag a room since I was late in applying."

Alex tilts his head, his smile growing. "How interesting. Well, I am looking forward to my little showdown with Garcia. It'll be nice to finally have a challenge."

Rachel's eyes widen. "Oh? I thought you two hated each other."

Alex shrugs. "Eh, more like a love-hate relationship for me." He leans in close, his lips nearly touching her ear. "You see, I love to hate him."

I scowl as I watch him straighten, wondering why he needs to get so close to my date. Rachel's face flushes, and I'm half inclined to drag her far away from Alex, friend or no. I know he's quite well liked, by both men and women. I don't need him finding a new challenge to conquer.

Alex looks at his Rolex, groaning and tossing his head back. "I've only been here ten minutes and I'm already dying to go. Please tell me you're staying for the next couple hours. I really don't want to talk to people."

Rachel chuckles. "Should I have even come? The way you and Lucas are talking about this event makes me think of walked through the gates of Hell."

Alex and I groan in unison and give each other a knowing look. Of course Rachel doesn't know about gluing on a charming smile and faking interest in stocks and bonds or boosting about clients and the latest new Porsche or tech equipment. Her parents have never made her carry on a conversation with someone she absolutely loathed. She doesn't have to hide her interests for fear someone will think her strange.

She can be true to herself.

"What?" Rachel asks while looking between us. "Is this party really that bad?" Her brow furrows, and she places her hands on her hips. "Oh, come on. We just got here. You both are just being negative nancies."

I sigh and run a hand through my hair, already needing a very stiff drink. "Where's the bar?"

Alex takes Rachel's hand and places it on his arm. My hand on her hip tightens once more, yet rather than taking her away from me, he gestures towards a crowd of people across from us with his champagne glass. "Just over there. Let's go. I need another." He downs his glass quickly before guiding us towards the bar.

"Did you hear about Morton and Co.?" I overhear, my jaw clenching as I pass a small group of middle-aged men and women.

"Oh, yes, just dreadful. Whatever shall they do?"

I scowl, hating the snobbiness in their tone, knowing deep down they find it funny that one of their "friend's" business is going down. I wonder what they say about the Brents when we don't arrive at events; or when I don't arrive. Do they talk about my rebelliousness, or my lack of drive? Or do my parents just lie about me?

Yeah, that sounds about right.

"Oh, Mr. Blake, I didn't know you were coming to this party."

I still, slowly turning around and finding two men about three feet from me. One is a man in about his sixties with snow white hair and a big bushy mustache. The other is a man in his early fifties, with greying dark hair. I have no clue which one is Mr. Blake, but I know if I am going to score Mr. Blake for Samuel's firm, I'm going to have to do it while I'm still sober.

Now is my chance.

I pat Rachel's side and lean towards her. "I will be right back."

"Oh?" She perks up while my hand slides away from her. "Where are you going?"

"I just need to speak with someone, and then I'm all yours," I promise, forcing a smile and trying not to notice her hand still on Alex's arm.

I know it's nothing. She likes me. She likes the bros. But I still can't help but feel agitated. There are so many other things I would rather be doing right now.

Like Rachel in the back of the limo.

Or having dinner with Rachel at the top of the Eiffel Tower.

Or playing video games with the bros while eating pizza.

I grind my teeth. I just need to get through this and then I'm home free. I stop several inches from the men, forcing my best charming smile. "Hello," I say, grimacing at the crack in my voice. What the fuck was that? It's like I'm fifteen all over again. "I'm Lucas Brent. I work for Samuel Allen's Firm." I hold out my hand, but both man stare at it as if it's a snake they'd rather slowly inch away from.

"Ah, you're Frank's kid," says the younger gentleman, thankfully taking my hand and giving it a firm shake. "I was wondering when I was going to meet you. Joe Blake."

My smile widens, happy to know the kinder of the men is the one I'm supposed to be speaking with. He stares at me with a sense of familiarity, yet I don't think I have ever met this man in my entire life.

"I'm Louis Clark," says the other, taking my hand hesitantly, watching me with narrowed eyes. "How come we never see you in New York? I feel like I've been to hundreds of Christina's events, yet you're never there."

I shrug, fighting off a grimace. My face feels like it's going to fall off by the amount of smiling I'm doing. Or maybe I will remain permanently stuck like this?

"I've been busy with school," I say with an awkward chuckle. "Prepping for law school and rowing meets tends to keep me a bit busy." I shove my hands into my pockets to keep myself from fidgeting.

Joe Blake tilts his head. He smiles at me, yet it looks forced. His eyes watch me as if he's grimacing. The aura around him changes, and I wonder if I've said anything to offend him. "So you're working with good ol' Sam this summer, huh? How come he's not here?" He looks around briefly before returning his shrewd gaze to me. "I thought he wanted to speak with me."

"Oh, he does," I rush out. I'm probably coming off to eager. I should have planned for this, yet my mind is all muddled. I have no clue what to say to get Joe Blake interested in working with Samuel. Part of me wants to dig out my phone and look at the notes Samuel sent.

Why didn't I do that on my way here? That would have been the smart thing to do; prepare for my meeting with Samuel's potential client. Instead I was…

My mind flashes to Rachel sitting next to me in that beautiful red dress, the high slit going up the skirt, displaying a wonderful view of her leg. My face flushes and I realize both men are staring at me, expecting me to finish my train of thought. I have no clue what I was going to say. What were we talking about? The party? The weather?

Allen.

"Um," I start, but Louis is chuckling and patting Joe's back.

"Kids these days," Louis mutters while shaking his head. "Their heads must be stuck in all these electronics."

His eyes swivel back to me. "Can't quite talk to people anymore."

Joe chuckles and starts turning around.

"Wait," I say a bit louder than I intended, grabbing Joe's arm and making him pause. His eyes narrow on my hand on him and I quickly withdraw it, wishing I could find a rock I could hide under for the next century. "Why don't you take my card?" I say, fishing out my wallet with trembling hands. "You're probably busy now, but you should give him or me a call. We can-"

"Sure, kid," says Joe, snatching the card from me and shoving it into his pocket without having a look at the contact info. "I'll probably see you around."

I frown, watching him leave with Louis. Louis whispers something in his ear and Joe tosses back his head, laughing. They're probably saying something about me; about how I totally bombed. Or they're probably comparing me to my father.

I grit my teeth, my hands fisting in frustration. I'm usually better than this. I can smile when needed and laugh when something isn't funny. I can make a conversation out of almost nothing. My hands shake and I turn on my heel, finding the men's sign and stalking towards the bathroom.

"Lucas?" I hear Rachel, but I don't turn around. If I do, I know I'll make a scene. I need to regroup in silence, where no one can see me.

I slam the door open and go to the sinks, turning on the faucet and splashing water on my heated face. My heart feels like it's going to ram out of my chest. I can't quite grasp my breath. My vision blurs and I lean against the sink, holding on as if the world will slip away from me. I claim my eyes close and inhale deeply.

"One, two, three," I whisper while forcing the memories out of my mind. I don't need to relieve my total fuck up with Joe, yet I can still remember the way they looked at me, as if they thought they were better than me. "Four, five, six." I groan, remembering how stupid I sounded. I force the dark thoughts away as I continue to count, "Seven, eight, nine." I wonder what this means if Joe doesn't call Samuel. Will he tell my father? Will my father come to the apartment and demand I leave? Will he take me back to New York?

Will I even have a home after this?

"Ten," I say while slowly opening my eyes.

I stare at my reflection in the mirror. By everyone's standards I'm young and attractive. My dark hair is styled perfectly, my tux looks immaculate. I look like I have everything, like I'm standing at the top of the world.

But I feel like I'm flailing. I feel like I am falling from the top to my death and no one is there to catch me. My hands shake as they grip the sink, my nails digging into the marble. I have nothing. I am nothing without my father, without the Brent family name to hold onto.

The thought makes me want to grab something and throw it into the mirror, watching it crack and shatter into tiny pieces.

The door opens and I straighten, watching Alex come into view through the mirror. He stands behind me, crossing his arms and watching me with worry filled eyes. "Is everything alright?" he asks, yet the tone of his voice implies he knows the answer.

I nod while turning around to face him, leaning against the sink. "I'm fine."

"You want to talk about it."

I scowl and push away from the sink. "No." I stalk towards the door.

Alex grabs my shoulder before I can reach for the handle. "You can talk to-"

I smack his hand away. "I'm fine," I say harshly, my gaze darkening. "There's nothing to talk about."

"Lucas-"

"Alex, shut the fuck up, and leave me the hell alone."

I shove him away from me and throw open the door, pausing in the doorway when I see Rachel waiting outside for me. She's holding a nearly empty glass of champagne. Her gaze widens on me, her brows pinching in worry. I don't know why, but it angers me even more. I shouldn't be angry. Not with her at least, but it still doesn't stop me from stomping past her and towards the entrance.

I need to get out of this place. I need to get some fresh air and calm down. If I'm around her, or anyone, I know I'm going to explode, and I can't do that. I must remain in control. I can't let anyone see me lose it.

"Lucas," I hear Rachel, but I ignore her as I hand my ticket to the guy in the front.

I snatch my jacket and run out the door, hearing footsteps following me, but not caring. The streets are busy with cars zipping past and limos pulling up to the venue. I feel as if hundreds of eyes are watching me and I can hear the gossip whispering to me:

"Did you see the Brent boy?"

"Yeah, didn't he leave early?"

"I wonder why. Do you think he's on drugs?"

"Poor Christina. She really tried with that boy, you know."

"And he still turned out like that. Completely rude and thoughtless."

"Lucas!"

I feel a hand on my shoulder and whirl around, finding Rachel standing in front of me with glimmering eyes. Alex is several feet behind her, slowing his pace, looking at me as if I've totally lost it.

"What's wrong?" she asks softly.

I hate the quiver in her voice. I hate the way she's staring up at me, with pity and remorse. "Nothing," I say harshly, turning around, but before I can move she grabs my hand and pulls me back to her.

"Please, tell me what's going on? Why are you-"

"Why am I acting like this?" I shout, shoving her hand off me and taking a step back. "Just leave me alone, Rachel. You shouldn't be around me right now."

"But why?" she asks while stepping towards me, a tear slipping from her eye. "Just tell me what's wrong. Maybe I can fix it."

I laugh bitterly. "You? Fix it?" I hate the way her bottom lip trembles, the way she sniffs and wipes her eyes, smearing her mascara. I hate the way I still find her so attractive when I know deep down this will never work. My parents will never allow us to be together. "You can't fix anything."

"What happened? Was it that guy you were talking to?"

"That guy?" I shout, feeling fire boil and seethe within me. "That guy is Joe Blake. A wealthy and potentially important client for Samuel. He is more than just 'that guy' Rachel."

She crosses her arms, and I can help but peer over her shoulder, scowling at Alex hovering there in the distance.

"What do you want?" I shout at him. "Do you want to take her?" I gesture to Rachel. "Perhaps take her back to your apartment and have your way with her like you have your way with everything."

Rachel's mouth parts and she gapes at me, looking horrified and angry. I know what I'm saying is cruel, but I'm too angry to stop. Too angry with myself. I don't know why, but I want to ruin everything. I want to ruin the good and just sit in the darkness by myself.

"Lucas," Alex starts, but stops when Rachel stomps towards me, closing the distance between us.

"Are you being serious?" she rushes out, her voice shrill. "You can't believe that I and-" she gestures to Alex- "him are-" she grits her teeth and stomps her foot- "I can't believe this. You are just trying to make something up to be angry about so you can avoid telling me what's really going on."

She's right.

"Oh, fuck off, I've seen the way you've been ogling him the whole night." I chuckle darkly while crossing my arms. "Well, go ahead, Rachel." I nod to Alex. "He's right there for the taking. I'm giving you permission."

I feel her hand against my cheek, my eyes widening. I barely saw her move. My heart stings more than the actual slap. She stares up at me with widened eyes, as if the hit surprised her, as well.

"I'm sorry," she breathes, taking a step away from me, a hand covering her mouth. More tears slip from her eyes. I reach for her, but she turns away from me, running back to Alex.

"Rachel," I call, taking a step towards her, but stopping when she turns around. I don't know what to say. I was a complete ass. I deserved to get smacked for the things I said to her.

I watch Alex rest an arm on her shoulder, leading her towards a waiting taxi. At least she'll get home safe. I turn on my heel and trudge down the sidewalk, wishing I could take back the last thirty minutes of this sucky night.

17

RACHEL

I sniff while staring out the window, trying to concentrate on the lights flashing by and not on Lucas being a freaking asshole. I don't know why he pulled a complete 180. We were having so much fun with the limo ride and meeting with Alex. Something must have happened with the men he was speaking with earlier, but what? What could they have possibly said that would make Lucas so upset? And why isn't he telling me what's going on? I thought we were in a relationship. Not everything has to be hunky-dory all the time. He can lean on me.

Why does he think he needs to be strong all the time?

"I have a handkerchief if you want?"

I turn to Alex. Seeing the white fabric in his hands, I quickly take it and wipe my eyes before blowing my nose. I frown at my reflection in the window. My mascara is smeared over my cheeks and eyes, giving me raccoon vibes, and my lipstick is nearly gone. I tried so hard to look like a beautiful princess for Lucas. And all of it had been wasted on a stupid fight.

I take the pins out of my hair, feeling my scalp relax as the tendrils fall to my shoulders. I kick off my shoes and place them in my lap, wondering if there's any way I can return them and my dress. With the way Lucas was acting, I don't think I should keep them. They were too expensive to begin with anyway.

I lean back in my seat, wondering what this means for our relationship. We already had a fight in the cafe and now this. If he doesn't want to talk to me about his troubles, what does that mean for us?

"Are you alright?" Alex asks softly.

I sigh, not knowing what to say. No? Yes? It's not like the world will end if Lucas Brent and I don't work out. It will definitely hurt, but I'll move on. Eventually. My bottom lip trembles at the thought, and I swallow a sob threatening to burst out from me.

I force a smile and nod at Alex. "I will be." I chuckle and shake the handkerchief. "Thanks for this. I suppose you won't be needing it back."

Alex makes a face and raises his hands. "Nope. Definitely yours."

I smile and nod. "Thank you for taking me home."

"I couldn't just let you wander around aimlessly."

I scoff. "I would have gotten a taxi myself."

Alex raises an eyebrow. "And then sobbed the entire way home with no-one to console you."

I purse my lips. He's not wrong there. "Well, either way I would have made it home."

Alex chuckles. "Although this is much better, right?" He takes my hand and gives it a gentle squeeze. Part of me wants to yank it from his grasp, worried that he will read into whatever this is, yet when I look up at him, I see only friendship in his gaze and not lust. "At least you can cry to me about how much of a fucking asshole Lucas is."

I sputter, trying to contain my laughter. I know Lucas isn't always a jerk, but right now all I want to do is laugh. I cover my mouth, allowing the giggles to take over.

"It's not that funny," says Alex while smiling widely. "Although, I'm happy to see you feel a bit better."

"Oh, I feel absolutely terrible."

Alex gives my hand a gentle squeeze again. "You can tell me. I guess things with you and Lucas haven't been perfect?"

I groan and press my free hand to my forehead. "It's not just him." I sigh. "I mean, yeah, this is our second fight, but things haven't been what I thought they would be."

Alex's brows pinch together. "Like how?"

I make a face, not knowing if I should spill my guts to Seth's arch rival and Lucas's kinda friend. Staring into his blue eyes, I feel as if all my pain is being absorbed. I'm too weak to say no. I open my mouth, knowing once I start, I will never stop. "Paris just isn't what I expected it to be. The internship program is hard."

Alex shrugs. "That makes sense. Good jobs and programs are supposed to be hard."

I wince, already hating myself for I'm about to say. "Well, I ended up skipping an afternoon to go to Samuel Allen's firm. You know, to do some photography for him. He's trying to do some advertising on Nstagram." I chuckle and run a hand through my hair. "I guess he wants to come off more modern and hip." I grimace, recalling the words he said to me in his office.

"I have a feeling Lucas will drop you eventually. Better sooner rather than later."

"Did he do anything to you?"

I turn to Alex and I see that horror in his gaze. "No," I say quickly, not wanting him to get the wrong idea. "He didn't do anything to me."

Alex's eyes narrow. "Really?"

I nod. "Really. It's more of what he said. It's kinda in line with what his mother said to me before, as well."

Alex chuckles. "Oh, so you met the great Christina Brent, did you? That must have been interesting."

I frown. "It was terrible."

Alex scoffs. "Oh, I can definitely believe it." He shudders, and his hand slips from mine, running through his hair. "She's always trying to see what she can get out of a situation. She's a bit of a drunk, but she's surprisingly smart. What did she say to you?"

"Oh, pretty much that I'm nothing and Lucas will drop me eventually." I shrug. "Samuel said about the same thing, although a little less cruel. More like I'm too driven."

Alex rolls his eyes, a bitter laugh escaping his lips. "Oh my God, these people." He shakes his head. "If I didn't have running, I wonder if I would turn out to be just like them."

The taxi stops and Alex opens the door, offering me a hand and helping out onto the sidewalk. I turn towards the apartment, frowning while my gaze travels all the way up to the top floor, wondering if Hunter is sleeping and if Seth is out for another run. The door slams shut, and I turn around to say goodbye to Alex, but I stop, my heart nearly leaping into my throat when I see the taxi driving off and Alex still on the sidewalk.

"Aren't you-"

"I'll walk you up," says Alex with a soft smile. "I wouldn't want you getting kidnapped on your way inside."

I raise an eyebrow. "You watch too many movies."

Alex scoffs. "I do not," he says while striding towards the door and typing in the code.

I blink, worry sinking into me before I realize Alex is a family friend. He's probably been to this place hundreds of times. Of course he knows the apartment code to get inside. I watch him pull the door open, holding it for me while giving me a wink. "After you, my dear."

I chuckle while shaking my head, striding inside. The lights flicker on at my movement. My gaze settles on the elevator, blinking away tears as I recall that barely two hours ago Lucas and I were right here. I had thought this was going to be a magical night.

So much for that.

Alex strides past me, but I remain glued in place, wondering if it's better to go for a walk in the park, clear my mind. Part of me wants to go for a run with Seth and talk about the fight, but I know he's training for the marathon. He won't want to slow his pace for me.

"Rachel?" Alex asks while standing in front of the elevator, his brows furrowing as he watches me. "You're not going to cry again are you? I don't have another handkerchief."

I sniff and wipe my eyes. "No," I say, my voice cracking.

"Oh, not again," I hear Alex say, his steps coming towards me while I lower my gaze towards the floor. I feel his arms wrap around me and I clutch onto him, burying my face into his chest while the sobs take over. I cry against him, knowing I shouldn't, but I'm too tired. All I can feel is pain tearing through me, ripping through my heart.

"It's going to be okay," says Alex while stroking my hair. "It was just a little fight. These things happen all the time between lovers."

I pull away from him, shaking my head. "What if he thinks nothing of me? What if Samuel and his mother are right, and he will just drop me in the next day or two? I'm not wealthy. I don't have anything."

Alex rolls his eyes and shakes his head. "You have more than both of those jerks combined. You're an artist right?"

I nod jerkily.

Alex smiles while stroking my hair behind my ear. "So that mean you must have passion. You're beautiful, inside and out. You show your true feelings, so that means you're honest. You have more to you thank you think, Rachel."

I smile, feeling a bit better. Alex's hands slip away from me, but his hand grabs mine and he gently tugs me towards the elevator. "You have to realize," he says while pressing the button, "that guys like me and Lucas have to pretend all the time. We have to be chameleons."

"Why?" I ask shakily, trying to control another sob threatening to break from me.

"It's what's expected of us. We can't actually be our real selves. We can't enjoy anything without our parents say so. I'm just glad I found running or else I would be like Marcus, burying myself in women and alcohol. It's the only thing we can really get away with."

The elevator opens and Alex guides me down the hall towards my apartment. "I wouldn't worry about Lucas," Alex continues. "I can tell he likes you. I just think he's having a hard time with his parents being here. He probably had different expectations for this summer, as well."

Alex reaches for the door, but it opens. My mouth gapes open as I watch Seth appear with his AirPods in, dressed in his running gear. His eyes widens for a moment as he stares at Alex before darkening into an angry glare.

"What the hell are you doing here?" he shouts, thrusting a finger into Alex's face.

"Ssh!" I shush, looking down the hall and wondering if anyone heard. It's too late to be this loud. I grab his finger and shove it down. "Not so loud. You could wake the neighbors."

"I don't fucking care!" Seth shouts.

I roll my eyes and grab his shoulders, pushing him inside. Alex chuckles while he follows in behind and the door slams closed, making me flinch.

"What the hell is he doing here, Rachel?" Seth asks, his voice a bit lower, thankfully.

"He-"

"I was seeing Rachel home. She ran into a bit of trouble."

Seth jerks towards me, looking me up and down before settling on my face. His hand strokes my cheek, taking in my swollen eyes and smeared makeup. "Are you alright? What happened?"

"Nothing," I say, not really wanting to get into it. I'm tired and all I want to do is get out these clothes and into the bath.

Seth scowls and jerks a thumb in Alex's direction. "Did this asshole do anything to you?"

Alex scoffs. "I assure you I did not. I just saw her home." Alex wrinkles his nose. "Also, why do you look like shit?"

"I do not look like shit!" Seth shouts, grabbing Alex's collar and dragging the man towards him.

My mouth gapes open, and I touch Seth's shoulder lightly, trying to pull him away from Alex. Alex is several inches taller than Seth with extra muscle around his arms, so I'm surprised he is able to grab him.

"Seth, let him go," I say, hoping he listens to reason.

Although, Alex does have a point. Seth has been looking a bit ill these days. His face is slightly sunken in, his skin pulled taut over his lanky arms and legs. I have a feeling it has to do with his new running and eating schedule. I've been noticing lately that his eyes are a bit sunken in, as well.

"Did you just hear what he said?" Seth whines.

I grimace, not wanting to agree with Alex. I'm not in the mood for another argument especially so soon after Lucas.

"Well, it's the truth," says Alex while grabbing Seth's hands and prying them off the color of his button-down shirt. "Don't train too hard, idiot."

"Idiot?" Seth shouts.

"I wouldn't want to outrun you in the first ten minutes of the race."

"Like hell you will!"

Alex nods towards me. "Alright, I'm heading out. Good luck with this one."

I smile. "Thank you, Alex."

I feel Seth's eyes on me while I watch Alex walk out the door. Out of the corner of my eye I see him gaping, looking shocked that I would treat his nemesis so kindly. As soon as the door closes, I turn around and head towards the living room, dumping my exhausted body into the sofa. The heels in my hand tumble to the floor, and I lean back against the cushions, closing my eyes while I watch the memories from the night unfold once more.

"So, what happened?" Seth asks. I feel the cushions dip and his arm comes around my shoulders, pulling me close. "I thought you and Lucas were heading somewhere fancy."

Opening my eyes, I turn towards Seth. All the anger and hate has left him, and he watches me with love and adoration. I haven't seen that look in so long. He's been so busy preparing for this race, I haven't really gotten to speak with him since the last time we got into an argument. I brush my fingertips against his brow, pushing the brown locks away from his gaze. He leans into the touch and I smile.

"Lucas and I," I say softly, but the door opens and slams shut.

I straighten in the sofa and Seth perks up, glancing over his shoulder. Lucas stalks inside, his dark scowl meeting mine for a brief moment before he strides towards the kitchen. I wait for some sort of response, maybe even a 'hello', as he grabs a glass and pours water inside it.

He remains stubbornly quiet.

"No hello?" Seth asks with an awkward chuckle.

Lucas slams down his glass and scowls over his shoulder at us. I sigh in frustration and jump out of the couch. I can't stand being in the same room as Lucas right now. Not after what he said. I can't believe he would accuse me of going after Alex. The track athlete had only been looking out for me and trying to make me feel included at an event that definitely wasn't up my alley of expertise.

"I'm going to bed," I announce, trying not to look at Lucas. I force a smile at Seth, who frowns while glancing between us. "Good night."

"Are you two fighting?"

"No," Lucas and I say in unison.

I flick my hair over my shoulder. "Why would you say that?"

Seth crosses his arms and leans against the island. "Because neither of you are talking to each other, and obviously you've been crying."

Lucas glances in my direction and I look away. "You know what, it's been a long night," I say while turning around. "I think it's best if-"

"So, Alex took you home," says Lucas in an accusatory tone.

I bristle, feeling a bit attacked. I'm not going to be made to feel guilty over a guy helping me home. A guy who is supposed to be his friend. "Yes," I say, drawing out the one word while watching Lucas's gaze darken. His hands clench, but I'm not going to back down. I frown at the red mark on his cheek, remembering how I slapped him. My palm still stung a bit from the hit.

Honestly, I hadn't realized I hit him until moments after it happened.

"Do you have a problem with that?"

Lucas smirks. "Actually, I'm kinda surprised you didn't wind up at his place. After all, you seemed like you were begging for it."

Seth gasps. "What the hell is going on?"

I scoff. "That's bullshit and you know it. Alex was just being nice to me."

Lucas laughs bitterly, tossing back his head like a drama king. "Yeah, yeah, whatever."

"You know what, I have no clue what corncob got stuck up your ass tonight, but I would be so happy if you pulled it out and talked to me like an actual adult."

"Alright, alright," says Seth, holding out his hands as if he's monitoring traffic and positioning himself between us. "Why don't the both of you just take a chill pill, go to bed and you'll resume this in the morning after some much needed sleep."

"Ha!" Shouts Lucas while crossing his arms. "Like that will actually happen."

I shake my head, stepping towards him.

Seth holds out his hands. "Alright, wait, Rachel. Just take a deep breath. You-"

"You're such a fucking asshole!" I shout while jabbing a finger in his direction. Tears prickle my eyes, threatening to fall, but I ignore them, not caring if he sees me act weak. "You know Alex has nothing to do with this. We were fine until you met with those men. Tell me what happened. Why are you so angry?"

Lucas looks away, which only angers me even more. "You won't understand."

I grind my teeth to keep from crying. Seth grabs my shoulders, trying to turn me around, but I hold my ground. "Is it because you don't want me anymore? Are Samuel and your mom right? Are you just going to drop me in the next few days?"

"Rachel," says Seth, stroking my hair away from my face. "I don't think you need to worry about that."

"How did my mom get dragged into this?" Lucas asks while staring at me as if I've completely lost my mind.

"When she was here in the kitchen with me," I sob, unable to control my tears any longer. "She said the meanest things. That I am nothing. That she knows girls like me, and I'm worth nothing."

"Rachel," Seth whispers. "Why don't I draw you a bath? You should relax and-"

"How are you not mad at her Seth?" Lucas asks darkly. "Wasn't she hanging out with your arch rival? How does that make you feel?"

"Well, it feels like shit," says Seth, sounding irritated. "But she's her own person."

"He's your friend, Lucas!" I shout, my voice shrill. "You were the one who introduced him to me in the first place."

Lucas smiles bitterly, leaning in close and in that moment I don't recognize this man standing in front of me. It's like Lucas has completely left, like he's been replaced by this cruel person who doesn't care about me at all.

"Still doesn't mean I like you hanging around him."

"Alright, enough!" Seth shouts. "Both of you to bed!"

Lucas and I don't move.

"I wanted to go for a run, but noooooooo!" Seth scowls while he looks between us. "Instead I have to act as middleman in your little battle or whatever you can call this." He jerks towards Lucas. "I don't care if Rachel hangs out with Alex. He's an asshole, but he's an asshole who got her home. Where the fuck were you man?"

Lucas lowers his gaze, his shoulders slumping, yet he doesn't say one word.

"Yeah, that's what I thought," Seth says bitterly. "And you." He swivels towards me, his gaze softening. "Go to bed. You have work in the morning. We can resolve this tomorrow."

I open my mouth, but Seth's eyes darken and he says darkly, "To bed. Now."

"Hey, guys."

All three of us turn towards the sound, finding Hunter standing meekly behind us. "I was wondering if you could keep it down? I'm trying to video chat with my dad and-"

Seth groans, smacking a hand to his forehead. "Yeah, yeah, yeah," he mutters while tugging me after him, pushing him into my room and closing my door. "Good night!" he shouts.

I stare at my room. Tears rush from my eyes once more and I cry while stripping the beautiful red dress from me, feeling so exhausted and weak from the events. I pad towards my bed, completely naked, not bothering to wash off my makeup while grabbing the blankets and pulling them towards me.

I close my eyes and will myself to sleep, trying to ignore the memories of the night resurfacing once more.

18

RACHEL

I blink while staring down at my lap on the metro, trying to ignore the pain swelling within my heart. I woke up late, not having much time to get ready let alone eat breakfast and make coffee. My stomach grumbles in response. I will have to buy something from the convenience store if I want to make it through this day.

Staring at my lap, I try to smooth out the wrinkles in my black skirt. I frown at the wrinkles in my white button down. This is my second time in the past week I'm wearing these clothes. I actually found them on the floor next to the laundry basket. I haven't done laundry in too long. Hopefully, Lauren and Dr. Arnaud won't say anything.

My face is barely wiped clean of all the makeup I slept in the night before. Bad move on my part. My flesh feels like it's trying to crawl away from my face and find a new host. I should listen to my mother more often.

'Always wash your face before going to bed.'

My eyes are still a bit red and swollen. It would have been nice to have some spoons in the freezer already prepared, but unfortunately I didn't think of that. I was too busy arguing with Lucas. Seth had been so kind, trying to break up our argument… And poor Hunter. He had no clue what had been going on.

I groan, lifting my gaze and trying to ignore the strange looks I get from the other commuters sitting with me. I really wish I didn't have to go in today. I'd rather wallow in my self-pity, eating ice cream out of the box while watching some stupid chick flick. Anything would be better than having to deal with Dr. Arnaud and Lauren today.

I can just imagine what Dr. Arnaud has waiting for me.

The metro stops and the doors open. I slowly stand and step out, following several other people heading to work, dressed in their finest. I try not to think of the red dress Lucas bought me, lying in a pile on the floor next to my bed; the finest dress I have ever worn in my entire life, only to be worn on one of the worst nights.

I sigh and shrug my bag up my shoulder. I have no clue what to do about Lucas. I didn't see him before I left, which I was kinda thankful for. I don't even understand why we were fighting. I didn't do anything. I also don't think this has anything to do with Alex.

It has to do with his family expectations. That makes more sense.

I just wish he would open up to me.

"Rachel?"

I turn around, my eyes widening when I see Dr. Arnaud standing behind me. She looks me up and down, wrinkling her nose before settling on my face. "Are you alright?"

My head bobs up and down as I watch her approach. What time is it? Am I too late? Too early? I thought I was running late this morning, but I could have been wrong. It's not like I got the best night's sleep in my life.

"Are you sure?" she asks while placing a hand on my shoulder. She leans in, her frown deepening. "Have you been crying?"

I sniff and pull away from her, quickly wiping my eyes. I know I'm going to cry if I open my mouth, so I turn away and step onto the escalator leading out of the metro system. I'm not ready to deal with my boss right now.

Unfortunately, there's only one way out of this place and she's about two people away from me.

I step off the escalator and stalk towards the Louvre. The beautiful glass pyramid glimmers under the morning light and I try to focus on the beauty of it rather than the pain racking through me.

"Wait, Rachel."

I stop when I hear Dr. Arnaud's voice. I'm being rude. She's my boss. I shouldn't just ignore her. Slowly, I turn around and force a smile. She stands in front of me, about a foot away, watching me with worry filled eyes. Worry I don't think she could ever possess. I've never seen her look more than annoyed or frustrated, so it's shocking to see any other emotion splayed on her face.

"Are you sure you're alright?"

My lips tremble, and I try to maintain my forced smile. It probably looks like more of a grimace, since I'm sure my eyes are still swollen. "I'm fine," I sob, hating the way my voice sounds. I inhale deeply as tears drip down my cheeks. Quickly, I wipe them away, feeling embarrassed that I'm breaking down in front of my boss, of all people.

I hear her sigh and assume she's probably frustrated with me. I expect her to send me away, or tell me to never go back, but instead I hear, "How about we get a cup of coffee?"

I perk up, my eyes widening when I see her soft smile.

"Will that make you feel better?"

My whole body feels numb. My head lulls up and down, and I feel myself following her to a cafe nearby, one with outdoor seating and a clear view of the Louvre. I lower myself in a floral cushioned chair, sitting at the edge of it while she dumps her body down. She flicks her hand towards the server and orders something in French. I watch as she drags out her pack of cigarettes, taking out one and lighting it promptly.

She nods towards the pack. "You want one?"

I shake my head numbly. "I don't smoke." My tongue feels heavy as I say the words.

She smiles while leaning close, holding out her cigarette to the side so the smoke doesn't blow my way. "Of course you don't."

I sit in silence, not knowing what to say to her. I always thought she hated me. Ever since I missed the first meeting. She's always given me the hardest jobs, sending me from one side of the museum to the next, ordering me around and hardly giving me any breaks.

Or maybe that's just the way she is?

The server sets the cups in front of us; two small cups filled with espresso with a smaller cup of milk. Not exactly what I am in the mood for, but I will take it. It's better than having no coffee.

Dr. Arnaud takes a sip from her espresso, not bothering with the milk. I watch her flick the ash from her cigarette into the tray, resting it there for a moment while inhaling the bitter scent.

"I can think of no better way to start the day, than with coffee and a cigarette."

I smile, mostly because it's all I can do. I can think of better ways to start the day; like drawing, taking photographs, making breakfast with the bros and laughing about something idiotic Seth said.

"I noticed you skipped an afternoon last week."

I bristle, cringing as I recalled running out of the museum to go meet Samuel. *Well, that afternoon hadn't gone to plan*, I think, remembering once more what he said about Lucas and our relationship.

"Yeah," I say simply, my voice extremely soft even for me. "I did."

"Care to explain why?"

I grimace. "I don't really have a good excuse."

"Try me."

I sigh, trying to think of the best words to explain why I skipped work to go to Samuel's firm. I guess there was nothing more I could say other than the truth.

"I was offered an opportunity to take pictures for a law firm's social media account."

Dr. Arnaud nods while grabbing her cigarette, taking a deep inhale and blowing it away from my face. "Sounds like a nice opportunity."

I shrug. "I guess. I don't plan to do it again."

"Why not?"

I stare back at Dr. Arnaud, trying not to gape. "Why aren't you angry?"

Dr. Arnaud shrugs. "Why would I be? You're an artist trying to make your way in the world. You should do everything you possibly can to get a position. Within reason of course."

"But," I pause, swallowing the lump in my throat, "I work for you. I signed up for this internship program. Don't you think I should see it through?"

"Well, that's up to you." Dr. Arnaud stabs her cigarette into the ashtray and leans towards me. "Rachel, I think you're actually doing quite an amazing job at the museum, given your start."

My heart leaps into my throat. "You do?"

She nods while smiling widely. "I do, but if you're not happy here, I'm not going to hold you by the ball and chain and make you stay here. It's completely up to you what you want to do."

"But I thought you hated me."

Dr. Arnaud chuckles and shakes her head. "Good heavens, no. Why would I hate you? I barely know you."

"Because, because," I frown, not knowing if I'm about to say will really make her hate me, "Because you're always so hard on me."

Dr. Arnaud's smile widens. "Of course, I am. I'm hard on everyone. Being an artist is hard. You have to really want it. I want you to succeed. That's why I'm so hard on you."

"So you really don't hate me?"

Dr. Arnaud shrugs. "Not yet. Give it time."

I chuckle and grab my espresso, pouring all the milk inside it and mixing it with the spoon.

"Is that why you look like a complete mess today?"

I groan, slumping over the table. "No," I say while focusing my gaze on the dark liquid. "It's not."

"Well, that's a relief. I'd hate to make someone cry yet again. You children are so easy these days to pick on. Now, quickly down that and let's get to work. Don't think I'll go easy on you today just because you look like you've been run over by a truck."

I smile, feeling joy glimmer within me once more while I quickly guzzle down my coffee. It's a good thing I ran into her this morning, otherwise I don't know what would have happened. I feel like I can actually get through this day, this internship.

Dr. Arnaud isn't a terrible person. She's actually looking out for me, for Lauren. It's good to know that. I watch Dr. Arnaud pay and follow her towards the museum. My phone vibrates in my bag and I stop.

"Rachel?" Dr. Arnaud asks while I take out my phone, frowning when I see Samuel's name on the caller ID.

"I'll be there in a minute."

"Well, hurry up. We don't have all day."

I flash her a bright smile and I nod, watching her leave while answering the phone.

"Hello?" I say into the receiver.

"Ah, Rachel. How are you doing this morning?"

"I'm fine, Mr. Allen. Did you get the photos I sent? Was everything to your liking?"

"They were absolutely perfect." He pauses and I grimace, already suspecting the reason why he called. "I was actually wondering if you could come down to the firm today?"

I shake my head even though he can't see me. "Sorry, Mr. Allen, but I'm actually busy with my internship program today."

"Well, what about tomorrow?"

"Mr. Allen, I think it's best if I focus on my internship. I thank you though for thinking of me, and I wish you all the best."

I hang up before he can say anything more, knowing that if he continued pestering me I would give in. I slide my phone back into my bag, happy with my decision. There's an extra skip to my step as I stride towards the museum.

"Well, look what the cat dragged in," says Lauren as she sidles close to me. "What were you doing last night? Out partying?"

I flash my badge, not bothering to look at Lauren as I enter inside.

"What? Not going to say anything to me?"

I shake my head. "I don't know why you can't just leave me alone, Lauren. I haven't done anything to you."

I hear her scoff behind me and turn around, finding her crossing her arms while she scowls back at me. "You must be kidding. It's about what you did to Josh. Not at all what you did to me."

I smile bitterly, slowly stepping towards her as if I'm a huntress and she's the prey. "Oh really," I say darkly. "So it's about Josh then? Are you still talking to that sexual predator?"

Lauren's mouth drops open. "You know-"

"Oh, I know very damn well," I say, stopping mere inches from her. "I know that you would rather side with a sexual predator than a girl like me, who you used to be friends with by the way. But no, because you like Josh, obviously he can do no wrong." I cross my arms, watching that stupid mouth of her shut while she stares at me with glimmering eyes. "How's that working out for you by the way?" I ask, leaning towards her.

Lauren takes a step back. "It's fine."

I chuckle bitterly. "Like, how can you sleep at night knowing that your crush can't take no for an answer?"

Lauren juts out her chin, yet remains pleasantly quiet.

"You should be ashamed of yourself," I whisper harshly before turning on my heel and striding down the hall.

I smile, feeling glee surge around me, taking hold. I can't believe I finally stood up to Lauren. I had a heart-to-heart with Dr. Arnaud. I discovered what is truly important to me, which is this internship.

What started out as a crappy day, is quickly turning into a good one.

19

LUCAS

I'm going to throw up. I am actually going to vomit all over Samuel Allen's carpet. My leg won't stop bouncing up and down as I wait outside his office for him to call me in. He's currently in a conference call with someone. At least that's what the receptionist said. It could very well be my father.

I lean back in my chair, bumping my head lightly against the wall and closing my eyes. Memories from the night before swim back to me and I grimace, wishing I could erase them. I was such an ass to Rachel. I had taken my initial jealousy and turned it into a whole thing when that hadn't been the problem in the first place.

The problem was me.

It is me.

It's always me. Why can't I be upfront with my parents? Why can't I be myself? Especially with Rachel. I shouldn't have acted the way I did. It wasn't her fault I failed with Joe Blake. And I should have just told her what happened. We would have had a laugh about it and continued on with hanging out with Alex.

My pride got in the way.

And my family.

I open my eyes and let out a frustrated sigh. I wish I had seen her this morning. I could hear her crying from the night before, and it broke my heart that I was the one responsible for it. Seth didn't really help. I hated how he pretty much swooped in like a knight in fucking armor.

Although, that guy is not looking good these days.

Someone needs to talk to him about his diet and exercise. He's overdoing it.

The door opens, and I jump, turning towards Samuel's bright smile.

"Come in, Lucas," he says before striding back into his office.

I follow him, feeling doom seep into me, strangling my insides. I pull at my collar, finding it difficult to breathe.

"That was Joe on the phone."

I still. My heart stops and I watch Samuel sit down at his desk, spinning around as if he's a little boy in a toy store.

"Joe Blake?" I rasp.

Samuel nods, looking smug as he stares back at me. "He's game. Good job, Lucas."

I clear my throat. "But, how?" I barely spoke with the man. His friend, Louis, thought I was a complete idiot. It didn't make any sense.

Samuel shrugs. "He can never turn down the Brent family." He chuckles. "Says if one of them is working for me, I must be good enough for him."

My insides twist around themselves and I seriously feel like I'm going to be sick. So that's it? Just flaunt my family name and I can get whatever I want? Then why do I need to even bother with law school? Why do I need to bother with anything? I can just wander from place to place, say my name, and get into anywhere I please.

Without even trying.

Why does that anger me so much?

"I expect you to be at the Gala at the end of August."

"The end of August?" I repeat, feeling as if I'm having an out-of-body experience, watching myself from above like I'm an angel replaying old events. "Why?"

"Well, I'll need you to speak to the Marksons and the Getties."

"You mean, you need me to introduce myself. That's really all I have to do."

Samuel snaps his fingers and his smile widens like a shark about to feast on several tons of fish. "Exactly." His gaze lowers to the papers on his desk and he waves a hand at me. "Now, out. I'm very busy. Go have a drink and celebrate."

I hardly feel like celebrating. Leaving his office, the only thing I can think about is trying to make amends with Rachel for all the hell I put her through last night. And for nothing. I was upset with myself, and I took it out on the one person who actually listened to me, cared for me.

I'm such an asshole.

She doesn't deserve me.

I ram into someone and stumble backwards. "I'm so sorry," I say, trying to straighten the person. "I wasn't paying attention." I pause, my mouth gaping as I see my father staring back at me, brushing the invisible lint from his suit jacket.

"It's fine, Lucas," he says gruffly. "I'm sure you're quite busy."

"What are you doing here?" I ask without thinking. I look over my shoulder in the direction of Samuel's office. "Do you have a meeting with Samuel?"

"Well, yes, but I was also wanting to see you."

I swallow the groan demanding to escape from me. Looking at my father, I watch him straighten his watch and jacket before looking at his pristinely manicured nails. I don't know if he does this due to anxiety, or if he's simply a vain man. Perhaps both.

"Is everything alright?" I ask, feigning interest. If anything is wrong, it's probably because they aren't happy with the hotel service or the food isn't posh enough for them.

"No, not at all. Your mother and I are returning to New York next week after the marathon, and we were hoping to meet with you for brunch before we leave."

I nod. If I need to get through one family brunch to be rid of them, then so be it. *It won't be that bad,* I think while forcing a smile. Probably just an hour or two and then I can negotiate something with Samuel. Maybe I can just go to that gala of his and then spend the rest of my summer with Rachel.

Maybe.

If she'll have me.

At this rate I don't even know if she wants to be with me anymore. I wouldn't want to if I was her considering I was very cruel.

Father clears his throat and forces a smile. "Perfect. I will have your mother send you the precise time and location." He snaps his fingers and something glimmers in his eyes. Something I don't like. "Why don't you invite that girl?"

That girl, I think darkly, trying very hard not to scowl. She's not 'that girl'.

"What was her name again? Raven? Raquel?"

"Rachel," I say, unable to hide the venom in my tone. How hard is it for anyone to remember Rachel? It's like the easiest name in the world.

"Ah, yes, Rachel. That's it."

My eyes narrow on him. I think he actually remembers her name. He's just being rude. I frown, remembering Rachel's words about my mother; how she had said some cruel things to her in the kitchen. Part of me wants to ask, but Father most likely will play dumb.

"I'll ask her," I say, forcing a smile I know doesn't reach my eyes. "Well, I need to get back to work. I'll see you then." I start to turn around, but stop when Father grabs my arm, jerking me backwards.

A shudder runs down my spine as I meet Father's cruel smirk. "Bring her," he whispers harshly, making me recall all those times I lived under his roof; the shouting, the hitting.

My head bobs up and down. "Okay," I breathe, feeling relief when he finally lets me go. I watch him stalk down the hall towards Samuel's office. My whole body shakes and I try to will the dark thoughts away, yet they linger, haunting me. I clench my fists and turn away, stalking past the receptionist and out the door, knowing fresh air is the only thing that can help me.

20

HUNTER

I groan as the volatile *beep beep beep* of the alarm clock on my phone goes off. I blink my eyes open, squinting at the sunlight blaring through my window. Grunting, I push myself up, scratching my head while looking at my phone. It's seven in the morning on a Saturday. Today is the day of Seth's big race, which he has been training like mad for. I should be excited for him, yet my stomach twists in worry as I slide my feet out of the bed and slowly pad my way out of the room, walking towards the bathroom for a quick shower. I can hear some thumping in the other rooms and suspect everyone else is already up and getting ready.

I start the shower and quickly strip, eyeing my muscles in the mirror for a moment. I've been gaining the weight back I lost from partying and doing drugs the previous semester. There is more color in my face. Thanks to my workout regime I've been able to keep my six pack, yet I'm not as bulky as I should be for the next year… my last year playing football for Aurora.

I will need to play well if I plan on playing for the NFL after graduating. I doubt this last term will look well in the eyes of scouts and coaches given I barely played in January and February. I will also need to prove myself to Coach, gain his trust again if I don't want to be benched.

I shake my head at my reflection, knowing these are worries I can't solve right now. I step into the shower, stifling a groan as the hot water hits my face and shoulders, washing away any of the stress lingering in my thoughts. I'll handle all those problems when I return I tell myself, trying to think of all the advice Dr. Forrester has given me over the past several months.

I just need to take one thing at a time.

Although, recently it's been difficult for me not to think of the future when things are a bit fucked up amongst our group. The mood has been quite sour since Lucas and Rachel's fight. We haven't been having dinner together like usual. The last few days I've felt like I've been walking on eggshells. Rachel and Lucas pretty much avoid each other while Seth spends all his time training. This will be our first time all together since the fight and I'm worried Lucas and Rachel will spend most of the race either pretending the other doesn't exist or making snide remarks.

I have no clue which I prefer.Both are awkward situations I kinda don't want to be in.

I turn off the water and dry myself off. After tying the towel around my waist, I fling open the door, making my way towards Seth's room. Pressing my ear against his door, I frown when I hear no movement. *Has he overslept?* I wonder while staring at the door. That wouldn't be like Seth. Maybe he's sitting on his bed, staring at the wall while trying to get his mind into the game like I know several players do. I think they call it meditation?

I open the door and my frown deepens when I don't find him inside. His room is mostly bare with only his backpack lying on the ground and a pile of dirty shorts, t-shirts, and underwear sitting in the corner of the room. His bed is unmade. The curtains are open and shining light inside.

Perhaps he's on another run?

But that doesn't make sense. Wouldn't that wear him out even more? Doesn't he need all his energy for the marathon?

"Hey, Hunter."

I turn, finding Rachel holding a sign. She lifts to her tiptoes, trying to peak over my shoulder.

"Is Seth there?" she whispers.

I shake my head while slowly striding towards her. "No, I don't know where he is."

Rachel frowns and returns inside her room. I follow her, pausing at the threshold. My gaze searches the room, landing on the large sign resting on her bed reading: GO SETH!!! Several red and pink hearts circle around his name, making it appear absolutely gaudy. Any other dude would probably find it absolutely embarrassing.

I think it's cute.

Now I kinda wish I'm participating in the race. It would be nice having Rachel cheer for me, making me cute signs with hearts all around my name. Maybe she'll do it for me when the football season starts again.

My gaze turns to Rachel, watching her pace back and forth while holding her cell to her ear. I can hear the ringing on the other line. After several minutes, she pulls the phone away from her, scowling at it before pressing the red hang up symbol. She sighs and pinches the bridge of her nose.

"I will call him again later."

I grimace. "Do you think he's okay? He's been looking a bit skinny these days."

Rachel shakes her head. "I don't know. I tried talking to him about it, but he got all defensive."

I lean against the doorframe, my stomach twisting in worry. "I don't know if he's going to be able to finish. I think he's been overtraining."

Rachel nods and dials her cell again, pressing her ear against it while continuing her pacing.

"You're not ready?"

I glance over my shoulder, finding Lucas standing on the other side of the hall wearing a white t-shirt with the Aurora University logo in the front. I clench my jaw to keep myself bursting into a fit of giggles as I stare at his face, painted in the school colors.

"I see you went all out," I say between clenched teeth.

Lucas's eyes narrow and he looks me up and down. "And I see you've decided to go in your towel."

I roll my eyes. Someone woke up in a bad mood. Is this how my day is going to be? Worrying about Seth and his crazy OCD-ness with Lucas being an absolute asshole? Part of me wants to dump my body back into bed, throw the blankets over my head, and return to sweet dreams.

Of course, I won't.

Rachel will probably ensure I actually go to the race.

"Seth?"

I whip around at the sound of Rachel's voice. She's no longer pacing, yet her brows are pinched together in worry and confusion.

"Hey, where are you? We're still at the apartment getting ready." Her frown deepens while she bobs her head up and down. "Oh, ok." I inch towards her, wondering what Seth is saying on the other line. "Well, I guess we'll just meet you there then. Is everything okay?" Her nose wrinkles. I hear the exasperated tone in Seth's voice, but can't make out the words. "Alright, alright. We'll see you soon, ok?" Rachel sighs and shakes her head while hanging up the phone. "Well, he's cranky."

"Where is he?" Lucas asks, now standing over my shoulder. "Why isn't he here? I thought we would go together."

Rachel crosses her arms. Her gaze slides to the cute sign she made for him. I notice the sadness gleaming in her gaze. Her jaw clenches, as if she's trying to keep it together.

"Rachel," I say while stepping towards her, wondering if she needs a hug.

She sniffs and blinks back the tears brimming in her eyes. "It's fine," she says, her voice quivering. "He's already there." She inhales deeply while rolling back her shoulders as if trying to roll the tension away. "He wanted to get there early to stretch. I told him we would meet him there."

I nod. "Alright, well, let me change and I'll get going."

Turning around, my gaze lands on Lucas, who is still watching Rachel. I see the pain in his eyes, notice the way his hands fist as he looks at her. He looks like he wants to offer some sort of support, yet he remains rooted to the ground, fighting himself. I sigh and shake my head, brushing past him.

He's on his own with this one. I know the nice guy thing to do would be to offer him so advice, but after the cruel things he said to Rachel, I don't know if there is any going back. And if there is, whatever is said, it needs to come from Lucas. It needs to come from his heart.

As soon as I'm in my room I grab the cleanest white shirt and jeans lying on the floor and shove on my tennis shoes. I wrinkle my nose, knowing I should probably do something festive for the race to show my support, but I don't feel festive. I feel like I am walking into some sort of war zone and I don't really feel like pretending. Rachel and Lucas can pretend everything is peachy all they want. It's their fight.

Stalking out the door, I sigh when I enter the kitchen, my shoulders slumping at the scene before me. Rachel waits silently with her sign in the living room, tapping her fingers against the cardboard while Lucas leans against the island with his arms crossed. Neither are looking at each other nor are they speaking.

Ugh. This is really going to be the worst day, now isn't it?

"Alright, let's go," I say, trying to stifle the annoyance in my voice, yet it still leaks out.

Somehow, I find myself leading the way out of the apartment, taking the stairs rather than the elevator. I don't think I can handle being in closed quarters with all the awkwardness and tension stifling the air. It is bad enough they are both trudging behind me. I just hope things will get better when we're in the crowds of people.

It's a short metro ride over to the start of the marathon. The streets and sidewalks are busy with racers stretching and the audience finding a good spot to watch from. Tourists weave in and out of the crowds. The streets are closed in preparation for the race.

"Do you see Seth anywhere?" Rachel asks while clutching onto my arm. She gasps as someone shoves past her, making her stumble into Lucas.

Lucas winces and my gaze lowers, finding that Rachel has accidentally stepped onto his foot.

"Sorry," Rachel murmurs softly.

Lucas doesn't say anything and I stifle a groan. He could at least be a bit nicer to her. Say 'It's okay' or 'No big deal'. Silence isn't going to help them.

"No, I don't," I say with a slight shake of my head. "I have a feeling we won't be able to see him at all in this-"

"There," says Lucas while shoving a finger towards something in the distance.

I follow his long finger, squinting at a familiar head covered in gravity defying brown locks.

"Seth!" Lucas shouts, making my ears ring due to how close he is.

I grimace and shake my head. The person standing several feet from us slowly turns around. His eyes lock with mine and he smiles brightly while waving his hand. I stifle my groan, hating the way his face appears so gaunt. His arms look so lanky in his t-shirt.

Seth really has lost too much weight.

He looks absolutely-

"Man does he look like shit," says Lucas, looking as if he's staring at a zombie rather than Seth.

Well, I guess Seth is pretty much like a zombie. He rarely eats. I only see him at nighttime when he's off for his second or third run. His body looks like it's eating itself for sustenance. And rather than shouting 'must eat brains, must eat brains', it's more like he's shouting for 'must run, must run'.

Seth doesn't bother coming towards us. I'm kinda miffed seeing how we are here, cheering for him, but I guess he already has number 36 pinned to his back and his chest. He's already getting into the zone. Well, he's been in the zone since we arrived in Paris. I don't think he can possibly get more prepared. We watch him stretch his arms and his legs. My stomach twists once more, knowing something bad is about to happen.

I feel someone tug on my arm and turn, meeting Rachel's fear-filled eyes. "I'm really worried about him," she whispers.

I take her hand, squeezing it gently before placing a kiss on her knuckles. "Don't worry. He'll be fine." I try to hide my grimace, knowing I'm lying to both her and myself. Seth really has taken training to the next level. He should know better. He should believe in himself. Out of his entire track crew, he's the best Aurora has. I feel like lately he hasn't thought so, which is crazy. Why does he think he need to prove himself? What has gotten into him? Ever since we arrived in Paris he's been acting like some OCD running freak.

I just hope he finishes the race without any injuries.

21

SETH

I'm exhausted. I don't think I've ever felt this exhausted, but I know I'm ready. I've reduced my mile running average from six minutes to five. I had been hoping to get to four, but at the same time, I know I will need to keep up the pace given this is a marathon. Four minutes would be fine if this was merely a 5k.

I put weight on my right foot. I'm hesitant at first. My heel keeps acting up, making it difficult for me to train, but the pain isn't unbearable. I walk forwards before walking backwards, careful to place the ball of my foot down first before my heel. My foot trembles while pain pierces through me, making it difficult to breathe.

I just won't put my heel down all the way.

I'll be fine, I tell myself while looking around at the crowds, wiping the tears from my eyes. I was able to run twenty-four miles the other day. A full marathon is twenty six. I can do this.

"Seth!" I hear someone call from behind.

I whirl around, searching the crowds of people standing behind the rope. I force a smile when I find Hunter, Lucas, and Rachel standing behind me. I wave my hands, trying to appear happy and excited. I know I should go to them, thank them for coming to support me, but I'm worried about my foot.

I need to save my energy for the race.

Lucas stares at me as if I've sprouted three heads while Hunter grimaces. Rachel looks worried and I quickly turn away from them, trying to focus on my stretches. I raise my knees to my chest, moving slowly so as not to irritate my heel. I don't need their worry. I'm fine. I can do this.

I need to do this or else Coach will take back the grant.

"Is that Garcia I see over there?"

I turn around, scowling when I find Alex Goode smiling at me with arms crossed. He's surrounded by a crowd of other runners. Some older, others younger, some even slightly overweight; probably wanting to relive their running days. They'll be easy to outrun once the race starts.

Alex wrinkles his nose, the joyful gleam in his gaze diminishing as he looks me up and down. "Well, I see half of Garcia. Where's the other half?" His smile vanishes, and he strides towards me, tilting his head from side to side.

If it wasn't for the crowd of onlookers watching us, I would probably punch him in the face. I don't know why, but Alex is probably the only person he can get under my skin. Well, him and Rachel.

"Are you sure you're good to run?"

I force a smile as he stops in front of me, hating the mockingly worried expression on his face. Like this guy ever cares about anyone but himself. Most likely, he's just looking down his nose at me, wanting to get to me so I trip up once the race begins. Lucky for me, I'm good at reading people like him. I know how to keep my mind in the game.

"Absolutely," I say bitterly while leaning towards him, my hands fisting. "Just you wait, Goode, it'll be my backside you see racing past you."

Alex's lips twitch and something mischievous glimmers in his gaze. "I look forward to it."

"Racers," came a voice on the microphone with a French accent. "Get into position. We will be starting shortly."

With one last scowl in Alex's direction, I turn around and carefully walk towards my spot in front of the starting line, finding the number thirty six drawn in chalk on the ground. I inhale deeply, trying to ignore the worry twisting my stomach. I have been training for this the past several weeks. I know I can do this. I've raced in so many track meets. I shouldn't be feeling nervous.

But I am.

I don't know why I'm so riled up. Sure, this marathon is a bit different than others. If I fail, I lose a ton of money and will have to pay back coach. I'll have to take on several jobs. It'll definitely suck.

Therefore, I won't lose.

I can't lose.

I inhale deeply while lifting my gaze, keeping my focus on that yellow ribbon. I can hear my heart pounding in my ears. My stomach grumbles angrily. I barely ate anything this morning for breakfast; just some banana and a tablespoon of peanut butter. My hands tremble while my legs wobble to keep me steady. As soon as I cross that finish line I plan on celebrating with a very large steak dinner.

Or a pizza.

A giant pizza covered in pepperoni just for me.

My mouth salivates just thinking about it.

"You can do it Seth!" I hear Rachel shout.

I turn towards the direction of her voice, my eyes widening as I find her with a sign in her hands. GO SETH!!! It reads with several hearts surrounding my name. My heart swells as I stare at it, finding it the most adorable thing anyone has ever done for me. Rachel meets my gaze and I find all the worry and anxiety dissipating as I gaze into her green eyes.

As soon as this is done with, I'm going to spend every possible moment with her. I'm going to drown her in kisses. I'm going to press my body into hers, make her cry out my name until I'm the only one she can possibly think about.

"On your mark!" A man shouts into the microphone.

I jerk my attentions forward. My hands fist as I lower my body into a running stance. I can do this, I tell myself once more, my fingers digging into my palms.

"Get set!"

I dig the balls of my feet into the cement. My breath calms. All sound leaves my ears as I focus all my thoughts, all my energies on the race before me.

"Go!"

I hear the sound of the starting pistol go off. The yellow ribbon falls and I surge forward, allowing my body to do what it's trained for these past several weeks. I weave around the first man in front of me, then the woman on my right. I continue weaving around the other racers until only five runners are in front of me. My body settles into a steady rhythm as I continue running forward, knowing I will need to keep up this pace for the next several miles.

I will have to save all my reserves for the end, when the others will be exhausted. I focus on my breathing, keeping it calm as I continue my run, turning down one street towards my left. A crowd of people stand behind the ropes, cheering and holding up signs. Someone in front of me stops to grab some water, allowing me to run past them.

Water already? I think, feeling cocky. We've barely been running ten minutes and they need water. I chuckle and shake my head.

"Water already?"

I scowl and look to my left, finding Alex running alongside me while glancing over his shoulder. He smiles brightly at me before giving me a wink. "I thought you were going to give me a glimpse of that backside of yours."

My scowl darkens as I watch Alex's gaze lower to my ass, nodding in appreciation.

"I suppose it looks good from this angle, too."

"Shut the fuck up, Alex," I rasp, trying to keep my pace steady no matter how much I want to surge forward. He's playing games with my head. He just wants me to use up all my energy now so he can pull to the front. I need to ignore him, push him out of my head.

"Ah, but I like talking to you. You're so much fun to tease."

I clench my jaw to keep from saying anything. I'll have about four hours of this nonsense to deal with. I can't let him get to me.

"Do you think Rachel and Lucas are breaking up?"

My fingernails dig into my palms while I try to ignore him. I can't pull forward. I need to save my energy for the last three miles. My right shoe feels uncomfortable, as if I tied it too tightly, but I ignore it. Everything is fine, I tell myself. Don't let this asshole get to you.

"If they are, I wonder if she'll be interested in dating me."

I growl, jerking my head in Alex's direction, hating that stupid smile on his lips. "You stay away from her, you fucking asshole."

Alex chuckles, the sound more like a choke given that he's running. "I thought you two were friends." He tilts his head to the side.

"I thought you and Lucas were friends," I grit out.

Alex nods. "Sure, yeah, we are, but Rachel is quite beautiful, and I'm quite the collector of rare beauties."

Stay calm, I tell myself. He's just trying to get in my head.

"Do you like her, Garcia?"

I ignore him, focusing my attentions forward as I turn onto the street to my right. The marker reads 10K, meaning there are 32 more kilometers of dealing with this assholes bullshit. I clamp my eyes closed, trying to listen to the sound of my own heart beating rather than Alex's grating voice.

"If you say you like her, I just might leave her alone."

My eyes snap open and I turn towards him, finding interest playing across his face. How can this asshole talk so easily while running a marathon? I'm dying here just trying to remain focused. My entire body is already beginning to slow. My muscles feel tight. I feel my legs wobble as I continue to push forward. Sweat drips down my flushed face.

"I like her," I rasp. "So stay away from her."

Alex's smile widens, but he doesn't say anything. He just stares at me, making me want to lunge and shove his body into the cement. I turn forward, seeing the marker for 15K and I push myself slightly harder, fighting my body. It begs me to slow, my muscles burn in my legs, my arms, but I ignore it. My mind feels like it's soaring into the sky and I relish in the runner's high, allowing it to seep into my veins.

Running past the 15K marker, I see someone holding out a water bottle. I reach for it, not bothering to stop as I run past. Quickly, I open it and douse my face in the chilled water, opening my mouth and allowing the droplets to soak my parched tongue. I barely have time to toss it into a trash can. Someone slows in front of me into a jog and I race past them, smiling at myself.

There's only two in front of me, and the asshole on my left.

I can do this.

I turn to Alex, noticing he's no longer looking at me and focusing on the race ahead of us. Thank fucking God. I don't think I can handle any more of his talking. How did Lucas every become friends with this guy? I don't even want to know how they met. Most likely it was at one of those fancy rich events where rich kids go to meet other rich kids.

The race continues quickly and my joy brims within me as I see the 20k marker. I pass it easily, stepping up my pace. Alex sidles next to me, urging forward. The bastard is probably going to pull the same bullshit he did when I first some him at the Eiffel Tower Park. I won't allow him to trick me this time. I'll save the last surge of energy for the end and leave him in the dust.

Then I see the 25K. We're more than halfway now. I smile brightly when another racer pulls to the side, taking a water bottle and chugging it down. A twinge of pain surges through my heel, but I ignore it. I'm almost there. Only 17K to go. That should take me another hour, maybe hour and a half.

It's nothing, just ignore the pain, I tell myself.

I bite my bottom lip as I feel pain piercing through my foot, reverberating up to my knee. I groan and urge forward. I can't quit now. Not after all the training and hard world I've put into this marathon. I pass the 30K marker. Tears stream down my cheeks as I feel a crunch in my heel.

I can do this, I think, feeling my body quiver. My feet stumble over each other and I land on my right foot, emitting a shriek as something cracks in my heel. Alex slows, whirling around with wide eyes as I feel my entire world tilting.

My body crashes into the ground and I burst into tears as I hold my foot, not knowing what's going on. I try to roll over, push my body up, but the pain is excruciating. I can't stop crying or screaming.

"Garcia!" Alex shouts while running towards me.

"I'm fine," I say while continuing to push myself up. I lead with my left foot, ignoring the shooting pain in my right.

Alex grabs my arm, throwing it over his shoulder while guiding me towards the ropes.

"Is he alright?" someone asks.

"I'm fine," I sob while struggling in Alex's arms. "Now let me go. I need to finish the race."

"You need a hospital."

"No!" I shout while squirming away from him, but I'm too exhausted and Alex is too strong.

Glancing over my shoulder I see runners race ahead. Their wide eyes drift to me. One runs towards us. "Do you need any help?" The racer asks while she looks me over, her brows pinched with worry.

Alex shakes his head. "I got it, thank you."

"I'm fine," I insist, watching in horror as everyone makes space beyond the ropes. Someone holds it up. I feel like I'm outside of my body and watching as Alex guides me underneath and towards the sidewalk. "I need to finish the race," I whimper, feeling the last bit of strength leave me.

"I'm a doctor," someone says, pushing through the crowd with wide, worrying eyes.

Alex gently positions me against the wall of some building. The doctor kneels in front of me, taking my shoe off my injured foot. He pulls at my sock, plopping it inside my shoe and I hiss as he takes my foot into his hands, turning it from side to side. I bite back a scream. Alex gasps while I clamp my eyes closed, not knowing if I really want to have a look at the damage.

"Oh my God," Alex whispers.

"Sir, you really need to go to the hospital."

"What is it?" I sniff. The pain is so bad I can't seem to stop crying or trembling. I feel like either vomiting or passing it. I grab at something soft. Opening my eyes, I see it's Alex's shoulder. His eyes are wide and staring at my foot while the doctor straightens, taking out his phone.

My gaze lowers and I bite back a whimper as I stare down at my swollen foot. The heel is completely black and blue. I can't even see the ankle, given the joint and tendons appear to be completely swollen, appearing as if my foot has become one large club.

The doctor says something in French on the phone, yet I'm not paying attention to him. I watch several other racers pass us by, hating myself for not being able to pull ahead, hating myself for this stupid injury.

What is Coach going to say?

What am I going to do?

"Alright, sir, I need for you to come with me," says the doctor while taking my hand and guiding through the crowd.

"I'll go with," says Alex while helping me hobble forward. "Where are we going? I'll call his friends."

"The American Hospital of Paris. They speak English there. Don't worry. They will take good care for you."

My grasp tightens on Alex. My vision blurs and I stumble forward as the pain takes hold of my body.

"Garcia?" I hear Alex while I lean against him, no longer having any control of my body. "Seth?" I hear the worry in Alex's voice, but I can't reply. All I can feel is the pain taking hold of me.

"He's going into shock," I hear the doctor say. "We need to hurry. Call his friends. Have them meet us there."

My eyes blink as the world continues to spin. I feel the darkness taking hold of me. Silence greets my ears until finally I close my eyes, my body falling numbly as I allow the shadows to swallow me whole.

22

RACHEL

I burst through the hospital doors, looking around at the yellow walls and the pristine white marble receptionist desk. I'm barely aware of Lucas and Hunter standing behind me as I rush towards the woman standing behind the desk. As soon as Alex called Lucas, informing us of Seth's injury, I dumped my sign and called for the nearest taxi. Traffic had been terrible. It took us forever to get the hospital, and I worried Seth would wake up in pain or feeling all alone.

"Bonjour," she starts, looking alarmed as she glances between us.

"We have a friend who was just admitted here," says Hunter.

"Seth Garcia," I rush out, tears prickling my eyes while I watch the receptionist type at her computer. "His name is Seth Garcia. He was in the marathon."

The woman nods while pushing back her dark curly hair. "Yes, he was admitted less than an hour ago. He's on the fourth floor in room 411."

I turn on my heel and run towards the elevators in the back, barely hearing Lucas's low, "Thank you."

I should have known something like this was going to happen. He was training too hard, barely eating anything. One of us should have talked to him weeks ago about his training. I stab my finger at the button over and over again, shifting from foot to foot while I watch the numbers displayed on the elevator lower.

There's no point in blaming myself now. What's done is done. Now I just hope nothing terrible has happened to him.

As soon as the doors open, we rush inside, my small body shoved between Hunter and Lucas. Lucas doesn't say anything while Hunter wraps an arm around my shoulders. We still haven't been on speaking terms since our fight days ago. I don't know if we will ever be the same.

Although, right now I can't gather the strength to care. Not when Seth is lying in a hospital bed injured.

"It's going to be fine," says Hunter while pressing his lips against my brow. "He got injured while running. These things happen all the time. It's not like he got hit by a car."

I nibble on my bottom lip while listening to Hunter.

"I mean, you should have seen me my sophomore year. I got three concussions and a broken nose. My shoulder is still all fucked up. These things happen."

"But this shouldn't have happened," mutters Lucas.

I lift my gaze, flinching when I see his dark scowl. Even with the school colors covering his face, he still has the ability to look absolutely terrifying when he's pissed off.

"Seth should have known better. He over trained." Lucas shakes his head. "And for what? All to win a stupid marathon."

My hands fist. "You know nothing," I breathe, my voice trembling. I swallow the lump in my throat while trying to stop myself from crying. I blink away the tears, trying to remain in control of my feelings. "He needed to win." I hiccup and swipe the tears from my eyes, feeling both stares on me. "Coach gave him a grant, telling him he had to bring back the trophy if he wanted to come." I feel myself breaking. A sob is demanding to escape my lips. I wipe my eyes again and sniff. "This is all my fault."

"Don't say that," says Hunter while pulling me towards him.

I nuzzle my face into his chest, clinging onto him and allowing his warmth to swallow me.

"It's not your fault," he whispers into my hair before kissing the top of my head. "Seth knew what he was getting himself into. He should have been more confident in himself."

The elevator dings and I push myself away from Hunter, wiping my eyes while turning towards the opening doors. Before I can catch Lucas, he's already stalking into the hallway with his back facing me. Hunter and I follow him out and I instantly look for 411, finding Alex standing on the opposite end of the hallway. He's still wearing his number 30 pinned to his chest. Worry etches his brow, and he holds up a hand, waving awkwardly.

"Hey," he says as we stride towards him. "I was just heading to the vending machine for some crappy coffee."

"How's Seth?" I ask while stopping in front of him. "Is he okay?"

Alex grimaces. "His foot is fucked."

I grind my teeth to keep myself from crying.

"Do you know what happened?" Asks Lucas.

Alex nods. "I was running alongside him. He was doing pretty well, but after the 30K marker I heard something snap. Next thing I know, Seth is on the ground, screaming and crying while clutching his foot." Alex chuckles while shaking his head. "The bastard still wanted to continue. Honestly, he probably would have won if he hadn't been in such bad shape. What the hell has he been doing to himself?"

Lucas, Hunter, and I share a knowing look.

"Training," says Hunter.

"Fuck loads of training," Lucas adds.

Alex winces. "I suspected he overdid it a bit," he groans while tossing back his head. "Well, he's safe. And he's awake. He passed out from the pain, but now the bastard won't stop talking, demanding for coffee and food." He nods towards the hallway. "I'm on coffee duty for now. You all will be here for a bit I'm assuming?"

Lucas, Hunter, and I nod.

"I'll be back then."

I watch Alex leave, feeling my heart swell with something as I watch him walk down the hall. This man, Seth's rival, had helped him in his time of need. I have no clue how I'm going to repay him. All I know is Alex Goode is an amazing guy. Seth should be lucky to have such an adversary, possibly a friend in disguise.

"Alright, let's see how bad it is then," says Lucas while grabbing the handle to door 411 and pushing it open.

We pause in the threshold staring at Seth with his foot hanging in a sling. The room is tiny with an old, small TV hanging on the wall. There's a soft *beep beep* from the machine resting next to Seth.

"You're back already?" Seth rasps while turning towards us, his eyes widening for a moment. An IV sticks out of his arm and he's dressed in a hospital gown rather than his running attire. Despite knowing he's fine, my eyes still prickle with tears and I run to him, throwing my arms around his neck.

"I was so worried," I sob against him, nuzzling my face against his cheek.

"I'm fine," Seth says softly while stroking my back. "You have nothing to worry about. I'm fine."

"You look like shit," says Hunter while I pull away.

Seth chuckles, pushing the locks away from his forehead. He buries himself deeper into his pillows. I notice his face is gaunt and there are dark circles under his eyes. "I definitely feel like shit. Thankfully, they gave me some drugs for the pain."

"What happened?" Asks Lucas, standing at the foot of the bed with arms crossed.

Seth squints at Lucas, making a face before quickly shaking his head. "Is it the drugs, or are you covered in paint, Lucas?"

Lucas's gaze darkens. "I did it for you numb nuts. To show support."

Seth sputters. "Some support. You look ridiculous."

"And you look like you could use a punch in the face."

The door opens and all four of us turn towards the sound. I'm expecting to see Alex with food and coffee, but instead a doctor stands in the doorway, holding a clipboard and reading through some papers. He lifts his gaze, flinching when he sees all four of us staring at him.

"Whoa," he starts. "I see you have some guests, Monsieur Garcia."

I sit at the foot of Seth's bed, fear taking hold of me while the doctor kicks the door closed and approach's Seth.

"Well, everything appears to be fine now," the doctor continues.

"What exactly happened?" Lucas asks.

"Monsieur Garcia has a fracture on his heel, specifically known as a calcaneal fracture."

"So his heel is broken?" asks Hunter while leaning against the bed frame. "How does that happen?"

"From overuse or repetitive stress on the heel bone. It's not uncommon for runners such as Monsieur Garcia to experience it if they are overtraining."

Hunter, Lucas, and I turn to Seth, who gives us a sheepish smile. "Whoops," he says simply while twiddling his fingers.

"Should we say I told you so?" Hunter asks.

Seth grimaces. "Please don't," he groans. "I already feel terrible enough as it is."

"Will he need surgery?" Lucas asks and my gaze turns to him, watching the worry play over his face before being replaced by that wall I've become so used to in the past several days.

The doctor shakes his head while moving his clipboard under his arm. "No, not at all. Although it will be quite painful. I'll prescribe a mild painkiller." He lowers his gaze to Seth. "No running," he says while pointing his finger at Seth. "No weight on that foot whatsoever. You'll need to get around on crutches for the next several weeks. Remember to ice and elevate."

"Will I be able to run again?" Seth asks, the fear plaguing his gaze making me want to wrap my arms around him and tell him everything will be alright. I know how much running means to him. It's the one thing that keeps him grounded, yet it's also the one thing that caused this mess to begin with.

Well, I guess it isn't really running, but Seth's obsessive nature to outdo everyone around him.

The doctor nods and Seth he releases his breath, leaning into the pillows behind him. "It will take three to four months to heal."

Seth's lips part, his eyes widening in horror. "Three to four months?" He asks, his voice shrill. "But that mean, that means," he turns to me and shakes his head, "my track meets begin in September. Are you saying-"

"You won't be able to run until October at the soonest. Most likely November."

"But-"

"Monsieur Garcia," says the doctor, looking very annoyed, "if you ever want to have full function in that foot; if you ever want to run again, you will head my advice. No weight on it until at least September, and no running until late October or early November."

"But-"

"No buts," says the doctor while shaking his head. "If you didn't want this to happen, then you should've practiced safe training." He looks at his watch before turning on his heel. "Now, if you excuse me, I have other patients to attend to. The nurse will be by in another hour or so to have you sign some forms. You can return home tonight. If anything happens, or your foot worsens, please return."

I take Seth's hand, giving it a gently squeeze while watching the doctor leave. As the door opens, I see Alex carrying several coffees and a croissant under his arm.

"So?" he asks while sliding into the room, setting the items onto the nightstand next to Seth's bed. "Is everything okay? Can you go home?"

"Yeah, he's fine," says Lucas.

"What?" Seth asks, his voice nearly a shout as he scowls at Lucas. "Everything is not fine." Tears brim his eyes while his grasp on my hand tightens. "Everything is fucking shit. Didn't you hear anything the doctor said?"

Hunter sighs. "I know it sucks now, but-"

Seth scoffs and shakes his head. "I don't want to hear it right now, Hunter."

"So you just want to sit here, feeling sorry for yourself?" Lucas says while throwing his hands into the air.

Seth sniffs and I worry he's going to burst into a fit of tears. I've never seen this side of him I don't know if he wants to be alone, or if he wants a hug so I remain on the bed, holding his hand, offering my support.

Seth nods his head while wiping his eyes. "That's exactly what I want to do."

Alex sighs and gives me a knowing look. "Maybe it's best if we wait outside," he says softly. "Let the two of you talk for a bit."

I offer him a small smile of gratitude and nod, watching as Hunter and Lucas follow him out of the room. Seth's hand slips from mine and he covers his face, his shoulders shaking I suspect he's crying quietly to himself. The news isn't terrible, yet I can understand that it's pretty much destroyed his running career for the next few months. It's nothing he can't return from, but it definitely puts a glitch in his plans.

I slide closer to him, wrapping my arms around his neck and pulling him towards me. He sobs while nuzzling his face into my neck. I feel his tears against my skin. His hands cling to me while he hides himself away. I stroke my fingers through his hair, shushing him while swaying from side to side.

"It's going to be okay," I whisper into his ear.

He shakes his head. "Nothing is ever going to be okay," he rasps.

"I know it feels terrible now, but things will work themselves out. They always do."

Seth pulls away from me, his swollen red eyes meeting mine. He wipes them, embarrassment splaying over his face while he quickly looks away from me. "I'm sorry," he says while making some space between us. "I don't mean to be so weak."

I shake my head while stroking his cheek. "You're not weak at all, Seth. You're exhausted. Physically and mentally. You can't be perfect all the time."

Seth inhales deeply, pushing the strands on his forehead away from his face. "It's the first time ever I didn't finish a race. What am I going to tell coach? How am I going to repay him?" He motions towards his leg. "How am I going to be able to keep my scholarship if I can't run?"

I take his hands and press my lips against his knuckles. "You don't need to figure everything out now. You still have time."

Seth grimaces. "What if this injury messes up my track career?"

I shake my head. "If you listen to the doctor, it'll heal. Just don't put weight on it and no running until November."

"My muscles will weaken." Seth gasps and I can tell he's having problems regaining his breath. I rest my hands on his shoulders, forcing him to look at me. "I won't be able to keep up with my running score. I'll lose-"

"Seth," I say while lightly tapping his cheek. "Stop. Don't worry about it now. Be glad nothing worse happened."

He shakes his head. "I can't not worry about it. Track is all I have."

I press my forehead against his. "You have me," I whisper while nuzzling my nose against his. "I'll help you through this."

Seth's frown deepens. "I can't ask that of you."

"I'm your girlfriend." I smile and kiss his forehead. "I'm supposed to lift you up when you're down."

Seth leans into me, resting his head against my shoulder. I stroke my hand through his hair, enjoying the silky feel of his locks against my flesh. "I'm so sorry I didn't listen to you," he whispers while nuzzling his head against me. "I'm so sorry I was such an asshole to you."

I shrug. "Definitely not the first time." I smile, remembering the first time we met. "And you've been worse."

Seth chuckles while raising his gaze towards me. His hand touches my cheek tenderly and he presses his lips against mine, kissing me gently.

"Do you forgive me?" he says between kisses.

I nod slowly. "Yes," I breathe.

I capture his lips, pushing him back against the bed. He falls easily and I climb on top of him, straddling his body. Seth moans as I continue kissing him, running my hands up and down the length of his body. He bucks gently against me, his cock pressing against my leg, tenting the hospital gown.

I pull away from him, a sly smile on my lips while I slowly lower myself down until I'm hovering just above the small tent. His cock twitches. He watches me, desperation glimmering in his gaze as I palm his tip.

"Rachel," he breathes while I push away the fabric, watching his hard, long length coming into view.

I grab it, moving slowly up and down while Seth shudders, his head lulling from side to side. My thumb plays with the sensitive flesh at his tip before my hand slides down. Precum dribbles from his slit, slicking my movements. His hands grip at the sheets as I continue my ministrations.

"God, Rachel," Seth rasps.

His hand grabs mine, urging me to move faster, but I fight him, ensuring I pump him slowly, enjoying every minute of this torture. I position my body until my mouth is hovering above his tip, breathing hot air against him and watching his cock twitch.

"You're terrible," Seth says between clenched teeth, his eyes glazed over, watching me intently.

He gasps as my tongue licks him, raveling around his length before sliding away. His body trembles while my hand pumps up and down. I take him again, just his tip in my mouth, sucking it tenderly before releasing him with a pop. He whimpers, bucking in desperation, needing my hot mouth on him again.

I answer his call, taking him all the way in, until I feel his pubic hairs against my lips. He gasps while I suck, moving up and down. His cock twitches against the back of my mouth. I feel my gag reflex kick in, but I fight it, moving faster now.

Seth moans. I glance at him, watching his head toss and turn. His dick thrusts into me, meeting each slide of my mouth. One hand grabs my hair, gripping it harder while I continue sucking him.

"God, Rachel, don't stop," he gasps while he continues thrusting into me.

I don't intend to. I want him forgetting all about his troubles. I want him to think of only me. I suck harder, moving faster, meeting each and every thrust of his dick. His moans heighten, growing shriller with each passing minute. I run my tongue up and down his shaft. I nibble on his tip, watching him spasm and grasp at the sheets. He's nearing his release. A part of me wants to torture him longer. I never knew giving blowjobs could be so enjoyable. I feel like I have control over him, playing him as if he's putty in my hands.

"Rachel," Seth whimpers while bucking against my mouth. "Rachel, please."

My hand rubs up and down him. His dick is completely soaked in my spit and his precum. More of it slides from his tip. I take it in my mouth once more, sucking harder and moving faster. He twitches, his whole body spasming. His groans are coming out louder and longer. We should probably stop. The nurse should be coming in soon, but I know he's past the point of return. I can feel his body shivering.

His hands grab my hair, holding my head still as he fucks my mouth, shouting his release as if it pains him. "Fuck, Rachel," he breathes, his hands sliding down to stroke my cheek. "So fucking good. You're so fucking good."

I swallow his cum, wiping my mouth while pushing my body up. His eyes are glossy, staring lazily back at me while I pull his hospital gown down. He moans while he watches me, looking completely satisfied.

I smile back at him. His lips remain parted while he breathes deeply. "I," Seth begins, but the door opens.

I turn, watching as Hunter, Lucas, and Alex enter with the nurse.

"Alright, Monsieur Garcia," says the nurse while handing him a clipboard. "Let's get you out of here and home in your own bed."

I rise from the bed and stride towards Hunter. He grabs my shoulders, his brows furrowed while he wipes something off my cheek. "You missed a little," he whispers into my ear, making my face flush.

I stride towards the door, wanting to see what else I missed in the bathroom. Glancing over my shoulder, I find Seth signing the forms and Lucas watching me, looking as if he has something to say.

We'll have to talk, eventually.
I just don't know if I'm ready.

23

LUCAS

"Alright, here you go," I say while helping Seth into his bed.

He grimaces as I take his arm off my shoulder. We were able to get him some crutches before we left, which we'll have to return to the hospital before we return to Colorado. They lie next to the door, nearly forgotten. I just hope Seth remembers he's not supposed to put any weight on that foot of his. I can just see us returning to the hospital with him screaming in pain in my ear and me yelling at him for being an idiot.

The pharmacy wasn't that far away either so we were able to pick up his pain medication, which was pretty much a European version of aspirin. Like that's really going to help him. However, it's probably better than being given anything stronger. I don't think I can handle another Hunter situation. Those harder pains meds are quite addictive. It's probably better this way. He'll also need to look into physical therapy when we return to Colorado. Most likely I will be nagging him day in and day out about all this annoying shit.

I sigh and rub my temples, already feeling annoyed and agitated like a fretful mother. Thinking of his mother, I wonder if someone should call her and tell her what happened, but I know Seth won't want to worry her. His family situation is just as complicated as mine. I don't want to get involved.

Watching him now, I can tell the drugs from the hospital are already wearing off. His whole body is trembling as if he's standing naked in Antarctica. Part of me wonders if it's too soon for him to be home, but then again the hospital isn't the nicest of places to be sleeping in. Thankfully, the bill wasn't too expensive. I was able to pay for it with the Brent family card.

I watch Seth roll over, not bothering to change out of his track clothes. He rests his head on the pillow and stares up at the ceiling, his hands gripping the sheets.

"Are you sure you're okay?" I ask while watching him clench and unclench his jaw.

Seth nods, but I can tell he's lying. I have never seen him this quiet in my entire three years of knowing him. I don't like it.

I sigh in frustration and rub the back of my head. "Do you want a warm bath? I'm sure Rachel will allow you to use hers."

Seth shakes his head.

"Are you sure?"

Seth groans and presses his hands against his face. "For fuck's sakes, Lucas," he says angrily. "I'm fine."

"Are you hungry?"

"No," Seth moans while smacking the bed. "I just want to be left alone."

I sigh and shake my head, grabbing the bag of medicine lying next to the door. "I'll get you some water to take with the painkillers. Then maybe you should get some sleep."

"Way ahead of you."

I stride past Hunter's door, hearing him talking with his therapist on video chat. My gaze slides to Rachel's door, noticing it's closed. She's probably reading a book or possibly drawing something. My parent's brunch is in a few days and I haven't found the courage to ask her to join us. I know we have a lot to talk about. I know I need to apologize, but everything has been weird since the fight.

I don't know how to fix it.

For the first time ever, I want to actually mend a relationship with a girl, but I don't know where to start or what to say. I'm worried I'm just going to make everything worse.

With a frustrated sigh, I turn away from her door and move to the kitchen, pausing when I see Rachel leaning against the island, staring out the balcony doors at the sun setting in the distance. She looks beautiful with her curly blond hair hanging over her shoulder, dressed in simple jeans and a t-shirt. All I want to do is go to her, grab her hand and pull her towards me, claim those sweet lips of hers, but I know I can't. She'll probably push me away or call me an asshole.

As if she senses my stare, Rachel turns to me, her eyes widening for a brief moment before she straightens herself and clears her throat. "Sorry," she murmurs. "I got lost in my own train of thought."

I chuckle awkwardly, not knowing what to do. "Happens to me sometimes," I say softly while striding into the kitchen.

"How is Seth?" she asks while I grab a glass and pour water into it, unable to look at her.

I nod and set the glass neatly on the counter. "He's in pain, but he's fine. Just bringing him some water so he can take his pills and go to sleep."

Silence greets my ears and I glance over my shoulder, finding her staring at me, looking confused. I slowly turn around, feeling my stomach twist with anxiety. Clearing my throat, I wince, knowing it's better to just apologize and get it done and over with. I don't want this silent treatment to continue. It can't continue. Not when I know I've been a jerk. She deserves so much more than me.

I don't want us pretending like the other doesn't exist, when all I want to do is kiss her.

"I'm sorry, Rachel," I rush out, my gaze dipping to the tiles in the floor. "I was a complete asshole to you at the party. I was upset with myself and took it out on you and I," I grind my teeth, feeling anger grasp hold of me for how stupid I've been acting these past few days. "I was a fucking jerk. I know that. And I know you're mad at me for the way I treated you."

I lift my gaze and close the distance between us, grabbing her hands and pressing them against my chest, where my heart resides. Her eyes widen in alarm, but she doesn't pull away from me.

Maybe we can still make this work?

"Please, tell me how I can make things better?" I say, unable to hide the desperation in my voice. "I have never felt this way with anyone before. I never thought I could. Just tell me what I can do to make things better between us."

Rachel's lips part, her eyes filling with tears. I feel my heart crack as I watch a tear slip down her cheek, her head slowly shakes.

"I don't know," she breathes, her bottom lip quivering.

She slowly steps away from me, her hands slipping from my chest. I feel like my heart is shattering into a million pieces. What is happening? How is this happening? It was only a small fight. Surely, there's some way we can make this work.

"I just need some space, Lucas. I'm not ready for us to talk about," she gestures between us as she says, "this."

I watch her wipe her tears, wishing I could simply kiss away the pain and make her mine once more. My head bobs up and down, knowing that sex isn't love. Lust isn't love. Supporting each other, listening to one another; that is what love is.

Trust is love, and I feel as if I have broken that trust by hurting her so terribly.

"If that's all, I need to get ready for bed," she says while briskly striding past me. "It's been quite a long day."

"Wait," I whisper while grabbing her hand, giving it a gentle squeeze.

Her brows furrow, her eyes fill with pain and confusion. "What is it?"

I swallow, knowing I need to get this over with, even if she says no. "My parents are having a brunch this week. They asked me to invite you."

Her shoulders slump and her gaze slides away from mine.

"You don't have to go," I rush out quickly.

"I don't want to go."

Those words make my heart twinge and I release her hand, knowing that I've fucked up big time. "Okay," I say, hating the way my voice sounds. My breath comes in rasps. I feel like my whole world is breaking as I stare at her.

Her eyes lift to mine, brimming with unshed tears. She tilts her head to the side, looking pained as she watches me. "But I will."

I blink. "You will?" I don't know why, but I feel as if I've been given a second chance.

I watch her nod. "If it means so much to you, I will go."

"Thank you," I say quickly, a smile curling my lips. "It means the world to me."

Rachel forces a smile while she slowly turns around. I watch her round the corner, feeling as if my heart is picking up the pieces. I will make this better, I vow to myself while turning, staring at the sun setting in the distance. Rachel means the world to me and I will prove it to her. I will prove to her that I love her and then she will be mine.

I reach for the glass, still resting on the counter next to the bag of pain medication. I stride towards Seth's room, feeling revived. Quickly, I wipe away the tears in my eyes, forcing a smile while I enter inside.

24

RACHEL

I sigh while looking at myself in the mirror, holding my two best dresses. Well, they are not as beautiful as the red dress Lucas bought for me. I frown at its reflection, staring at me through the mirror, haunting me with memories of the fight I had with Lucas. It's my best dress, but I think it's a bit too fancy for a brunch, no matter how wealthy Lucas's parents are and how nice the place is.

Lucas told me the name of the restaurant that we are meeting Christina and Frank Brent. My heart instantly dropped to my stomach and my insides went cold when I saw the photographs on their websites. It's one of those places where they have a chandelier hanging every few feet from each other, the tables and chairs are gold plated, and there are at least seven forks and spoons to decipher between.

According to *Pretty Woman,* I should start with the outer silverware and move inwards. Hopefully, Julia Roberts won't steer me wrong, because that is the only advice I have in order to get through the next few hours. That and keeping my mouth as quiet as possible. I already suspect Christina will be a bit passive aggressive towards me and Frank will probably hound me with questions I don't know how to answer.

I inhale deeply in order to calm myself. I shouldn't be thinking so negatively. They were the ones who invited me, therefore they'll probably be on their best behavior. My frown deepens in my reflection, recalling my last interaction with Christina.

I raise the baby blue dress up once more. It's a little short, but it has puffy sleeves and a high collar. I can wear it with my nude heels and some faux gold jewelry with my hair up. That will certainly look nice. Although, I don't know Christina's opinion on short dresses, considering last time I saw her I was in my bunny pajamas and slippers.

I hold up the white t-shirt dress. It's a bit longer, ending just above the knee. It's more like a long collared, button down with a belt to cinch in the waist. A bit more casual, but I can spruce it up with my pink pumps and some more gold costume jewelry. I tilt my head to the side, switching the garments back and forth, before tilting my head up to the ceiling and emitting a frustrated groan.

Both dresses are nice. Both dresses will look super cute and can be styled nicely. I toss the blue dress onto the bed, opting for the white t-shirt dress, given that it is longer. When in doubt, always go a bit more conservative, at least that's what Mom always told me.

I belt the waist and slide on my pink pumps before pulling my hair into a high bun. I tug a few strands down to frame my face and dab on a bit of gloss. Smiling at myself, I turn around, deciding this is quite cute for a formal brunch with the parents.

There's a soft rap at my door followed by Lucas peaking inside. His eyes widen and traveling over the length of my body while he pushes the door open. I notice his white button-down shirt and his jeans, which makes me feel better about my dress choice. I guess it won't be that fancy.

"Wow," he murmurs while striding towards me. "You look beautiful."

I try to hold my smile, yet these days I don't know how to react around Lucas. I'm still upset with him. We still need to talk and I don't think sharing a meal with his parents is really the greatest way to mend the rift growing between us. Actually, I'm absolutely positive it's going to make the rift bigger, but it's important to him, and I want to show him I'm still in this relationship.

"Are you sure this will be fine for where we're going?" I ask while crossing my arms, feeling a little self-conscious.

Lucas smiles and rests his hands on my shoulders, nuzzling his nose against mine. I feel a spark in the pit of my stomach and close my eye, enjoying this close proximity.

"Definitely," he murmurs.

I open my eyes while his hand laces with mine, allowing him to tug me out of my room and into the kitchen. My purse is still on the counter where I last left it; a small pink bag that barely contains my wallet and cellphone let alone my keys.

Seth and Hunter are sitting on the sofa, talking about something I don't catch as their voices lower. Hunter keeps glancing at me and my eyes narrow, suspecting they had been talking about us.

Seth glances over his shoulder, whistling as his eyes rake over me. "Don't you look mighty fine."

I roll my eyes and groan. "That's not exactly what I was going for, Seth."

Seth smirks, yet it quickly dissipates as he lifts his body from the sofa, grimacing as he tries to get a better look of me.

"Don't overdo it," Hunter mutters while reaching for Seth, but his hand is quickly pushed away.

"I'm fine," says Seth with an eye roll.

I chuckle at Hunter's scowl. "We won't be long," I say, feeling Lucas's hand give me a gentle squeeze. "I expect the both of you will stay out of trouble. Don't move around too much." I waggle my finger at Seth, who rolls his eyes once more.

"Yeah, yeah, yeah," he mutters while turning around.

"Have fun!" Hunter calls while Lucas guides me out of the apartment.

I'm partly surprised, and yet thankful, when Lucas escorts me outside the apartment complex towards the awaiting taxi. I expected a limo, knowing Lucas and his family. It seems like this will be a bit more of a casual meeting; only the venue and food are fancy. The food is supposed to be amazing. My stomach grumbles in response as I buckle my seatbelt, turning my attentions to the window while the driver begins the commute.

The silence is deafening. Other than Lucas tapping on his knee there is nothing. No music. No weird conversations with the driver. Nothing. I glance at Lucas, seeing that he's also staring out the window. His leg bounces up and down.

Is he just as nervous as I am? I wonder, but don't ask.

My hand grabs his tapping fingers and he jerks towards me, looking surprised before a smile takes hold. "Don't worry," he says, as if I'm the one fidgeting nonstop in the car. "It should be fun. If not the food is supposed to be great."

I nod, not knowing what to say. His voice is cracking. He's definitely nervous about something. I've never been this nervous in front of my parents, but then again we had an open discussion. They always told me to call them if I had been drinking, because they didn't want me drinking and driving. I asked Mom to be on the pill and she was very proud of my maturity. I think the only time I had been nervous around my parents, was when I told them I was going to Colorado for school, rather than staying in New York.

I had been nervous, but not this nervous.

If I didn't know Lucas, I would suspect he was going to a job interview, not meeting his parents.

"We're here," says the driver before stopping in front of the restaurant.

I peak outside, my eyes widening when I see the gold plated doors. Two ladies dressed in the tallest black stilettos I've ever seen wearing matching brown Gucci, tight fitting dresses, enter inside. The door is held open by a butler in a tuxedo.

A tuxedo in this heat?

He must get paid well.

"Rachel?"

I flinch and turn towards Lucas, already standing on the sidewalk, offering me a hand. Tentatively, I grab it and slide out of the car, wishing I had gone with the blue dress, or maybe even the red dress. The butler opens the door for us and I'm suddenly smacked in the face by a cold wave created by the air-conditioning humming in the corners of the restaurant.

Or maybe I should have brought a jacket, I think while rubbing my frigid shoulders.

I stare in awe at the place. It's better than the photos with red carpeting everywhere. Red and gold seems to be the theme with waiters dressed in tuxes, minus the jackets, hovering near their customer's tables with a white towel hanging from their arm.

"Do you have a reservation, Monsieur?" asked the man at the front desk.

I shrivel in front of him as his shrewd eyes rake over me, stopping for a moment at my ten dollar pink pumps before giving a slight shake of his head.

"I'm afraid we aren't taking walk-ins at this time."

All I want to do is pull up the carpet and hide underneath it, or perhaps turn around and head to the closest and cheapest cafe. Obviously, I did not choose the correct dress for today's brunch. I really should have asked Lucas for the dress code.

"We are meeting with Christina and Franklin Brent," says Lucas with a smile that doesn't quite reach his eyes. His shoulders are tense and his back is rod straight and once again I get the sense that he's attending an important job interview.

The man's eyes narrow on Lucas before turning to me. I wonder if he's going to send us away, but instead he turns on his heel, saying curtly, "Follow me."

I grab Lucas's hand, my grip tight as I follow him further inside this beautiful place. With each and every step, I feel my stomach twist. All hunger leaves me as my eyes meet Christina's. Frank's back is facing us, but I can tell he's dressed in a suit. Christina is wearing a pink pencil skirt with a matching blazer and button-down shirt. The buttons look gold. They probably are gold, knowing Lucas's family.

"Excuse me, Monsieur," says the man softly, "you have visitors."

Frank turns around, his gaze meeting mine and traveling down the length of my body. Yet, it's not desire I see in his gaze. It's that judgmental look I haven't been able to rid myself since walking into this place. I swallow and raise my hand, twiddling my fingers. My voice cracks as I say, "Hello." I clear my throat and turn to Christina, who hasn't stopped staring at me. "I hope the both of you are well."

Christina's eyes narrow, yet she doesn't say anything.

Frank rises from his chair, offering Lucas his hand. "Good to see you, son."

Lucas takes the offered hand, shaking it firmly. "Likewise."

"And it's so nice for you to join us, Raven," says Frank while gesturing towards an empty seat next to Christina.

"Dad, its Rachel."

Frank shakes his head while pinching the bridge of his nose. "So, sorry, Rachel. Of course it's Rachel. Please, take a seat."

The man before, who stared at me as if he thought I was an irritating bee buzzing around him, quickly moves to pull out the chair.

"Thank you," I murmur softly, sorry to leave the safety at Lucas's side.

I clench my jaw, watching Lucas take his seat across from me, wanting to be next to him so I can take his hand for some support. Instead, I keep my hands in my lap, fighting the need to pick at my fingernails.

"I hope the both of you don't mind, but we ordered for you," says Christina with a thin smile. "This place is supposed to have amazing food."

Well, at least that's something I can talk about, I think while offering my best, charming smile. "Yes, that's what I read on Tripster. The chef is supposed to have a Michelin star."

Christina purses her lips while she turns towards me, raising an eyebrow. "Tripster? This place is on Tripster?" She chuckles bitterly. "You must be teasing me. Isn't Tripster for those backpacking sorts?"

"Mom," says Lucas, his tone warning.

"Times have changed, Dear," says Frank before lifting his glass of what I suspect to be champagne.

I look around, wondering where I can get a glass of one of those. If Christina is going to be picking at everything I say, I may need a drink to get through this.

Christina flicks her hair over her shoulder. "Well, I'll say. Did you hear that Samuel's daughter, Lucy, is backpacking through Asia? Not even bothering to pursue an actual career." Christina shakes her head. "Really, such a pity. She had so much potential."

Lucas's brows furrow. "Well, isn't she paying her own way?"

Frank leans back in his chair, taking a sip from his champagne while he eyes his son. "That's what I heard."

"So, she can't be doing that bad, right?"

Frank purses his lips before his gaze swivels back to me. "You're supposed to be doing some internship here, right?"

I straighten in my chair, feeling like I'm on the spot. Why do I feel like this every time I'm around Lucas's family? "Yes, I'm working at the Louvre."

"Weren't you also working with Samuel?"

I nod. "Yes, I took some photos for his Nstagram."

"And then you just dropped him, right after that?"

I feel like the whole world has frozen over as I stare back at Frank. That's not how that happened. I didn't drop Samuel. "Uh-I," I say, trying to form the words, but Frank's gaze darkens and I lose all capacity of speaking. I turn to Lucas, wondering what I should do, but he's also staring at me, with worry in his eyes.

"I-I," I begin again. "That's not quite how it-"

"I'm quite surprised you dropped Samuel," says Christina while looking at her nails. "I thought artists needed their clients. Samuel was probably one of your best opportunities of making it in the art world." Christina sighs and shakes her head. "But I suppose you will never know."

"Rachel already had an internship, Mom," Lucas rushes out. "She needed to-"

"But what are you doing at that internship?" Frank asks.

I can't stop myself from picking at my nails. I'm too nervous to stop. "Well, I help with restoring the paintings."

A slow, bitter smile lifts Frank's lips. "Restoring paintings?" He shares a look with his wife. "How will that ever pay the bills?"

"That's not all Rachel does," says Lucas, jutting his chin out and straightening his back. "She also provides tourists with directions, leads informative tours-"

Christina scoffs. "So she will be a tour guide once she graduates." She tosses back her head, laughing for a few minutes before grabbing the handkerchief in front of her and dabbing at her eyes. "I didn't think you could go to college for that."

Lucas opens his mouth, but before he can say anything several waiters swarm around us, carrying covered platters of food in their hands.

"Excuse me, Monsieur and Madame," one waiter says

In unison, they lift the lids, as if choreographed, and lower the food in front of us. I stare at the small plate. A veal, coated in bread crumbs and grilled very lightly, rests in the middle with a small touch of red berry sauce. On the side is a dollop of pureed sweet potato. It looks absolutely beautiful, but I'm not hungry.

I sniff, feeling like I am going to burst into tears. As soon as the waiters leave, I quickly shove my chair backwards.

"Excuse me," I say, my voice breathless as I try to control myself. A sob is demanding to break through, but I won't let these people know they got to me. "I should go wash my hands before I eat," I say, turning on my heel and not even bothering to hear their response.

Tears stream down my cheeks as I walk away, looking vaguely around for some kind of sign. As soon as

I see the WC sign with an image of a person in a dress, I turn the corner, nearly running into the bathroom.

I slam my hands onto the marble sink and sob. Staring at myself in the mirror, I watch the tears leave my eyes, making them look more like a misty green. I take my bun down, throwing the tie in front of me, not caring if I lose it. My mascara is already running down my flushed face. Bending over, I splash water onto it, not caring if I ruin my makeup. It's already ruined anyway.

I don't know what I was thinking when I agreed to this. Of course they didn't really want me here. Of course they were going to use this opportunity to drag me down. And why did they care anyway? It's my life. I can do what I want.

I inhale deeply, lifting my gaze and staring back at myself. It's not me, I tell myself. It's them and Lucas. They are upset that Lucas is dating me, someone they think is below them.

It's not about me at all.

25

LUCAS

"Why do you have to be so cruel?" I say while watching Rachel practically run away from our table. I jerk my attentions back to my parents, glaring at both of them.

Mom stares back at me with wide eyes, looking confused, as if she doesn't know that she is being mean to Rachel. Dad crosses his arms while leaning further back in his chair.

"We weren't being cruel," says Dad, his gaze hardening on me. "We were being realistic."

"How can anyone make a living with an art degree?" Mom asks while gesturing towards Rachel's empty chair. "She needs to know the truth."

"Turning down Samuel's help wasn't the smartest choice."

My hands fist and my glare darkens. "She already made a commitment to her program. She's honest, dedicated, and sees things through."

Dad scoffs, tossing back his head while Mom shakes her head.

"Honest doesn't pay the bills," says Dad.

"If she was smart, she would have dumped the program and worked with Samuel," adds Mom. "You know how he opens doors. Look what he's done for you."

I groan and shake my head. "Samuel has done shit for me."

"What's that supposed to mean?" Mom asks, her voice shrill. She glances at Dad before turning back to me. Her hand rests on mine, but I jerk it away, not wanting to be touched right now. I can't believe I just witnessed both my parents pretty much attacking Rachel. They were the ones who invited her.

It's completely uncalled for.

"Honey," says Mom, her voice uneasy while she turns towards me, "Samuel really is a great way to enter this field. And then after, when you graduate, you will be better prepared to help your father in Manhattan."

"I don't want to help Dad," I rush out, my eyes widening when I realize I just uttered those words. Am I really doing this? My gaze lifts, landing on my father scowling at me. I take in his greying hair, his beer gut, his pristinely ironed suit and realize he's not so terrifying.

He's just a man.

"I didn't come here to work with Samuel," I say, holding my ground.

Dad sighs, straightening before taking a sip from his glass. "I know," he says darkly.

My heart stops, plummets into my stomach. "You know?" I breathe.

I hear Mom sigh and turn toward her. "Why else do you think we came?"

My eyes widen. "All this time, you knew I came here to fuck around."

"Language!" Dad shouts.

Mom bobs her head up and down, her gaze remaining on the table. "We were planning on taking you home, but when we spoke with Samuel, we thought you had finally realized what is best for you."

"That's until we met your new play thing."

"She's not a play thing!" I shout while slamming my fist on the table. "Her name is Rachel, and she's a wonderful person. She's the only one who makes me feel like I- like I-"

"Like what?" Dad asks, tilting his head to the side, a bitter gleam flashing at me. "Is she the sun in the sky? Does she make butterflies flutter in your stomach? Your heart twitter?"

I jut out my chin. "Yes. That's exactly what she does."

Dad scoffs. "All of that is pathetic nonsense. It doesn't mean anything."

"Well, it means everything to me."

"And what about in five years? No, ten?" Dad smiles bitterly while leaning in. "What about then? What will you be doing? Writing?"

I nod. "Yes, that's exactly what I will be doing."

Dad chuckles bitterly. I turn to Mom and see she isn't looking at me. "And she will be an artist? You'll both be starving, living on the streets, unable to provide for yourselves."

"You don't know that."

"I do know that."

"Lucas, please," says Mom while grabbing my hand. I try to lurch my hand away from hers, but her grasp tightens. "Listen to us. We know what's best for you. We just don't want you making the same mistakes as-"

"As who, Mom? You?"

Mom flinches and she instantly releases me. "What's that supposed to mean?"

I laugh darkly, watching her eyes widen in horror as she leans away from me. "You know exactly what that means. You don't love Dad, you just use him for his money."

"That's not true," she breathes, her eyes glimmering with unshed tears.

"How can it not be true when he cheats on you every chance he gets?"

"Now, you listen here, you little shit!" Dad shouts while grabbing my collar and shaking me. "You are going to break up with that girl, finish your program with Samuel, and when your senior year ends, you are returning to Manhattan. Got it?"

"No." I grab his hand and shove it off me. I shove my chair back, not caring if the waiters and the other guests are staring at me while I rise, towering over my father. "I'm not doing any of that."

Dad's face is going red as he sputters, thinking of what to say. His eyes are wide, filled with anger and hate. Has this man every loved me? Or has he only seen me as a means to an end? I don't think he's ever told me he loves me.

I don't think I've ever loved him.

"Sorry," I hear a wonderful voice.

Turning around, I see Rachel walking towards us, her eyes red and swollen, most likely from crying. Her makeup is smeared around her eyes. She forces a smile while glancing between my parents. Her brows tent in confusion for a moment before softening.

"I think I've caught some sort of stomach bug," she says softly, her gaze moving to the floor. "I don't want to get you sick. I think I should get going."

I nod and close the distance between us, looping my arm with hers. "I'll be going with you. I seem to have caught the same stomach bug."

Rachel lifts her gaze, her eyes widening for a moment before a genuine smile takes hold of her. She doesn't say anything as I turn us towards the direction of the door, striding briskly towards it.

"Don't think you can use the family name after this!" Dad calls after me.

I shrug, not bothering to turn around. "Fine!"

"Don't let him just leave like this," I hear Mom say. "Go after him. You can't just let him leave with nothing resolved."

"I've given that little shit so many chances," I hear Dad say.

"Are you ok?" Rachel asks.

I gaze down at her, knowing this is where I belong, by her side, taking on the world together.

"Don't you dare think you can be part of this family ever again!" Dad shouts after me, as I open the door and step out into the light.

Of course, I'm worried. It's only a matter of time before I get cut off, or Dad shows up on my doorstep, demanding I return. But right now I feel reborn, re-energized. I know this is the right path for me. No more sitting in an office, being bored out of my mind. No more listening to my parents telling me what to do and what to say.

I can finally be myself and do what I want.

I feel like I'm finally leaving the nest and on my path towards becoming an adult.

I press my lips against Rachel's, enjoying the feeling of her against me after so long of being apart. She opens for me, sliding her tongue against mine. I feel her hands in my hair, stroking the strands softly.

Pulling away from her, I smile down at her misty green eyes, stroking the side of her cheek.

"I'm fine," I whisper while lacing my fingers with hers. She smiles up to me and I swear, it's difficult to breathe. I'm unable to look away from her. I never knew I could feel so much love for someone.

I place another kiss against her brow, murmuring, "I'm exactly where I need to be."

26

RACHEL

"I'm so sorry, for everything," says Lucas while facing me and holding my hand in the taxi back to our apartment.

I feel exhausted and giddy at the same time. It's probably from crying, and also from the fact that Lucas finally stood up for himself. Well, he also stood up for me, which is all I can really ask for. It's everything I wanted him to do. I know we still need to talk about what happened, but I feel like everything will be fine from now on.

"I can't believe they said those things to you."

"Its fine," I say while giving Lucas a gentle squeeze. "Thank you for sticking up for me."

Lucas shakes his head. "It was bound to happen. This, I mean," he says while nodding at me. "I know they hate outsiders and they hate me not following all their orders. It will probably be hard from now," he grimaces. "And different."

"We'll get through it together, Lucas."

I press my lips against his, but the car stops, making the kiss short lived. We slide out of the car and I watch Lucas hand the driver some euros from his wallet before grabbing my hand and tugging me inside. His lips are on mine as soon as we are through the doors, stumbling through the hallway towards the elevator.

"I just want to be with you," Lucas murmurs against my lips.

My hands are in his hair, tugging him towards me, never wanting to let him go. His tongue strokes mine, stoking the fires within, making that pit in my stomach twist in desire. I moan, meeting his demands, twining my tongue around his and enjoying the soft groan escaping his lips.

The elevator dings and we stumble inside, refusing to part from one another. I'm vaguely aware of him slamming his hand against the buttons before shoving me against the wall. He grabs my leg and grinds himself against my core while the doors slide shut. A whimper escapes my lips and my mouth slides from his, lulling to the side while he kisses a path down the length of my neck towards my chest. My shoe is barely hanging onto my foot. I cling to his hair as his teeth graze against the sensitive flesh at my nape, sucking lightly before sliding back up to seize my mouth.

I hear something plop onto the ground and release it's my heel. I'll need to retrieve it. I can't forget. They're cheap, but they're also cute. Lucas's hand going down my front makes me forget all about my shoe and my body pulls taut as I feel his hand slide under my dress and rub against my panties.

My mouth releases him and I lean against the wall, my leg pulling him closer to me as his fingers increase their pressure. My lips part as I gaze back at him, his eyes lingering on my lips before lifting to me.

"You're so beautiful," he breathes.

I pull him towards me, wanting my mouth on his, but the elevator dings and the doors slide open. Lucas slowly kneels before me, grabbing my shoe and sliding it onto my foot. I like this look, with him in front of me, on his knees, gaze up at me while putting on my shoe. It makes me feel powerful, and I can't wait to have him back at the apartment.

He rises and grabs my hand, pulling me down the hallways towards our apartment. His fingers fumble with the keys in his pocket as our pace quickens. I'm desperate to be out of these clothes and on top of him.

Stopping in front of our door, I watch his hands tremble as he shoves the key towards the lock, missing a couple times before gliding it inside. I bite my lip as he shoves the door open. Kicking off my shoes, my hands wrap around his shoulders. He picks me up easily, as if I weigh nothing and slams me against the wall. I moan as his mouth finds my neck, sucking lightly while he grinds his hard cock against me.

"Hello?"

Both Lucas and I jerk towards the sound, finding Hunter standing with Seth peaking around the corner, their mouths agape either in shock or arousal.

"So, I guess you're not fighting anymore?" Seth asks while waggling his eyebrows. He wobbles to stand next to Hunter, holding onto his crutches with a white knuckled grasp.

Lucas chuckles and we turn towards each other. An easy smile comes over my lips while my head lulls lazily up and down. "We're not fighting anymore," I murmur while nuzzling my nose against his.

Lucas's grip on my bottom tightens, and he carries me from the foyer through the kitchen, towards my bedroom, where he dumps me unceremoniously on the bed. Seth and Hunter tag along with Seth propping his crutches against my bed before rolling over next to me.

"I'm ready," says Seth while throwing his arms out.

With one dark look at his shoes from Lucas, Seth kicks them off.

"You shouldn't be moving," I say while turning towards Seth, who gives me a mischievous smile.

"Oh, I know." He waggles his eyebrows and my face flushes at the implication. His hand tugs at my shirt before moving towards my knee, stroking it with up and down motions.

I lean towards him, my stomach fluttering as I lick my lips, desperately wanting his hands on me. His hands continue upwards, nearly touching my underwear before moving down towards me knee once more. He grabs it gently, before moving upwards, his knuckles brushing against my panties only slightly.

I whimper and wiggle towards him, needing more. There's movement in the bed and glancing over my shoulder I see Lucas crawling towards the head of the bed while Hunter is at the bottom. I bite my lip when I feel Seth's hands on my underwear once more, this time with more pressure. Slipping my hands under my dress I tug my panties down and kick them off my feet before moving to straddle Seth.

I meet Lucas's gaze, glossy with desire. He reaches for me and I grab his hands, pulling him towards me until his lips are on mine. I feel Hunter's hands on my waist, undoing my belt while Lucas continues to kiss me. His teeth graze against my tongue and I moan when I feel him suck tenderly before releasing it.

Seth's hands massage up my leg, sending tingles through me. His hands grip my bottom, tugging me towards him. I stumble forward, my arms circling around Lucas's while Hunter's hands massage my breasts. My legs shake as I keep myself balanced, not knowing how much longer I can handle this sweet torture.

Hunter's fingers deftly unbutton my dress. Seth pushes the fabric apart. My gaze lowers, watching him continue nudging me forward, his tongue licking his lips, making my face flush. I'm nearly above him. I can feel Seth's breath on my womanhood. My body trembles while Lucas sucks my earlobe and Hunter tugs at my bra. My dress is now fully open. Only my bra covers me while my men continue worshipping my body, fully clothed.

I push Lucas away, grabbing his shirt and pulling it over his head. Biting my lip, I run my hands over his chest. My gaze rakes over him, lingering on his washboard abs. I lean towards him, pressing my mouth against his chest while I hear movement behind me. Hunter's hands slide up my back, deftly undoing my bra while Seth's tongue glides against my clit. My teeth sink into Lucas's chest. A soft hiss emits from his lips while Hunter's hands grab my breasts, his fingers toying with my nipples. My legs shake as Seth continues licking me, his hands playing with my bottom before moving towards me front.

I continue kissing a path from Lucas's chest towards his mouth while I hear him undoing his belt. Hunter tugs at my dress, pulling it from my arms until I'm completely naked. I toss back my head, moaning as Seth's finger enters me.

"Yes," I murmur while Hunter grabs my breasts, his mouth pressing slopping kisses against my neck. I feel his hard cock pressing into me through his jeans.

Seth is sucking on my clit even more, adding another finger and pushing deep inside me. Lucas claims my lips, sucking on my tongue. I feel like I'm being taken from each side. My attentions are being pulled here and there. Hands slide up my front and from the back, stroking me, biting me, sucking me until I'm shaking with desire and yearning for release.

Lucas seizes my mouth once more and my hands dip inside his unbelted and unbuttoned pants. His cock twitches in my hand. The precum slickens my movements as I pump him. He moves in my hand. A gasp escapes him as I play with his slit.

I feel something hot and hard pressing against my butt. I realize it is Hunter's dick and wiggle against him. He moans in my ear, spurring me on. I'm tempted to wiggle again but Seth's tongue provides more pressure against my clit, making it impossible for me to pay attention. I feel so wet. My walls constrict around Seth's fingers, wanting something bigger and harder deep inside me.

"Seth, more," I whimper against Lucas's lips.

Seth continues sucking and kissing, yet I feel movement behind me. Glancing over my shoulder, I see Seth is tugging his shorts down. His hard cock springs out. Precum leaks down his length. Hunter hands him a condom, and he quickly slides it on while I hover above him, desperate to have him inside me.

Hunter's fingers move from my breasts towards my clit, circling around my little nub, pulled so taut. I lower myself onto Seth, tossing my head back against Hunter's shoulders as Seth fills me deep inside. Lucas's lips move down to my breasts, sucking on them tenderly before nipping them. My whole body tingles in response, wanting and needing more.

I feel Hunter shifting and turn towards him, realizing he's switching places with Lucas.

"Dude," says Hunter with a sly grin. "You should fuck her. You've been fighting so long, I'm sure you want to be deep inside her." His fingers grab my chin, his thumb stroking against my bottom lip before the top. "I want this mouth of yours."

I smile back at Hunter, watching him tug his jeans further down while Lucas moves to stand behind me. Seth thrusts slowly into me, his head lulling from side to side. His hands pat against my hips.

"Move," he mutters, his face strained as if he's in pain. "Move."

"Wait, you idiot," says Lucas, his hands massaging my butt cheeks while his cock slides in between. "You are always so impatient."

Seth grits his teeth, not saying anything. His face is flushed and his eyes stare up at me, pleading for more. My attentions are taken when I feel Lucas sink his teeth into my neck, his head right at the entrance to my ass.

"You want this?" he whispers darkly.

My head lulls open and down. He shoves himself deep inside, making me lose my balance and fall forward, my breasts dangling in Seth's face. Seth thrusts into me, his hands taking my breasts while he sucks on one nipple. Seth tries to speed up the rhythm, but Lucas keeps it slow, sliding in and out of me, making me feel every inch of his hard length.

Hunter grabs my chin, lifting me up until I'm level with his cock, twitching in front of me. My mouth parts and I take his head, sucking lightly and mouthing the slit.

"Good," Hunter murmurs, his hands stroking my face. His cock slides in and out of me, but only the tip. I suck on it as I feel Lucas move slightly faster. Seth's teeth graze against my nipple, making me gasp.

"More," Hunter groans, grabbing my face and shoving himself deep inside my mouth.

I gag, but I control myself as he moves in and out of me, shoving himself harder into me while Lucas quickens the pace behind me. Seth grabs my hips, moving faster while one hand slides between us, circling around my little nub.

I can't moan or gasp. My mouth is full of Hunter's dick. All I can do is let him use me until he's had his fill. I don't know why, but it turns me on so much, being filled from every angle. Seth grinds his cock against me while Lucas moans from behind. I can feel Lucas's full length entering me. He moves harder, faster, jolting me with each pounding he gives me. It hurts, but at the same time the pain blends with the pleasure and I can no longer decipher between them.

"Yes," Hunter groans, shoving his cock into me once more, holding my face tight on either side while he twitches inside me.

I gaze up at him, watching his mouth part into an 'O' shape while his whole body trembles. His cum explodes into my mouth and all I can taste is him as I watch his shoulders relax. His hands stroke my hair away from my face and he leans back, sitting on his knees while his cock slides out of his mouth.

"Faster," Seth groans, his hands on my hips tightening as he thrusts into me.

Lucas grabs my arms, pulling me backwards until I feel his chest against me. It's so hot. Sweat drips down the side of my face while I continue grinding myself against Seth. Lucas kisses my jaw, my neck, my shoulder. His cock is hard and deep in me, yet he seems controlled unlike Seth.

"Fuck!" Seth shouts, thrusting into me harder until finally he stills. I feel his cock twitch, watch as his hands grip the sheets while his head moves from side to side, contorted in pain as he empties.

Seth becomes relaxed under me. His breath comes in pants. I lean forward and place my lips upon his, chastely kissing him. I hardly have time for more as Lucas tugs me back towards him, thrusting harder into me. I moan while his hands come around me, one stroking my clit while the other pinches my nipple.

"I want to hear you screaming," Lucas whispers darkly in my ear, sending shivers down my spine.

He grabs my arms, pulling them backwards. I bend forward, unable to be upright as he pounds into me harder. My mouth gapes open. I want to call out his name, but my voice remains silent as I gasp into the blankets in front of me.

"Fuck, Rachel," Lucas mutters, enunciating each syllable with a thrust. "Say my name."

"Lucas," I cry, my body trembling as I feel it soaring higher towards that sweet release.

"Louder."

"Lucas!" I shout, feeling myself getting closer, like I'm about to explode into a million tiny pieces. My whole body shakes and I bury my head into the bed, unable to control myself any more as I feel my body falling over the edge.

"Lucas!" I scream. Stars explode beyond my eyes. I can't stop myself from screaming as my orgasm takes hold of me. Lucas shouts, his body stilling behind me and I feel his cum flow through me.

I topple onto the bed, next to Hunter and Seth. Lucas lands on top of me, kissing my shoulders, the crown of my head, my cheek. It's like he can't get enough of me.

"I love you," he whispers in my ear, nuzzling my cheek with his nose.

I smile and turn towards him. I take a moment and stroke his hair back before I whisper, "I love you, too."

We stay like that for a long time, cradling each other with Hunter and Seth on either side. Lucas moves off of me, squeezing himself between me and Hunter. Seth sighs next to me and I turn, seeing that he's staring up at the ceiling with his hands on his stomach. My gaze travels down his body towards his injured foot, still bandaged from his time at the hospital.

"Are you okay?" I whisper while nudging his shoulder.

He turns towards me and smiles. "Yes," Seth says while stroking my hair behind my ear. "There's just one problem."

My brow furrows, wondering if our activity had somehow damaged his foot even more. Although, we were careful. At least, I thought we were.

"What?" I ask, fear seizing hold of me.

Seth sticks out his bottom lip. "I'm hungry."

I chuckle and smack his shoulder before turning away from him. "And I thought it was serious," I mutter while closing my eyes.

"It is serious," says Seth while poking me in the shoulder. "I'm starving. My stomach is eating my insides."

"Should we order pizza?" I hear Hunter ask.

"No, I have a better idea," says Lucas. My eyes open and I see he's smiling brightly at me.

"What?" I ask, but without saying anything more, I watch Lucas rise from the bed.

"Put on your nicest clothes," he says while getting out of the bed. "There's something I've been wanting to do since we got here."

***

I stare down at the delicious food. The view of Paris is absolutely amazing here. I never knew there was a restaurant near the top of the Eiffel Tower. It's probably one of the most romantic places I have ever been to. The restaurant is on the second floor, but based on the information given on the menu, the second floor means 410 feet up from the ground. The city lights twinkle around us.

I groan, feeling slightly uncomfortable from all the food we ate. Lucas didn't spare any expense. He made each of us order the eight course meal. I'm now definitely paying for it. I probably should have worn the white dress out, but seeing how I already wore it to a very dismal brunch, I thought it best to go for the blue dress.

Maybe it's the area, or the fact tons of tourists are here all the time, but the service is definitely better. The waiters linger near our table, offering us more wine or water. No one has given me judgmental looks.

They're definitely getting an excellent review from me.

My gaze turns towards Hunter, leaning back in his seat with his hands over his stomach, groaning while his head lulls from side to side. "So full," he whines while grimacing.

I'm tempted to shove another bite into my mouth. The curried crab was to die for, the lamb in the cream sauce was exquisite, and I can definitely see myself eating the chocolate soufflé for the rest of my life.

But I don't think there's any way I can cram any more inside.

"I still think pizza would have been better," Seth grumbles from my other side.

I scowl at him, sitting there in his t-shirt and running shorts. That's all he brought. Lucas offered to loan him something nice to wear, but Seth refused, not wanting to take any charity. If he wasn't already in crutches, I would have smacked him on the top of the head and made him change into something nicer.

"Do you want to have a look on the top floor?" Lucas asks, already sliding his chair out and offering a hand in my direction.

I smile and take it, leaving Seth and Hunter groaning and grumbling in their seats. Lucas pauses in front of the waiter, who gathers up our half eaten plates and empty glasses.

"Can you charge everything to this card?" Lucas asks while handing him a credit card from his wallet.

"Of course, Monsieur," says the waiter with a curt nod. "Was everything to your liking?"

"Yes," Lucas, Hunter, and I answer in unison.

Seth grumbles in his seat.

I shake my head while Lucas guides me to the elevator. There's a short line to go to the top floor and so we stop and wait. My gaze lingers on the room once more, enjoying the simple classiness of the restaurant.

"I want to thank you for today," says Lucas while we follow the other guests onto the elevator.

I shake my head. "I don't think I did anything."

"If you hadn't been there, I don't think I would have ever stood up to my parents."

The doors to the elevator slide close and I wait to respond while we go up to the top floor, my hand on Lucas's tightening. As soon as the door dings open, we follow the group of people out. It's windy at the top and my skirt blows, nearly exposing my panties to the tourists surrounding us.

Lucas chuckles and takes off his suit jacket, putting it on my shoulders, but I doubt it will help all that much. Well, at least it's dark. I don't want to give up this beautiful view. I'll just tell Charlie when I return that everyone got to see my undies on top of the Eiffel Tower.

It's not everyday someone can say that.

"All I did was run into the bathroom crying," I say while leaning towards Lucas. We find an open spot near the railing. My eyes widen while I stare down at all the city lights.

Paris really is beautiful. Whether in the dark or the light.

It's been a difficult start, but this place really is amazing.

"You make me want to be more than what my parents expect of me," Lucas murmurs in my ear. "You make me want to stand up for what's right."

I chuckle and push my hair away from my face. "I should have said something to your parents."

Lucas nods, a mischievous glimmer in his eyes. "Next time."

I scoff. "There will be a next time?"

Lucas nods vigorously. "I have not heard the last of them. They'll probably cut me off, make it difficult for me to survive. Once I show them I can live on my own, they'll relentlessly call me, demanding for me to be a good boy and listen to them."

I frown. "Will you be okay?"

Lucas sighs. "I hope so. I've never lived without their money or the Brent family name to flaunt. It will definitely be different."

I lean my head against his shoulders. His hand strokes my back and he turns us away. "I guess we should get going before Hunter passes out and Seth causes a scene."

I chuckle and follow him towards the elevator. "I suppose you're right."

There's no line to the elevator and we're back in less than five minutes, but the waiter stands at our table, looking nervous while Hunter and Seth are frowning at each other.

"I'm afraid, Monsieur," starts the waiter while handing the credit back to Lucas, "your card has been declined."

Lucas's eyes widen while I glance at Seth and Hunter. They look nervously between themselves.

"Shit," breathed Lucas while stuffing his card back into his wallet. He stares at the cards inside, as if trying to figure out a maze. "I doubt any of these will work." He turns to me, his eyes filled with worry. "I didn't expect Dad to cut me off so soon. I don't think I have any money to pay."

I open my mouth to say something, but Hunter speaks instead, "I got it."

All eyes jerk towards Hunter while he takes out his wallet.

"You're sure?" Lucas asks.

Hunter shrugs. "My dad gave me a budget and I've barely spent it. I'm sure one fancy meal isn't going to put me back that much. How much is it?"

The waiter hands the bill to Hunter. His eyes bug out of his head when he opens the small black folder. "Holy fuck," Hunter nearly shouts. "Jesus fucking Christ, Lucas. Why didn't you say anything?"

Lucas groans and pinches the bridge of his nose. "I didn't think Dad was going to cut me off so soon."

Hunter shoves his card into the folder and hands it back to the waiter. I pat Hunter's shoulder. "I'll handle the tip."

"I will, too," says Seth, perking up in his seat.

Lucas dumps his body into an empty chair, pressing his hands against his eyes. "I really didn't think this was going to happen."

"Well, it has," says Hunter. "No point in crying about it now. We got you covered."

"And in the meantime," says Seth while slapping Lucas's back, earning a sharp scowl. "You're going to have to get a job." Seth smiles brightly while Lucas groans. "Welcome to my world, Lucas."

"I hate your world," Lucas mutters.

Seth chuckles. "You'll get used to it."

"Yeah, you have us to help you out," Hunter adds.

Lucas turns his gaze to me and smiles. I can see the worry in his gaze, yet he looks a bit more relaxed. He has us to take care of him.

We're his family now.

27

RACHEL

I stretch my arms over my head while I sit in the back of the shuttle bus. A yawn escapes me. Seth's head lies on one shoulder while Hunter's head lies on the other. My gaze shifts to Lucas, who looks antsy. His leg is bobbing up and down and I notice he hasn't stopped playing with his fingers since we left the plane.

The internship program finished a few days ago. We left Paris what felt like yesterday, but I guess by time zone standards, it was this morning? I blink my exhausted eyes. I didn't sleep at all on the airplane. Lucas sat up in first class, having bought the tickets before his father cut him off.

I kinda wish he sat in economy with us. Even in first class, I don't think he slept at all. Dark circles shroud his eyes. His skin looks more pale than usual. I know he's worried about the semester being paid for, paying for rent at the brohouse, and being able to afford rowing, since it's an expensive sport. I told him I'd help him look for a job, but it seems like my promises and assurances that he will be okay have completely missed him.

I know he will be fine. I think it will just take him time to adjust to life without his father's money.

I'm happy the summer is over. The internship in Paris was amazing, but I'm happy to be returning to life in Colorado. I smile at the mountains in the distance, recalling the final weeks of my internship. Dr. Arnaud really took me under her wing and Lauren pretty much left me alone.

Which was all I could really ask for.

"Do you know if your running store is hiring, Seth?" Lucas asks. His bloodshot eyes land on me and my heart pulls. I wish he was sitting next to me so I could hold his hand or give him a hug, but Hunter and Seth both staked a claim on my shoulders.

Seth opens one eye. "Bro, I have no clue. You'll have to wait until we get home."

Lucas's frown deepens. "How much longer do we have?"

I grimace and look at my watch. "About thirty minutes."

Lucas groans, turning his attentions towards the window.

"Bro, I told you my dad could have picked us up," Hunter says while straightening himself. He cracks his neck before slinging an arm around my shoulder.

"I didn't want to bother him. He already paid for that expensive meal."

Hunter shakes his head. "Dad was just happy it wasn't hookers or drugs."

Seth chuckles. "I wonder what he would do if it was hookers or drugs."

Hunter shrugs. "Hunt me down and drag my ass back."

"What about that cafe you always go to, Rachel?" Lucas asks, his voice shaking. "Do you think they're hiring?"

"Bro, calm down," says Hunter. "My therapist always tells me to handle one problem at a time. What problem should you be handling right now?"

Lucas's brows furrow. "Getting home?"

"Wrong," says Hunter while raising one finger. "You should be handling your boredom. Right now, you are solving your boredom by worrying nonstop about something you can't fix right now. Why don't you think of all the exciting things we can do this year?"

Lucas frowns. "Honestly, I can't think of anything."

Hunter scoffs. "You must be kidding me. It's your senior year." He pulls me closer to him and nuzzles the top of my head. "I'm excited for the new football season. I'm going to play hard and ensure I got spotted by a coach of the NFL."

I kiss his jaw. "Of course you are."

"You'll go to all my games, right?"

I make a face. "I don't know about that."

Hunter frowns. "Really? You won't go to them?"

"I'll go to five total," I say while holding up five fingers.

Hunter's eyes narrow. "Ten."

"Five."

"Ten."

I jut out my chin. "Four."

Hunter's eyes widen and he shakes my hand vigorously. "Five then."

I chuckle and bat his hand away.

"What about you, Seth?" Hunter asks.

Seth groans and nuzzles his head against my shoulder. "I'm not excited about anything." His eyes open and he scowls at the seat in front of him. "Gotta talk to fucking coach about how I fucking fucked up and my leg us fucked and I won't be able to fucking run."

The elderly lady in front of us turns around and scowls at Seth, making his face flush. "Sorry, ma'am," he murmurs.

She gives a curt nod before turning back around.

Seth groans and turns towards Hunter. "Not to mention getting around campus is going to be a bi-bummer," he quickly corrects as the elderly lady begins turning around once more.

"You're off the crutches though," I say while nodding at his foot, which is freshly bandaged. He's been off crutches for the past week after his check up at the hospital. He still can't run though, and he needs to keep walking to a minimum.

"Yeah, but I still hobble around. I can't walk fast."

"You'll be fine," I say while giving Seth a pat on his shoulder.

Seth catches my hand and presses his lips against my knuckles. "I do look forward to spending all my free time with you."

I roll my eyes. "How is that any different?"

"Well, now you have to do all the work." Seth waggles his eyebrows and my face flushes.

"Alright, Lucas, your turn," says Hunter while leaning over and peeking at Lucas.

Lucas sighs and shakes his head. "I'm looking forward to being off this freaking bus."

Hunter purses his lips. "Not exactly what I'm looking for there, Bro."

Lucas runs his hands through his hair, giving another exasperated sigh. "I don't know. Maybe my writing class. If I can even take it. Who knows at this rate?"

I reach over and take Lucas's hand, giving it a pat. "Don't worry about that now. You'll get it figured out. Besides, I'll help you."

Lucas forces a smile and slides his hand away from mine, turning his gaze towards the window. After talking for so long, I begin to recognize where we are. We're almost in Aurora University. The bus should stop about five-minute walk from our apartment, which made this commute nearly perfect.

If only it didn't take nearly two hours from the airport.

I perk up when I see our neighborhood coming into view. We pass by the running store and The Coffee Shop, which I see is already busy with returning college students. The bus continues straight until it reaches a crosswalk with a bus sign. The doors open and we grab our suitcases and bags shoved above us before shuffling out into the humid air.

I inhale deeply. "Home sweet home," I say while dragging my suitcase over the cement.

"Sure," grumbles Lucas.

Hunter and Seth follow behind as I lead the way home, stopping when I see someone sitting on the steps leading upstairs. My eyes widen. Hunter and Lucas brush past me, busy talking amongst themselves about something I vaguely hear.

"What is it?" Seth asks, stopping next to me.

I shake my head, not believing my eyes. Well, it actually makes sense. I haven't been home since the winter holidays. And I even cut that short in order to go skiing with the bros. I decided to go to Paris for the summer.

I should have expected this.

The woman on the stairs rises as Hunter and Lucas stop in front of her.

"Hey, are you lost?" Lucas asks.

"Do you need directions?" asks Hunter.

The woman turns towards me, her green eyes wide as she takes a step towards me. "Rachel?" She calls.

I grimace and stride briskly towards her, wishing she had called me before. Although, knowing her, that would never fly. She is her own person. Always was and always will be.

"Hey, Mom," I say, unable to hide the disappointment in my voice. How am I going to explain the bros to her?

"Mom?" I hear Lucas, Hunter, and Seth say in unison.

Mom runs towards me, throwing her arms around my neck and giving me a tight hug. "I thought I missed you. I know you're busy these days." She pulls away from me, looking me over. "Well, it looks like you've been taking care of yourself." She pushes my hair away from my face. "I'm so excited to finally meet your roommates. Maybe after you unpack we can all go for dinner?"

I wince. "Um, ok."

"Well, where are they?" Mom asks while looking around.

My frown deepens. "They're… here." I nod towards Hunter and Lucas, still standing at the staircase. "The dark-haired one is Lucas. The one who looks like Thor is Hunter." My stomach twists as I see my mom's brows tenting in confusion. I turn towards Seth, currently hobbling towards us with his backpack slung over his shoulder. "And that's Seth."

Mom turns her attentions back to me, her chin jutting out. Her hands plant onto her hips and I stifle a groan, already knowing I'm in for a very long lecture.

"You're living with a bunch of men?"

I nod. I don't know if I'm going to vomit or pass out. I don't know which would be better right about now.

"Under one roof?"

I nod again, my stomach churning.

Before I can get sick everywhere, my mom's scowl dissipates, and she smiles brightly, throwing an arm around my shoulders and guiding me towards the apartment. "Why didn't you say so?" She waves at the bros excitedly while I stare at them in confusion. "Let's unpack and get some food. I'm starving. I can't wait to hear all about Paris."

I allow her to guide me inside, feeling numb as I listen to her talk about family and New York. It's great that she's okay with my roommates, but what will she say when I tell her about our relationship? A part of me wants to ask how long she is staying and where?

I have no clue how long I will be able to keep this secret from her.

I'm surprised I've kept it secret this long.

I feel a chill come over me as I watch her look around our apartment, releasing it's only a matter of time before she finds out.

Made in the USA
Columbia, SC
26 July 2021